The Vc Cranberry Club

Barry Lillie

Copyright © Barry Lillie 2025

Cover design © Flatfield

The moral right of Barry Lillie to be identified as the author of this work has been asserted in accordance with the Copyright, Designs and Patents Act of 1988.

All rights reserved. No part of this publication may be reproduced, stored in a retrieval system, or transmitted in any form or by any means, electronic, mechanical, photocopying, recording, or otherwise, without the prior permission of the copyright owner of this book.

This novel is entirely a work of fiction. The names, characters and incidents portrayed within are the product of the author's imagination. Any resemblance to actual people living or dead is entirely coincidental.

For Karon
Who thankfully never drank vodka and cranberry juice.

…all great ideas are dangerous
Oscar Wilde

You can follow Barry on the following platforms:
www.facebook.com/barrylillieauthor
www.instagram.com/barrylillie2
https://www.youtube.com/@barrylillieauthor

For news about new releases and free content
sign up for the newsletter here:
barry@barrylillie.com

1

~ Circles ~

As the old-school comedian wrapped up his outdated and painfully unfunny routine, the half-hearted applause from the audience quickly faded away and music kicked in again from the hotel's PA system.

Leaving their wives and mistresses sitting at the overpriced tables of the charity event, the male audience members started to rise and head towards the bar. The compere leapt onto the stage where the lights illuminated the lint on his green velvet jacket, giving him the look of a leprechaun with psoriasis.

"The auction will begin in twenty minutes," he said after tapping the mic, dispatching a squeal of feedback into the room.

"Heaven save us," said the woman with hair the colour of tar, and with a white streak at the left temple to no one in particular as she waited for the bar staff to notice her. She looked over the heads of the men clamouring for drinks and caught sight of her husband laughing with his cronies. "I see they've served you already," she muttered.

A man wearing a supercilious smile and Hugo Boss turned and said, "Waiting at this bar is like... what's his name's, first circle of hell?" she tried to ignore him but he nudged her and added, "Limbo, the state whereby–"

"I know what limbo is," she said, baring her teeth as she smiled at him, "and if you're going to quote Dante, at least use his name. This, however, is like his seventh circle."

The man's brow knitted itself into a widow's peak as he looked at her, confused, and she knew he was out of his depth. Didn't expect the little lady to know The Divine Comedy, she thought, before she said, "Violence. The circle I'll be creating if that fucking barman ignores me one more time." Hugo Boss gave a weak smile and sidled away as the man in the white shirt with what looked like a blackcurrant cordial stain down the front asked her what she'd like to drink. "At last. A large vodka and cranberry juice, no ice." Waiting, she ran her fingers through her hair, the luminescence of the black fanning out from the white giving her the look of a magpie, and like the bird, her eyes shone like jet in the subdued lighting.

Picking up her drink, she turned and walked to the back of the room and observed the auction beginning to take place. Fat men with fat wallets were bidding for celebrity cast-offs to mollify their bored wives, and luxury hotel breaks to share with the flirty piece of skirt in the office. A man who'd removed his jacket and rolled up his shirt sleeves whooped as he won a pair of gloves allegedly worn by Florence Hunt in the TV series, Bridgerton.

"For God's sake," the vodka-drinking magpie said, and turning she downed her drink, left the function suite and headed towards the intimate bar across the hotel corridor.

The bar was small, but welcoming, unlike the claustrophobic atmosphere she'd just left. She looked across at a woman sitting beside the artificial log burner before addressing the young man behind the bar.

Taking the drink she'd ordered; she turned around and looked again at the woman sitting alone. She looked out of place. Here everyone wore their finery, and she stood out, dressed in her ordinary day-to-day clothing.

"Do you mind if I join you? I'd appreciate some company."

The woman at the table looked up. She was wearing no

make-up and with her hair tied back, she looked tired and drawn and the woman with the white streak noticed she tugged the cuffs of her blouse down over her wrists.

"I'm sorry, how rude of me, I've not introduced myself," the stranger offered her hand, "Emilia Hart."

"Selena Cavendish," the shy-looking woman replied, accepting a firm handshake.

There was a long pause before Emilia said, "Would you like a drink… Selena Cavendish?"

Selena looked up through her eyelashes and said, "Thank you. I'll have whatever you're having." Emilia raised her hand, the diamond bracelet on her wrist catching the light as she grabbed the barman's attention. Signalling with a spiralling motion over the table, he nodded his understanding.

They sat in companionable silence as the barman delivered their drinks with a wink and a smile. "Probably fancies his chances," Emilia said. "A pair of cougars. Or what is it young men call an older woman now… milf? He's probably hoping for a milf experience."

"I'm not in the market for a casual dalliance," Selena said, before taking a sip of her drink.

"Me neither. Shame really, look how good his arse looks in those tight trousers."

Emilia lifted her glass in salute to Selena and surreptitiously assessed her. An angular face of pale, almost translucent skin with shadowed circles beneath each of the eyes gave her a washed-out appearance, an almost gothic look.

"I take it you're not here for the fiasco across the corridor?"

"No, I've escaped for the weekend," a longer pause and then, "So what's happening across the corridor?"

Emilia explained about the charity gala being hosted at the hotel, and how the room was full of businessmen waving their wallets around like elephant seals squabbling over a mate. "It's a gaggle of bored wives in old diamonds mixed with younger second wives wearing tanzanite the size of walnuts. Puts me in mind of a modern-day Sodom and Gomorrah."

"I take it you're not a fan of these events?"

"Goodness, no. I'd much rather peel the skin off my face without an anaesthetic."

"So, who have you come with?"

"Husband. Iain ... that's who I'm saddled with ... for my sins."

"And what does he do?"

"At the moment he's propping up the bar, surrounded by a group of like-minded men, all trying to outdo each other in the skiing slash golf holiday and high-performance car arena. When all they're really interested in, is who has the largest bank balance. It's penis envy for the business community." Selena laughed a little, and Emilia continued. "Iain is in property development. When we first married, I was involved with the business, but not so much now. When he talks about it I pretend to be interested, but in all honesty, I'm as interested in the minutia of his day as I am in the plight of families with Japanese knotweed invading their gardens. I like to think we live separate lives, but that's not the case. He's like microwaved fish, always hanging around making its presence felt."

Another small laugh from Selena. "What about you?"

Emilia watched as she thought about answering her question, and at first thought, being so direct she'd maybe scared her into silence.

"Married to Andrew. It's always Andrew, never Andy. He's in imports." Selena took a sip of her drink, eyes on the table. "Antiques." She shifted her gaze to Emilia.

"He's at home packing for another trip to China at the moment... at least I hope he is. There's been a sudden surge of interest in anything from the Orient... Oh shit, can we still say Orient, or is it on the list of words that have become demonised for the sake of political correctness?"

"I think you're safe," Emilia said.

Applause trickled over from the gala, followed by music. A group of men in the corner polished off their drinks and left, talking loudly about the band that was about to take to the stage.

"A 1990s pop group has been coaxed out of retirement for the evening. The men..." she nodded towards those leaving the bar, "are all going back to their seats to check if the singer still has legs up to her armpits. You can guarantee if she's looked after herself, there'll be more than a few erections beneath the linen tablecloths." Emilia laughed then rose from her seat, said she ought to show willing and return to her husband. "It's been lovely to meet you, Selena. We're staying over, so I'll maybe bump into you at breakfast."

"Sadly, no, I'm leaving quite early. I need to catch a train to Stansted. I'm escaping to Milan for a couple of days."

Escaping, thought Emilia. There's that word again.

"Well, have a lovely time," she rolled her eyes, smiled and said, "Duty calls," and left the bar.

2

~ Selena ~

So far, Milan hadn't lived up to her expectations, although in truth, Selena wasn't sure what she expected from the city. Was it sufficient to visit another country to escape? She could have gone to Aberdeen or Truro to be free for a while, for temporary solitude. The reminder on her phone pinged, telling her that Andrew was boarding his flight to China.

"Shanghai has the world's busiest port," he'd once told her. "Perfect for shipping antiques to the UK."

Selena couldn't care less.

Goodness me, she thought, pulling her coat around her as she shivered in Milan's infamous morning fog. Having left early to spend more than just a morning visiting the Pinacoteca di Brera, she'd booked a Brera card in advance, to allow her as much time as she needed to walk around the galleries.

Selena was specifically looking forward to viewing *The Kiss* by Francesco Hayez and Modigliani's, *Enfant Gras*, and so, giving herself a whole day meant she could wait until there was a lull in the crowds and enjoy an unspoilt view of these works.

It was only a fifteen-minute walk from the hotel, but she opted to take a bus from the central station.

She punched her bus ticket and chose a window seat; unenamoured by the endless landscape of buildings with balconies that clung like limpets.

After collecting her admission card, she took her time strolling around the galleries. She was studying *Ritratto di*

Uomo; a portrait of a solemn-looking man. Out of nowhere, a woman appeared beside her and started to jabber away in Italian. Feeling hemmed in by the woman's insistence for information, Selena made her apologies, saying she was English, and walked away.

Standing away from the other visitors, she looked across the room at the image of the morose man, thinking that he looked as miserable as she felt.

~ ~ ~

Life for Selena had become a constant battle against not having an opinion and keeping her own counsel. She knew she would pay the price for these few days away, but lately, she had reached her limit. Like an elastic band stretched until it could give no more, in danger of snapping.

Andrew had been everything she had wanted in a husband, handsome, successful, the life and soul of any party: Everyone loved him and told her she was so lucky to have him and that thought had comforted her.

They'd settled in a small village in the Derbyshire Peak District and at first, the cottage garden, hiking and local book club filled her days. But after a year, they ceased to fulfil her, or her initial ideas of how village life would be. She craved the challenges of employment and longed for discussions with colleagues, but Andrew was adamant no wife of his would go to work. "Why would you?" he'd said, "I can support the both of us."

"I just want to get out of the house. There must be more to life than flower arranging and making a shepherd's pie every Wednesday."

That was the first time it had happened since their wedding and he had put the conversation to bed.

~ ~ ~

The fog had dissolved, replaced by a high Italian sun and as she stepped outside, she smiled as she watched three boys sitting eating panini beneath the statue of Napoleon in the palazzo.

Selena took shelter in the shaded portico. Leaning against a column, she ate her sandwich, dreaming about how her life could have been different. She thought back to her time at university studying history and fine art and often wondered how her friends from the course were and how many of them had followed up a career in their chosen subject. She recalled plates of historical artworks in dusty tomes in the university library and how she'd sit soaking up the wonder of the skilled artists within the pages.

Many times she would regret never having pursued the career she craved and often fantasised about sharing her knowledge with enquiring minds. But she knew outside of her private thoughts this could never be. Not now she was married to Andrew.

~ ~ ~

Born into a working-class family, Selena had been a friendly girl with a close group of friends and had been popular with the other students at high school. She took part in a range of activities and after-school clubs, and her parents often joked about her moving her bed into the school because she spent so much time there. How happy and full of fun those teenage years had been. Selena never lacked confidence, and her laughter had been loud and joyous.

Of course, there had been boyfriends; teenage affairs, but nothing serious.

Except for Racer Ralph, the first boy in the school to pass his driving test. While sitting on the back seat of his Ford Escort, she'd allowed him to put his hand up her jumper and under her bra. He had wanted to take things further, but when Selena said no, he moved on to another girl.

Putting Racer Ralph behind her, she knuckled down to her studies and, after leaving college with an impressive clutch of exam results, gained entry to her chosen university and embraced the opportunity of new friendships and the specialised education that academia promised.

University brought her new experiences, new hobbies, and a new boyfriend, Andrew Cavendish.

Spending her evenings listening to him rehearse with his student indie band, she encouraged his aspirations of a music career that never materialised. She had worked locally in a fashion shop, a job she'd liked; the girls were great fun, and while Andrew spent his days with his head in the clouds, she opted to put aside some savings.

Mortified to discover she was pregnant at twenty, Andrew blamed Selena. Every time they met up they argued, "You've spoiled my life," he'd say, "Taken the joy from these years, how can I be a successful recording artist chained to a kid I don't want?" One particular argument became more heated and Selena, tired of his accusations and continuous self-pitying, told him their relationship was over. Andrew raged and pushed her hard against a lamppost, his hands around her throat. Her reaction was to bring her knee up into his groin just before he punched her in the stomach. The altercation was brief and ended with tears and snot sliding down Andrew's face as he delivered a snivelling apology. Two days later, in the bathroom, Selena's pregnancy ended. Relief replaced her sadness and so began the rollercoaster of her on-and-off relationship with Andrew.

Months passed. He had been on his best behaviour, even managed to hold down a part-time job, and then out of nowhere, one evening, he proposed. He'd got down on one knee in the local pub. What could she do? Embarrassed, her only option was to say yes. Selena had already learned never to humiliate him in front of their friends.

~ ~ ~

With the museum closing time looming, she made her way to view the Hayez painting depicting two young lovers in a passionate embrace. Arriving at the artwork, the only other onlookers were an aged couple holding hands. As they surveyed the kissing couple in the castle hallway, Selena smiled inwardly, thinking of them as the lovers in the picture. Her eyes roamed the canvas and stopped at the sinister-looking shadow in the recess to the left of the painting, and her thoughts once again returned to her husband.

3

~ Il Duomo ~

Emilia pushed back the bedclothes and stretched. After wrapping herself in a sheer negligee, she looked out of the window and down on to the city below. Thanks to the hotel's soundproofed windows, cars and buses jostled for space noiselessly. Students raced through the streets clutching books and men with briefcases walked to office jobs with a brisk but fashionable gait. There was a knock at the door, followed by a voice calling, "Servizio in camera." She opened the door to allow the young woman delivering her room service to enter and stood watching as she placed a tray of pastries and a pot of coffee on the table beside the window. "Buongiorno," the maid said, followed by, "Grazie signora," when given a ten-euro tip.

Emilia sipped her coffee and pulled flaky pieces of the cornetto apart, dropping the morsels into her mouth as she opened a tour guide and planned her day. The hot water from the shower needled her skin, washing away the remnants of sleep and airport fatigue and with her hair tied back, the white flash tucked behind an ear, she chose a pair of navy trousers and teamed them with an embroidered Valentino blouse. After applying a slash of red to her lips, she slid her feet into her sandals and picked up her Lulu Guinness handbag before leaving the room.

Outside, the motionless air carried a tang of diesel that competed with the aroma of coffee from open-fronted bars. Emilia looked through a tabacchi window at the array of truffles on display but opted to purchase a small bag of sugared almonds, thinking that chocolate may not fare well if the temperature increases. She sashayed through the Rinascente where mannequins tempted her, but she held onto her resolve. She stopped briefly to gaze enviously at the shoes a window dresser behind the glass was wearing before leaving the store. Outside, the sun was almost at its zenith and in the piazza, she stopped to look up at the pinnacles and spires of the impressive cathedral. The only thing spoiling this vision of Italian architecture was the MacDonalds, on one side of the square. The queue for the Duomo entrance was long and wound around the side of the cathedral, and Emilia decided if she wanted to see inside, she would book a tour in advance. Sightseeing could take a back seat to – what was it the woman in the bar had said? – oh yes, escaping.

Emilia sat on a bench looking at the crowds gathered around the cathedral; mostly tourists, the majority being Italian and British. Nearby was a stall that sold souvenirs and a small boy was watching out for the Carabinieri while the stallholder took euros from the travellers.

A woman carrying shopping bags with store names Emilia approved of walked past, fanning herself with a street map of Milan. The midday heat was becoming unbearable, so Emilia stood up and wandered away from the main piazza into a shaded vico and pushed open the door to a gelateria. She breathed in the sweet aroma and ordered a glass of prosecco and a tub of amaro cherry ice cream.

Sitting at a table by the window, she watched as people strolled past. Some looked like Milanese, but most appeared to be tourists.

About to gesture to the waitress for another glass of prosecco, Emilia became distracted by a tapping on the window. Turning around, she saw the woman she had met days before in the hotel's small bar. She beckoned her in, ordered a bottle and two glasses.

Selena joined her at the table as the waitress opened the

bottle of prosecco and poured two tall flutes. With her hair pulled away from her face. Emilia noticed that Selena's skin, which was devoid of any make-up, looked paler than she remembered. This woman has an air of sadness about her, Emilia thought as she watched her take a seat opposite.

"What are you doing here in Milan?" Selena asked.

"I took a leaf out of your book and thought I'd treat myself to a break."

"Why Milan?" Selena said, picking up her glass clumsily, spilling a little wine.

"Why not? You must have sown the germ of an idea when we met at that god-awful charity event."

"How did it end?"

"As they usually do. Drunken men clambering for autographs from retired pop stars while catty wives and girlfriends out bitched each other on the way to the late night bar." Emilia pulled a napkin from the dispenser and mopped up the wine from the table. "So, what have you been up to?"

"Art gallery yesterday and today I did the cathedral tour."

"Good?"

"Would have been if the couple from Wigan had stopped asking pointless questions and slowing down the guide."

"I quite fancy the tour, but not the rooftop viewing. Me and heights don't get along."

"Here." Selena took out her mobile and showed Emilia the photos she had taken from the rooftop, and together they chatted like they'd been friends for years before they agreed to meet at Selena's hotel for dinner that evening.

~ ~ ~

Enjoying the luxury of a large power shower, Selena washed away the hours and sitting at the dressing table, she thought about her day. The cathedral experience had been informative, and she'd enjoyed it as much as the constant interruptions had allowed. Then, spotting Emilia in the ice cream parlour had been a pleasant surprise. If not a little disturbing. Why was she in Milan? Had Andrew employed Emilia to follow her?

Why am I being so paranoid?

Putting the hairbrush down, she walked over to the bed and picked up the emerald-green A-line dress that matched her eyes and held it up against herself looking at the short lace sleeves; she usually wore them long. Putting the dress down, she checked her arms and, seeing the remnants of an old bruise, applied a spot of foundation. Satisfied she had concealed it, she stepped into the dress and looked in the mirror. Her hair fell in giant curves over her shoulders and her lips, painted in a pale coral, gave her an ethereal, almost Gaelic look. She also noted that the sun had caught her, giving her skin a healthy glow.

Being tall, she rarely wore heels and so slipped her feet into a pair of green pumps and made her way to the hotel lift.

Walking down the steps into the sunken restaurant, the Maître d showed her to a table near the entrance and snapped his fingers. A young waiter delivered her a complimentary glass of prosecco. She hadn't yet taken a sip when Emilia appeared at the top of the steps, dressed in a lilac, Azazie, off the shoulder gown, perfectly matched with Eliza lilac heels, that gave her an air of northern Italian elegance she looked like she was gliding rather than walking.

"Sorry, I'm a little late. Bloody Italian taxis, never on time." Emilia's hair was loose with the white streak snaking over her shoulder; her smoky eyes and signature red lips complimented it.

"I've ordered you a drink," Selena said as the earlier waiter delivered a second complimentary glass of fizz to the table, and another deposited two tumblers of red liquid.

"Vodka and cranberry. You remembered."

"I've become quite partial to it." They each picked up the menu but hadn't a chance to look at it when there was a commotion on the steps, as a petite blonde tumbled down. The restaurant fell silent.

Selena was out of her chair in an instant and helped the woman to her feet. She guided her towards a spare chair at the table. "Are you all right?" she asked, watching the young woman brush down her fashionably torn jeans before tucking in the copper-coloured blouse that stretched across her small breasts, the nipples showing she was braless.

"It's these bloody shoes," both Selena and Emilia looked down at bare feet with pink painted toenails inside a pair of Alexander McQueen double buckle punk mules. "When I saw them in London, I just had to have them, but they didn't have my size, so I bought the next size up and this is the second time I've tripped in them. But will it stop me wearing them, will it buggery." The woman blushed and then said, "Sorry, didn't mean to swear."

"If I'd just fallen down steps in front of a packed restaurant, I'd do more than swear," Emilia said, offering her hand, "Emilia Hart. I think I saw you earlier near the cathedral with shopping bags."

"Yes, I'd been buying a few pieces for my autumn wardrobe. Sorry, where are my manners?" she shook Emilia's hand and said, "Melanie Rothman."

"This is my friend, Selena," Emilia nodded towards her. "Would you like a drink?"

"What are you two drinking?" Melanie was now sitting with her knees tucked under the table.

"Vodka and cranberry," Selena said, noticing the light reflect from a small gold stud in Melanie's nose. "Have you eaten?"

"Not yet. I'm staying at the sister hotel across the road and decided I'd give this place a try."

"Why don't you join us?" Emilia said, looking at Selena. Her eyes asked if it was okay and Selena smiled a yes across the table.

"So, where are you ladies from?" Melanie asked as a waiter delivered a fresh round of drinks to the table. Selena explained she lived in Derbyshire, and Melanie said she was from Worcester. "We're not near the river, so luckily, we don't get flooded when it rises. What about you Emilia?"

"Saffron Walden."

"Nice..." Melanie said. "Is that where saffron comes from?"

"I don't think so," Selena said, a smile itching at the corners of her mouth.

"Crocuses," Emilia said, "I believe saffron is a crocus stamen."

Melanie laughed. "Looks like my expensive boarding school fees weren't in vain." Polite amusement followed before she continued, "I love your dress. I thought at first you were Milanese." Emilia smiled as Melanie spoke. "I can't wear anything long, because I'm so short, I look like a goblin in a chocolate box bow. Mind you, the Italians are so stylish."

"I'm not so sure. Style is on its deathbed, what with the birth of sports casual wear."

"How do you mean?" Melanie drained her glass.

"The younger generation seems more influenced by music videos and celebrity culture. Gone are the sharp suits and pressed shirt fronts, replaced by low-slung jeans and jogging bottoms."

"In fairness, the top designers have branded sportswear now."

"Money Melanie. It's all about money. If the younger generation wanted to wear pizza boxes, then the likes of Gucci and Prada would produce their own range."

Dinner was divine. Expensive but divine. Scallops with a lemon and caper sauce, vitello tonnato with a sun-blush tomato salad, and as they waited for dessert, Melanie asked them if their husbands were with them in Milan. Emilia said Iain was in London, while Selena said Andrew was in Shanghai. "A work thing."

"Interesting," said Melanie. She caught the waiter's eye, held her glass aloft, and showed him three fingers. "I wish mine was in Shanghai… without a passport. Husbands," she pouted. "At least a vibrator doesn't want conversation afterwards, and you can lock it away in a drawer."

"I could cheerfully lock mine away," Selena said, blushing.

"Me too," Emilia said, and with their refreshed glasses raised, they chinked again as three plates of crostata frutti di bosco arrived. After they had ordered digestivi, the waiter cleared their dessert dishes and leaving, he gave Selena a wink, spotting it Emilia sighed and said, "Sometimes the Italian men are walking stereotypes."

"As I've said before, I've sworn off men," Selena said. "Why would I want another one?"

"Me too," Melanie added, "I'd rather be bobbing for apples in a deep-fat fryer."

"Here we are three like-minded ladies with one thing in common."

"What's that?" said Selena.

"Isn't it obvious? We'd all be much happier if we were single."

"We could divorce our husbands." Selena's eyes opened wider, as if the idea thrilled her.

"I'm not giving half of what's mine to the waste of space I married," Melanie said.

"Men always get the better deal," Emilia said before swallowing the last of her drink.

"It's a shame we can't kill them off." Selena said, then rose from her seat and added, "More drinks, everyone."

4

~ Melanie ~

Melanie shook her head as she looked down at the gravel strewn across the outdoor mat. She knew how it had got there. Putting her key in the front door, she paused and took a breath, wondering what she'd find on the inside. Experience had told her it wouldn't be good. Seeing the trail of dirty boot-prints walked into the hall's cream carpet, she left off surveying the rest of the house until she'd put away her purchases from Milan.

After removing the tags, she hung the clothes in her bedroom. Dresses to the left, skirts, and trousers on the right with another wardrobe housing her vast assortment of blouses, these were what she called her function clothes, suitable for formal affairs and family dinners. A third wardrobe held her everyday wear. Designer jeans folded and placed on shelves, funky shirts on hangers with shoes below. Some of these items, although fashionably distressed, had to be arranged neatly, because Melanie liked order. In her heart, she wished for the rest of the house to be as organised and tidy upon her return, but she knew that would be too much to ask for. Closing the wardrobe door, she left the bedroom and headed downstairs to see what state her home was in.

Before leaving for Italy, there hadn't been a cushion out of place, no dishes in the sink; even the dishwasher was empty and cleaned.

The bathrooms were fresh and floral scented and now,

after just three days away, the bathrooms – even hers – smelled like she imagined an abattoir to smell. Towels on the floor, indescribable stains, yellow water inside the toilet bowls and toothpaste on the mirrors. "Well, at least Paul has cleaned his teeth, even if his underpants were now lying on the floor where he'd stepped out of them."

Her nostrils flared and her mouth puckered when she entered the sitting room. A mess of newspapers and PlayStation cables littered the carpet, evidence that Paul had had friends over to play FC24 or some other computer game. One of her merino wool and cashmere throws lay discarded, a yellow stain, she assumed to be curry sauce at odds with the cool cream of the herringbone.

Her body craved caffeine and walking into the kitchen, she was dumbstruck at the sight that greeted her. Foil trays and takeaway containers littered her travertine work surfaces. A trail of rice led from the microwave to the sink where stacked dishes looked like a child's endeavour at rocket making. The top oven door to the Aga was open and what looked a home cremation lay inside, charred and blackened. She picked up her Italian coffee maker and looked inside; it was full of black, noxious smelling sludge. It was all too much.

No surprise.

But too much.

Emptying what looked like stale, cold pee into the sink, she knew she'd have to resort to instant coffee.

As the kettle hummed, she thought back to how she had got together with Paul. He'd been an exciting prospect when she had met him more years ago than she cared to remember.

She was sharing a small, boxy flat with Chrissie; a girl she'd met a few months before. Chrissie, who worked at the local stables, was full of confidence and experience. She swore and smoked and often had boys staying over, her noisy lovemaking keeping Melanie awake. Chrissie was so different to the shy and naïve Melanie and this made her exciting to be around.

One evening while lighting a cigarette, Chrissie said, "I need you to do me a favour."

"What?"

"I've got a date on Friday with a lad named Jez. I'm meeting him in the King's Arms but he's bringing his mate along, so will you come with me to keep him entertained?"

"What, like on a date?"

"No, just so his mate, Paul, isn't sitting with us like a gooseberry. Please say you'll come."

And after more cajoling, Melanie agreed to Chrissie's request, making it clear she was not romantically interested in her date's mate.

The bar was a fog of cigarette smoke, sticky carpets and voices, conversations that were comforting to the ears, the sound of sociability. The girls spotted Jez and Paul standing beside a fruit machine, watching as a man, still in his work overalls, fed coins into the slot and pushed the button to set the reels spinning.

Leaning on the bar, a nervous Melanie said, "I like your new top."

"It's what's under it Jez will be more interested in," Chrissie laughed. She had already pointed out to Melanie that the landlord couldn't care less if they were underage. Melanie had just ordered half of cider for Chrissie and an orange juice for herself when Jez sauntered over.

"Let me get those," he said. "Why don't you girls find us a table?"

"I'd like a pint," Chrissie said before walking away.

Sitting in a banquette that had seen better days around a copper-topped table, Melanie smiled as the boys joined them with the drinks. Chrissie's face fell when she saw that her half hadn't upgraded to a pint, and she shuffled over as Paul squeezed himself between her and Melanie.

The evening went well, Melanie thought. Jez was the

quiet one, while Paul told some of the rudest jokes she had ever heard, but she laughed in all the right places and it seemed to please him. Chrissie flirted with Jez, laughing at his work-related anecdotes. Later, Paul said he'd get another round in and Melanie offered to help him carry the drinks back.

"Your mate's getting on well with Jez," he said as they waited at the bar.

"Yes, seems that way."

"Maybe it's his finger action."

"What do you mean?" Paul nodded towards their table and Melanie could see Jez had a hand beneath the table. "What's he doing?"

"He's fingering her. No wonder she's smiling." He gave a small laugh and Jez looked over towards them both and winked as if confirming the action taking place beneath the table.

They arrived back with the drinks, and Jez's hand was back in view. Chrissie said she needed the toilet and the two girls rose and went together. As she sat on the loo, Chrissie told Melanie she wasn't too keen on Jez. "He's okay, but not proper boyfriend material. Rather common, but I bet he's like a skinny dog in bed."

"What do you mean?"

"All prick and ribs." Chrissie laughed as she flushed the toilet. Melanie behind the closed door of her cubicle shook her head in disbelief.

After last orders, the boy's walked them home and at the door Paul asked Melanie if he could see her again, she turned to speak to Chrissie who was several steps behind but she and Jez were sucking at each other's faces while his hand was now up her top. "Sure," she said, "that would be nice." Paul leant in and tried to kiss her and she pulled away.

"Sorry," he stammered.

"It's okay, you just startled me." His head moved towards hers and their lips met and she moaned a little as his tongue entered her mouth. Later that evening, when she told Chrissie about the kiss, she said, "French kissing, he must be really into you."

"Do you think so?"

"Next time he'll have his hands on your tits." Melanie blushed, making Chrissie laugh. "Where have you been until now, Mel? A nunnery."

"St Columba's Girls' Boarding School," Melanie laughed. "Might as well have been a convent."

"So, didn't you get a sex education?"

"Sort of. Sister Norma told us 'when you get married', a man plants his seed to create the miracle of a new life."

"Bloody hell, it's shagging not sowing courgettes."

The sound of gravel skittering against the front door brought her back to the present. Paul was home. Looking through the window, Melanie watched as he got out of his car, his mobile pressed to his ear. The door opened, and he strode into the hall without removing his shoes and made his way into the kitchen where she was standing. "Must you brake so hard on the drive?" Melanie said.

"I'm on the fucking phone," Paul replied.

Feeling her annoyance rising, Melanie picked up her coffee and made her way upstairs. She was sitting at her dressing table when the door opened and Paul entered the bedroom. "Good trip?"

"Yes, it was nice." Knowing he wasn't interested, she didn't go into any details but said, "I've only been away for three days and the house looks like a bloody bombsite."

"Chill out Mel, can't a bloke get some time to just be a…" he paused, "a bloke."

"Does being a bloke mean you lose the ability to clean up after yourself?"

"Shut up Mel. You've only been back five minutes and you're pecking my head as usual." He turned and left the bedroom and stomped downstairs. The front door slammed shut and, hearing the engine turn over, she watched as he reversed forcefully out of the driveway, scattering gravel into the floral borders. Melanie's blood boiled and she screamed into a pillow.

5

~ Don José~

Selena smoothed the arnica cream over the bruises on her arms where Andrew had held her while he'd shouted into her face. His trip to China hadn't been as successful as he'd hoped and so he used this as an excuse to blame her for all the problems in his life and their marriage.

On the day of Andrew's return, she'd set about furnishing each downstairs room with flowers and scented pot-pourri to create a welcoming space. She'd even bought him a bottle of his favourite whisky as a welcome home gift. He'd sent a text earlier saying that he had cleared customs, despite a horrendous wait in passport control, and now his taxi was late. His message had made her heart race, and she noticed her hand was shaking as she poured him a glass of whisky in readiness.

She was already waiting anxiously in the hall, listening for his taxi. Headlights filled the hall with light as it arrived, and she took a deep breath as the front door opened. Andrew gave her a half smile as he walked inside and she watched him place his hand luggage down before removing his shoes and stepping inside his slippers. He walked over, kissed her briefly, just a peck on the cheek, and she revealed the glass of amber liquid she was hiding behind her back. "I bet you could do with one of these," she said.

"Too right," he replied, taking the whisky and swallowing it in one mouthful. "I'm off for a shower. Can you put my things in the washing machine?" he nodded towards his carry-on luggage before he passed back the glass and set off up the stairs.

As the washing machine began its cycle, she stood and listened to the sound of the shower upstairs. She tugged at her bottom lip and nervously fidgeted with her hair, hoping the water would soothe him and he'd return in an amenable mood.

Hearing him come down the stairs, she began pouring him another drink. She didn't hear him enter the kitchen and walking up behind her; he placed his hands on her shoulders and she flinched. "What's wrong?" he asked.

"Nothing. You startled me. I didn't hear you come in." He lifted her hair and kissed the back of her neck; standing behind her, he couldn't see the anxiety stamped across her face. "I've ordered in dinner from the Star of Bengal. I know how much you like their food. Why don't you sit down and I'll put it in the oven to warm through."

Dinner was pleasant. She drank a glass of chilled Sauvignon Blanc and Andrew replaced his whisky with lager. He told her all about his trip, how he'd travelled for three hours to an appointment where the dealer hadn't bothered to turn up. "Good job really. I saw Colin Brook... Remember Colin?" Selena nodded. "A few days later, he told me that Mr Tung, our trader, had been arrested for selling counterfeit goods."

"Looks like he did you a favour not turning up."

"Still cost me a bloody fortune on a round trip with nothing in return." His volume rose, causing an unwelcome flutter in her chest. "Anyway," his voice calming, he continued, "Enough of my disastrous trip to China. What did you get up to in my absence?"

"I did a little shopping," she said then told him about her visit to the duomo and art gallery, she omitted the drinks and dinner with Emilia and Melanie, knowing he'd make a fuss, thinking she'd arranged in advance to meet up with friends – Andrew wasn't keen on Selena having friends he didn't know, or hadn't vetted.

She opened another can of lager for him before clearing away the dinner dishes. "Are you trying to get me drunk?"

"Not at all," she answered a little too quickly.

"Is there something you're not telling me?" his voice remained calm. It was this calmness at the start of his rages that frightened her the most, asserting his control. "Are you sure you were alone in Milan? You weren't meeting a man, were you?" He tried to make his question sound like a joke, just an inconsequential remark topped with a smile.

"Of course I wasn't meeting a man. I've told you I went on my own."

"Long way to go on a shopping trip."

"And to do some sightseeing. I've always wanted to go to the Pinocoteca. It was…" her voice trailed off. He'd stopped listening to her and resumed with his own conversation until they retired to bed.

Lying beside him, she could feel his stiffness, the tension in his body that was mixed with alcohol. Once again, he brought up the subject of her being with another man, a regular accusation of Andrew's. His voice grew louder and more aggressive with every denial she made. Her protestations seemed to fuel the impending rage, and she pulled back the duvet and got out of bed.

"Where the fuck are you going?"

"I'm going to sleep in the other bedroom."

"No, you're not. Get back into this bed. Now!"

Selena did as he asked, and after pulling up her nightdress, he rolled on top of her. She lay there as he went through the motions, momentarily her mind and body shut down.

"Does your lover like doing this to you?" he said through gritted teeth. Selena refused to answer, wishing he'd finish and roll over and go to sleep. "Does he?" he shouted. His hands were around her arms, pressing down and pinching her flesh. "Well, does he, or do you do other things with him, things that you don't do for me?" his breath was hot against her face as he spat out each word. His breathing became ragged and his thrusting more urgent, and then without a sound, he finished and rolled off her.

Selena waited until he had fallen asleep before she pulled her nightdress down, turned over, and noiselessly wept.

~ ~ ~

After preparing breakfast the following day, Selena was listening to Radio Three. The station was concluding a program of highlights from Carmen. In a jealous rage, Don José, the disgraced soldier turned bandit, had stabbed Carmen. Looking up, Selena saw Andrew standing in the doorway, watching her before he walked over and opened the fridge. With his back to her, she glanced across at the knife block on the counter and then again at her husband. She felt nothing for him, not even anger. Her heart was empty.

6

~ Emilia ~

When the letter written in a hand, she was unfamiliar with had arrived, Emilia became intrigued. Upon reading it, her interest turned to anger. It was from Selena explaining that she couldn't call as Andrew checked her phone regularly, even to the point of having her request an itemised bill. The letter had started off cordially, thanking her for the lovely time they had had in Milan and for buying dinner, but quickly it documented Selena's experience since she'd returned. The letter had also stated that Andrew would be away again at the weekend, and so she was 'escaping' to a cottage in Cumbria for a few days. "I can't bear to be in this house even when he's not here," she had written. The letter closed with, "I enjoyed our chat in Milan. It would be nice to continue it at a later date."

Later, Emilia re-read it and realised that Selena was asking her to come to Cumbria. She turned over the last page and written on the reverse was the name of a cottage and an address. She recalled the conversation the three of them had held in the restaurant in Milan, and after checking her calendar, she made plans. But first, there was something she needed to do.

Mundane tasks had occupied the rest of her day. The grocery shopping and bed linen change hadn't taken her mind off Selena's words and, despite being in a stale marriage herself, she searched herself for a way to help her new friend.

Arriving home that evening, Iain saw an overnight bag in the hall. "Are you going somewhere?"

"Tomorrow. Just a weekend away, a friend is having an impromptu birthday bash."

"Sounds like fun. What's for dinner?"

"There's a shoulder of lamb in the oven."

"Great, I'll grab a shower and be back down," Iain left the room then called back, "By the way, I'll be away this weekend, too."

As he stepped out of the shower, he was surprised to see Emilia packing his overnight bag. "Which shirts would you like?"

"What are you doing?"

"I'm packing your bag for you. You've had a busy day, so I thought I'd save you the trouble." Iain patted her on the bottom, told her she was a good wife, and, turning away, her nostrils flared in anger. She thought, good wife indeed, I've been more than a good wife to you over the years.

They sat down for dinner, Iain poured two glasses of a Montepulciano and held his up and said, "To you, have a good time with your friends." Emilia smiled back and lifted her glass in response thinking, no doubt you'll be having a good time too.

Emilia cleared away the dishes as Iain poured two generous glasses of brandy and they retired to the sitting room. "How has work been?" she asked.

"The usual, over-priced legal reps and idle trades. What have you been up to?"

"Not much, just pootled about in the garden and did a little grocery shopping. I was chatting with the woman in the Post Office earlier and she told me that the academy is looking for teaching assistants."

"Bloody thankless task, if you ask me," Iain took a swig of his brandy, "remember when we met, you said you wanted to be a teacher? I bet you're glad you didn't go down that road now."

"I –"

"Think about it, all that studying wasted standing up in front of a roomful of ungrateful fucking teenagers." Iain finished his brandy in one gulp and opened the bottle to pour another. "So, what's planned for this birthday bash?"

"Just drinks, then dinner, then more drinks, I guess. It'll be nice to meet everyone."

"Anyone I know?"

"I don't think so, love."

"Never mind, I'll be stuck in town, endless meetings with the accountants." Emilia became irritated when Iain referred to London as 'in town' as if he was a Londoner himself, but rather than show it she made to return to the kitchen and asked if he'd like some cheese and crackers, "I picked up a nice piece of Stilton in Waitrose today."

"Sounds nice," Iain said.

Walking into the kitchen, Emilia thought, meetings with the accountants, my arse.

7

~ Truth Be Told ~

The drive from Saffron Walden had been long and uneventful. Traffic on the A14 had moved along slowly, at its usual trudging pace. Cars and lorries; huge caterpillars with no apparent urgency. The central reservation was, as always, littered with plastic bottles filled with noxious yellow liquid tossed out of cabs by lorry drivers on timetables that didn't allow for regular toilet breaks. The M6 had also been dreary, almost at a standstill and so when she was able, Emilia had taken the toll road, leaving much of the tailback behind. Now as she left the motorway and continued on her journey, the dual carriageway slimmed down to a single road and then a rural lane with a 'please drive carefully through our village' sign. She stopped and switched on her sat nav and the automated voice told her she was ten-minutes from her destination.

The cottage was at the end of a single-track, bordered on one side by hawthorn hedging and on the other, fencing that afforded views over a collage of countryside.

The holiday rental was situated alone, with an open aspect of the valley. Built from a local stone with mullioned windows and a recessed door covered by a wooden canopy, it looked both inviting and set apart.

Pulling into the drive, she saw two cars and parking alongside; she checked herself in the rear-view mirror before opening the door and climbing out.

She was stretching, easing away the hours of driving, when the front door opened and Selena stepped outside, followed by Melanie, who stood behind her. That explains the second car, she thought before a combination of hugs and air kisses preceded her entry inside.

"It's like stepping back in time," Emilia said, taking in the tiled fireplace, cottage suite and abundance of dark wood furniture. Selena took her overnight bag while Melanie stepped into the kitchen then called, "Tea or coffee?"

"Is that the best you can do? There's a bottle of vodka and a carton of cranberry juice in my bag."

Melanie popped around the door jamb brandishing a bottle and carton, and said, "Great minds and all that jazz."

Over drinks, sitting in a high-backed armchair, the kind that nursing homes seem to have in abundance, Selena said, "I hope you both didn't mind me writing to you. I needed to reach out after Andrew's return and... well, you know what happened."

Emilia and Melanie listened as she gave them a litany of similar experiences she had endured over the years. "I know people say that women in my situation should just face up to it and get out, but it's not as simple as that."

"Not everything is black and white," Melanie said, reaching over and squeezing Selena's knee.

"In the past, afterwards, he would be remorseful. Full of apologies and swearing he'll never do it again. Now he says nothing, he's indifferent."

Selena removed a tissue from under the cuff of her cardigan and patted at her eyes.

"I used to hope he would change. But nothing ever changes. Now I'm no longer looking for him to change. I'm hoping he will go away on business and never come home. I don't even care why he never comes home, just as long as he is out of my life for good."

"Let me refresh everyone's glass," Emilia said, "and then we can have some lunch."

"Sorry to dull the atmosphere," Selena said.

"Nonsense. After we've had something to eat, we can take a walk in the fresh air, maybe."

"Blow away the cobwebs," Melanie added as Emilia collected the glasses.

July had arrived with highs of twenty-four degrees and the three friends donned sunglasses but left off jackets as they strolled along the lane towards the brow of the hill. In the hedgerow, lesser knapweed flowered, its purple crowns buzzing with hoverflies. Cornflowers and buttercups floated in the flaccid breeze, their yellow and blue heads complementing each other.

Melanie was striding ahead and stopped abruptly and gasped as the others joined her. Below them was Esthwaite Water, a smaller lake than its nearest companion, Windemere. "Look how peaceful that is," Melanie said.

Walking towards the lake, the sheep grazing on the bank moved away from them and ducks noisily entered the water. A footpath led them to the water's edge and a bench. They sat together in silence, just looking at the glassy surface of the water. Emilia wondered who the nearby moored boat belonged to, briefly fantasising about an idyllic life in the embrace of nature. But she knew life wasn't that simple and that when they returned, it would be her turn to tell the others about the failings within her marriage and her loathing for the man she had married.

Each of the women held their breath as a heron landed nearby, its head erect and its grey wings coming to rest. It waded into the shallows, the long neck stretching forward until abruptly its head shot under the surface of the water, returning with a small silver fish in its beak and the women inhaled again.

Back at the cottage, Selena fixed the drinks while Melanie poured crisps into a bowl.

"I've not known anyone named Emilia before," Melanie offered the crisps, and Emilia took a handful.

"It was mother's idea," she said. "I'm named after Iago's

wife in Othello."

"And she had a horror of a husband too," Selena said, handing out the drinks.

"Oh, the irony," joked Emilia. "Mother was an English teacher at a secondary school, and my father a university professor. They introduced me to the classics, Shakespeare and Marlowe. The Brontës and Wilde and once, I had dreamt of following in their footsteps."

"But you didn't?" Melanie asked. Emilia shook her head, and Selena asked her why.

"Iain happened. How dreams diminish when love enters the heart. We met by chance at a friend's engagement party, and despite his yobbish behaviour, I found myself attracted to his ambition. He had plans, had his future mapped out. We soon became a couple, and I realised he had the drive, but not the ability to make it happen. I recall confessing to my mother that I would help Iain achieve his goals."

"And how did she feel about that?"

"She just smiled and quoted Sophocles, saying, the most beautiful human deed, is to be useful to others. Mother was like that, forever sprinkling her speech with literary quotes.

"Iain's dream was to develop property. To build a portfolio of rentals, but his educational ability let him down. So we teamed up and worked on his idea together. At the start, I was hungry for success. As fired up as he was. We began our first project with him managing the tradespeople while I looked after the accounts. By the time we had married, we already had three small rental properties." Stopping to take a sip of her drink, she looked at the faces of her new friends, noting that they were focusing on her words.

"Years passed, and the business changed. My role became reduced as Iain moved into a partnership that focussed on property development on a larger scale."

"Did you think of going into teacher training at that point?"

"I did, but Iain said that it was too late and that he thought younger graduates would always be preferred over me. So I just accepted it and went about filling my time with the mundane and became a stay at home wife."

"That's a real shame," Selena said picking up the vodka and pouring herself another glass, only to stop when she realised she was the only one of them who had finished their drink, she blushed and Melanie necked her glass and held it out for a refill and Emilia mirrored her.

"The company has been very successful and Iain has never denied me anything, but it's not his dedication to the business that I detest."

"So, what's the beef?" Melanie said.

"It's two things. One is his attitude towards women. He's a serial shagger, always has been. If it's not a piece of skirt from his office, it's an escort he's hired to help make stays at hotels more entertaining."

"What a rat," Melanie said.

"How do you feel about that?" Selena said, less judgemental.

"At first it bothered me, but now it doesn't. I think it's rather sad to tell the truth."

"So, why do you stay with him?"

"The business."

Emilia took a sip of her vodka and cranberry and continued, "I've worked just as hard as him to build up our portfolio. I negotiated deals with councils and landowners, builders and contractors. I'm not prepared to get a pittance of a payout in the divorce courts. Lately he's opened new bank accounts."

She paused, thinking before continuing.

"Why I'm not sure yet, but I will find out. But I have to be careful. I can guarantee one sniff of a divorce lawyer and Iain will shift the assets around faster than a kestrel on a vole, hiding the truth from me and reducing my alimony."

"How do you know he hasn't done that already?"

Melanie asked.

"Because he doesn't trust anyone, not his partners, accountants, lawyers, none of them. He's unaware that I know all of his passwords and so I can log into his balance sheets and bank accounts. For the past two years, I've been keeping copies of everything. The funny thing… well, not actually funny, but strange, is he's not even aware that I'm privy to his extra marital proclivities." Emilia laughed, a knowing laugh that told the others that she wasn't a victim in this situation.

The timer on the oven pinged, putting a stop to Emilia's tale and so Melanie laid the table while Emilia refreshed their glasses. Selena served up fat portions of shepherd's pie with roasted carrots and the dinner conversation was light. They discussed TV shows they had watched recently and Melanie talked about a current shopping trip to Cheltenham to purchase a handbag to match the boots she'd bought in Milan. The dinner ended with them laughing after Selena told them that a freak July hailstorm had spoiled her village's summer fete.

After washing and putting away the dishes, they returned to the sitting room and two expectant faces looked at Melanie. "So, what's your marital gripe, then?" Selena said as she put a CD into the player and Take That played at a discrete volume in the background.

"Blackmail." Emilia and Selena looked at each other, their faces expectant and open.

"So," Melanie continued after taking a large gulp of her drink, "I knew Paul was a wanker even before I married him. A waste of oxygen, my father had said, but I was determined not to have a husband chosen for me from a 'suitable' family – for suitable, I mean boring. Well, not exactly boring, but traditional, you know the sort, boarding school, rugby and a job in the city." Melanie gave an outrageous fake yawn, her humour brightening up the mood in the room.

"Paul was funny, exhilarating, dangerous, everything that the boys in our family's social circle weren't."

Another fake yawn.

"I knew he'd never amount to much. How he had kept his job as a mechanic for as long as he did was beyond belief. Forever turning up late or hungover, if he bothered to turn up at all. In Paul's world, there was always something more exciting to occupy him than the everyday existence everyone else seemed to just get on with. My marrying him was fifty per cent adventure and fifty per cent two-fingers up at convention. When we got married, Paul was happy to flit from job to job, living in a world supported financially by his wife and, to be honest, life wasn't too bad. Things changed when my father went from being a local councillor to becoming an MP. A few months later, Paul stopped working all together, and then one day out of the blue he said he wanted an allowance from my father to buy his silence about, in his words, 'dad's dodgy property deals and council backhanders.'"

"You're right," Emilia said. "He is a wanker."

The three women nodded their heads in agreement, exchanged smiles, and sat in silence, digesting each other's revelations.

The CD ended and Melanie breathed out, "Thank God for that. I bloody hate Take That. Paul imagines he's like Robbie bloody Williams, the class clown, the comedian, the loveable rogue, when in all honesty he's just an arsehole." Selena laughed, a raucous, hearty sound that encouraged Emilia to join her, and in the middle of the laughter, Melanie said, "So, are we going to do it, then?" The room went silent, and they all looked at each other as if daring another to speak first. "Selena's idea in Milan."

"Well," Emilia said, "I, for one, would relish the idea of Iain being disposed of, leaving our fortune intact."

"Me too," Selena said. "Not Iain… Andrew."

"It would take a lot of planning."

"Are you serious, Emilia?"

"Yes, but let's have some time to mull it over and meet up again in, say, a week's time. What do you think?"

"What harm can our thinking about it do?" Melanie said.

"None," added Selena.

"Well then, that's settled. We'll take some time out to think about... let's call it, for now, erasing our problems. Let's reconvene in a week with our decisions."

"Until then," Melanie said as she raised her glass and laughed, "To dead spouses." Emilia held her drink aloft and repeated the salute while Selena remained silent.

8

~ Burner ~

A driver in a Citroen flashed and Melanie crossed the oncoming traffic and drove through the gates into a yard where she pulled up alongside a portable cabin. The building behind looked derelict. Possibly neglected for years; its doors and windows covered with metal security shuttering. Sited in a rundown area of town where the houses were visibly empty and shops boarded up, Melanie double checked the central locking had activated as she left her car. This wasn't an area where expensive cars usually parked.

Emilia had already mentioned that the address was one of Iain's current projects. "A council funded, white elephant. A proposed regeneration area where there is no visible CCTV."

Pushing the cabin door open, Melanie saw Emilia and Selena sitting on white plastic patio chairs and the table minus its umbrella was between them. Selena looked up from her phone to acknowledge Melanie, while Emilia unscrewed the lid from a flask and poured coffee into a plastic mug. Dragging a spare chair over, Melanie sensed an air of awkwardness as she watched the other women. Selena's scrolling, and Emilia's fiddling with the flask. It felt like each of them was waiting for the other to speak first.

"The traffic on the ring road was murder," Melanie said, and then chuckled, "Sorry if that was an unfortunate turn of phrase."

The cloying silence evaporated, and Emilia said, "Okay. So we're here to talk about our thoughts and any decisions we've made regarding our marital situations. I'm sure the both of you haven't travelled this far to drink lukewarm coffee from a plastic beaker. So what have we decided?"

"You're making it sound quite formal," Selena said, her attention finally in the room rather than her screen.

"If we say no, then this ends here," Emilia added.

"Emilia's right. We have to talk about this sensibly," Melanie said, "Especially if we plan to get away with it. So, I'll get the ball rolling. I have given it a lot of thought and I'm happy to go ahead if it's what we all agree on."

"Me too." Selena whispered as she pulled her sleeve down to cover her wrist. Melanie spotted the fresh bruise.

"We need to be confident, but not cocky, and certainly not complacent." Emilia said.

"I agree," Melanie added, "and for what it's worth, I've thought long and hard about it and think I need to let you all know my reasons for wanting to do away with Paul. It is more than just his being a tosser."

Selena glanced across at Emilia and shrugged and Emilia nodded and said, "If you feel comfortable telling us, then we'll listen and what we all need to remember is, each of us has a valid reason and there is no need for any of us to be judgemental."

"Agreed," Selena said.

Melanie placed her handbag on the floor, placing her car keys beside it and said, "I think I have to tell you why I'm ready to become part of this plan."

After taking a deep breath, she told them briefly how she had met Paul, talking about her friend Chrissie and his mate, Jez. When she paused, Emilia gave her an encouraging smile. "Before Paul started his shit, he was working on and off as a labourer for a reclamation company clearing a derelict site, a disused factory."

Melanie nodded when Emilia said, "Similar to this one."

"Yes. One day, Paul came home saying the site was going up for sale. My father was a local councillor at the time and, after looking at the location, he suggested it would be ideal for a small housing estate. But being a member of the local planning committee, he couldn't bid for the contract because of a conflict of interest. Long story short. I set up a company and put in a bid that was accepted and, using my father's money, we built on the site and made a tidy profit from the sale of the properties. We thought that, that would be it. But then a patch of green space owned by the council came up for sale and was open to tenders. Once again, I bid and won the contract and we built three properties, one of which is the house that we now live in."

Melanie needed a minute to think before she continued with her story, so she paused and took a sip of her coffee.

"Paul was interested in the business and I let him help me. Nothing taxing, just some simple admin, and at first it was great to be working alongside him in the office. He fooled everyone though, working so closely he was well aware of my father's involvement in the planning applications and tendering process, and yes, before anyone says anything, we knew what we were doing was illegal, but as my father had said, it's a dog-eat-dog world and we need to look out for number one. Paul did his research about our involvement and made sure his own actions were not unlawful. 'I'm just an office boy,' he called himself when he first suggested being paid for his silence."

"What did your father say?"

"He tried to point out that he was part of our family, but Paul just scoffed, saying he'd not grown up with an enviable bank account like I had and being part of the family, he needed his own recompense. So, as you can see, he has us over the proverbial barrel and divorcing him would be disastrous."

"Wouldn't it be a case of his word against yours?" Selena said and Melanie shook her head.

"My family's bank accounts were used to siphon all the funds to and from a bogus business listed at Companies House, where I'm detailed as the owner of said property development company. It's an open and shut case of fraud. What started off as a get rich quick scheme has snowballed into a nightmare. I'm just glad my mother isn't alive to see the mess we're in." Melanie sniffed loudly and Selena handed her a tissue.

"I suggested buying Paul's silence, but my father dismissed him as a snake and someone we couldn't trust. He said that none of Paul's promises would provide us with any security, because a snake may shed its skin, but underneath, it's just a bigger snake."

Following Melanie's revelation, the room remained hushed until Emilia said, "Thank you Melanie, it was very brave of you to tell us your story. And without taking away from your experience, I can say that it's remarkably similar to mine now."

"Has something happened?" Selena asked.

Emilia nodded, rose and opened the flask again. Melanie and Selena declined another coffee, leaving Emilia to pour one for herself. "I've discovered Iain has been moving money from the primary account recently."

"Could it be for a new project?"

"I don't think so Melanie, he's moved it via a foreign exchange company, so chances are it's out of the country already."

"What will you do?" asked Selena.

"There's nothing I can do. If I mention it, Iain will know I am still accessing the company accounts and keeping tabs on him. I need to make sure I can take over the business and stop him. I just need to be as devious as Iain."

"Looks like we actually all have a good enough reason to do away with the bastards we married." Melanie said, "So, getting back to the business at hand, how do we envisage our plan taking shape?"

"I think we should each focus on one of each other's husbands rather than our own," Emilia replied. "That will enable us – the wives' to develop cast iron alibis."

"How will we do it?" Selena said.

"I think that's something that we should keep to ourselves. Too much knowledge might prove dangerous and we can't let anything trip us up." Melanie said.

Emilia agreed. "We will need more preparation too," and reaching inside her handbag, she removed two small mobile phones. "I've taken the liberty of buying us all one of these."

She handed them out.

"Burner phones. Pay as you go. I used mine to arrange this meeting with you both and from now on, this must be the only way we can contact each other. We must delete each other's phone numbers and addresses from our other phones. Melanie, you must destroy the letter that Selena sent. There must be nothing to link us together, no matter how small."

Emilia put her burner and private phone on the table before showing them they were both switched off. "One thing to be aware of is, if you are going to use the burner phone, turn your other phone off. Better still, leave it at home. You don't want both phones registering on the same mast at the same time. It's tricky, I know, but just give it some thought." She gave the two women a look to make sure they'd understood her. "We have to be conscious of CCTV and public spaces. Remember, no electronic communication, from now on apart from through these phones. Once we have achieved our goal, we can get rid of them."

"Emilia, you're very organised," Melanie said. "Anyone would think you've done this sort of thing before."

"I grew up reading Agatha Christie, so know the pitfalls of not planning. Besides, it's just common sense, really."

"Perhaps we should use disguises. Something real,

nothing silly like false noses and moustaches," chuckled Melanie, pulling a comedy face. "Wigs, sunglasses, hats."

"Spot on, we'll need to give this some serious thought, like Melanie says it's got to be believable."

"Who is going to get who?" Selena asked, her question causing the conversation to halt coldly, leaving them all looking at each other for an answer.

"I have an idea," Melanie said. "We could each write our husband's name on a piece of paper, fold it up and pick one out. Call it a husband lottery."

Each of the women took a sheet of paper from Melanie and wrote a name on it and folded it in half. "Okay," Melanie picked up a cement covered bucket, "Here we go."

"What if we pick our own husband?"

"Then we put it back and pick again."

Emilia and Selena looked at each other, neither one wanting to go first and so Melanie took control and dipped her hand into the bucket and removed a piece of paper, opened it and showing it to the others she said, "Andrew."

"So, that determines the other choices. No need for us to pick now." Selena said.

"Come on, pick. It's more fun this way." Melanie shook the bucket like a fundraiser in a shopping centre.

Emilia went next, showing her paper to the others. Following suit, Selena chose the last one and revealed it. "What next?"

"I'll have a think and be in touch in a day or two about the next stage." Emilia said, tucking her piece of paper inside a pocket in her jeans, while Selena folded hers into a small square and put it inside her purse.

Without a word, they all reached across to each other and clasped their hands together and nodded their agreement.

"So it's settled. No going back now," said Melanie.

Selena was the first to leave, her goodbye barely audible, and as Emilia locked up the cabin, Melanie said goodbye and climbed into her car.

After closing the door and before starting the ignition, she unfolded her piece of paper and looked at Andrew's name again.

9

~ Picking Over Bones ~

Selena hadn't passed another car for a long time as she drove to the meeting point mentioned in Emilia's earlier text. Coming around a bend, she spotted the layby tucked away behind some scrubby bushes and spindly trees. She parked up beside the other two cars on the gravelled pathway. Emilia was sitting inside her car with the driver's door open, talking to Melanie, who clutched a green folder to her chest. They both looked at Selena as she left her car and walked towards them.

Emilia, who was wearing a large-brimmed hat and sunglasses, left her car. I see she's embracing the idea of disguising herself, thought Selena as she leant into her car and picked up the plastic wallet she'd brought with her. The thought of greeting the others with an embrace, maybe an air kiss, was forgotten, as Emilia said. "Shall we get this over and done with?" her formality dictated the atmosphere.

"I'm going shopping in Market Harborough. No doubt the traffic cameras will register my car en route, so I need to give myself a reason to be there." She placed the envelope she was holding on the car bonnet, and the others followed her lead. Melanie picked up the plastic folder Selena had delivered and, without a word, she got into her car and drove away.

Emilia handed her envelope to Selena and said, "You sure about this?"

"Absolutely." She lifted her skirt to reveal the boot shaped bruise on her thigh.

"I'll always have a reminder like this to tell me why it's essential." Taking the envelope, she said goodbye and left Emilia with the green folder. As she drove, she continually glanced at the envelope lying on the passenger seat, wondering what it contained inside. She parked her car in a city centre multi-storey, knowing that the CCTV cameras would capture her image, so after putting the envelope inside the glove compartment, she fed coins into the parking meter before walking away thinking she might buy Andrew something nice, giving herself a good excuse to be filmed."

~~~

While making breakfast, Selena couldn't stop thinking about her idea that had initially been a throwaway comment in Milan, realising that it was in danger of becoming a reality. Was she having second thoughts? What if Melanie and Emilia were having second thoughts? Andrew brought her back to the present as he walked into the kitchen and asked if she'd made coffee yet? "I have to be in Leeds by 10:00 for my meeting."

Selena pointed to the espresso pot on the stove and placed his favourite mug on the counter before cracking an egg into the pan. "Is a bacon and egg sandwich, okay?" she asked, and Andrew grunted a response as he checked the morning news on his iPad.

Looking through the kitchen window, Selena saw the postman coming along the road and left Andrew to his breakfast. She stepped outside and met him at the gate and took the mail from him. Andrew, standing at the sink when she returned, said, "What were you talking to the postman about?" her heart lurched, he'd obviously been watching her.

Why don't I ever learn, she thought, knowing any interaction with a man would create tension, regardless of how innocent it seemed. Trying to make light of Andrew's question, Selena dismissed it. "Just passing the time, the weather and stuff. Nothing of any substance."

"It must have been something. You were out there talking for over ten-minutes, laughing and flirting."

"Andrew, I wasn't flirting. He was telling me about his daughter who has joined a drama club. It's just chat, passing the time of day."

"Don't patronise me." He grabbed her and pushed her against the wall and, bringing his face in close to hers, he growled, "I bet you pass the time of day when I'm away, don't you?" Selena shook her head, the pressure of his hands making it hard to speak. "Does he make... special deliveries when I'm away? Does he? Hey!" He released his grip and picking up his keys stormed out of the house, as the front door slammed shut, she slipped down the wall resting on the kitchen floor with anger rising in her chest, lessening any second thoughts she'd been having.

More thoughts invaded her head. How had it come to this? How had her life become so tragic? Picking herself up, she muttered to herself, "I used to be a confident person, full of adventure, and now look at me. Look at what he has done to me." She was familiar with the questions that people typically asked women in her situation. She knew the answers too. The offers of advice. Leave him, escape, call the police. All the things she had wanted to do so many times, but thinking and doing, are opposite ends of the spectrum. "It's like being caged," she said as she dropped his breakfast dishes into soapy water. An image of pushing him down under the water flooded her imagination. "I have known for a long time that I need to put a stop to this, and now I know how."

Reaching behind the fridge, she removed the burner phone and envelope that Emilia had given her and, pulling on a light summer jacket, she went outside for a walk.

Walking along the leafy footpaths of the Peak District National Park eased her soul, tempered her mood. She often wished she had a dog, something to care for that would care for her unconditionally, something soft-mouthed and gentle like a Cocker Spaniel. But Andrew wouldn't let her have a dog. He'd said they were more trouble than they're worth. Besides, she couldn't spend her time worrying about a pet's safety along with her own.

With her husband back in her thoughts, she brought her hand up to her throat; it was sore, and she knew in a few hours his fingers would show as another set of bruises. With quiet determination, she took out the phone and sent a text to Emilia and Melanie that read simply:

all systems go

Climbing over a stile, she moved towards an oak and, sitting in the shade, she removed the folded envelope from her pocket and tore it open. She tipped out the contents, laying them on the ground beside her, and stared at the two photographs, a credit card statement and a list of bullet points Emilia had thought she would be interested in. She pored over the contents, digesting the information with an odd feeling of picking over Iain's carcass as she made plans in her head.

~~~

In her Essex kitchen, Emilia sat at the breakfast bar, a mug of coffee by her side and a plate of biscuits in front. She opened the green folder and took out its contents. Several sheets of printed paper and three photographs.

"So, you're the blackmailer then," she said, looking at Paul's smiling face.

In another photograph he was sitting on a ride-on lawnmower, a bandana tied around his head and a can of beer in his hand. In the background was a red brick house with two large windows on the ground floor separated by a front door flanked by two bay trees in pots: nice, but unoriginal. At least two reception rooms, she thought as her eyes returned to the subject of the photograph. Paul was shirtless, tanned, and lithe, with a glory trail of dark hair from the waistband of his shorts to his navel. She had expected a workshy wastrel to have been pasty and podgy from sitting around doing nothing. Gazing at his image, she could imagine why Melanie had fallen for him. "He is handsome in an impish way," she said aloud before dunking a biscuit into her coffee, "and we all know how troublesome an imp can be." She picked up the last photograph. It showed him holding up a pint standing beside a dart board, a typical bloke in the pub shot. It said a lot about his character.

Looking closely at the photograph of him astride the mower, she noted he had pale blue eyes fringed by long blond eyelashes. His nose was slender above thin pink lips that were parted to reveal straight white teeth. "A wanker you may be," she said to the image, "but a wanker with good dental hygiene."

Melanie had only included one page of details. Paul likes beer, darts and curry. Dislikes supermarkets, early mornings, and romantic comedies. "Sees himself as some kind of rebel, does he?" Emilia whispered to herself. The rest of the document listed the places he visited regularly. Emilia noted that most were pubs or clubs, she guessed to play darts and drink beer.

Melanie had also listed Paul's favourite Indian restaurant and his preferred meal. She had also underlined, Usually has a delivery as can't be arsed to fetch it himself.

And one piece of information proved very useful. Paul has a peanut allergy.

~~~

Melanie had opted for a visit to her local spa to study the

contents of Selena's plastic wallet. As she lay on a lounger wrapped in a thick towelling dressing gown, she popped open the press-stud and removed a sheet of paper. It contained similar information to that she had printed out about Paul, giving details of antique fairs that Andrew would visit, including the flights he had booked for the next few months. She removed his photograph, and to disguise it, slid it between the pages of her paperback. She looked at the face staring out from between the pages of the latest bestseller. Andrew had thin, arching eyebrows that looked cosmetically shaped and heavy-lidded eyes that gave him a brooding countenance. Definitely the look of a wife beater, Melanie thought, although she knew hostile partners didn't come in a one size fits all.

Selena's information about Andrew told her when he wasn't at work, he rarely strayed far from the family home, choosing to stay home with his wife rather than socialise. He hadn't any real preferences regarding entertainment or hobbies, his life seemed to be mostly work and keeping Selena close.

Melanie looked at his work address thinking, that will be the best place to interact with him. Could be a godsend, she thought, as long as he hasn't got some nosy office assistant.

The idea of undertaking the role of a killer was exciting Melanie. It was almost as if she was in the pages of the book on her lap. She was aware she'd have to keep a rein on the thrill she was feeling, but for now she was enjoying the planning process. I need to figure out how to dispatch him, she thought – 'dispatch.' – get me, I even sound like a hit-woman now.

Google would probably have information on ways to kill someone. Even authors must look online for ideas, but Melanie knew that would be a stupid road to go down. Maybe I could use an internet café, she thought, then dismissed that idea too because of the possibility of cameras and IP address trails and other electronic shit she didn't understand.

"Is that any good?" a woman in a white robe asked, cutting into Melanie's thoughts. Realising she was asking about the book, Melanie told her she'd only just started it, so couldn't really say. "I'll maybe borrow it from the library. Have a lovely day." The woman sloped off as Melanie could almost feel the idea saturating her brain with electrical pulses.

"The local library," she said, then looked around and lowered her voice as she made her way to the changing rooms. "They'll probably have a good reference section I can exploit in my search for the ideal way to kill someone."

10

~ Iain ~

Iain stepped from the shower wearing just a towel; his commitment to his health and the years' had been good to him; he could still tie a hand towel around his waist. Not an inch of body fat hung from his fifty-one-year-old toned frame. His wet hair was shining like jet and taking the towel away to reveal the manscaping below his waist as fashion dictated, he dried his hair. Shaking it until it fell into a tousled mass of black spikes. After admiring himself in the full-length mirror, turning to view himself from different angles, he smiled. Some would say an arrogant smile, but it was a self-appreciative one. He knew he looked good. Growing from an awkward teen into a handsome man, Iain had grown to accept that women, and a handful of men, judged his look attractive. He pulled on a robe and sat down at the dressing table he shared with Emilia and squeezed out an inch of male moisturiser and applied it to his face; he brushed his eyebrows, adding a small amount of gel to keep them in place and after rubbing some product into his hair, styled it. Happy with his work, he dropped the robe and pulled on a pair of bamboo boxers, rearranged his bulge before sitting and then slipped his feet into the Ted Baker socks he preferred.

Dressed for the office, he walked into the kitchen, slid his arm around Emilia's waist, and planted a kiss on the back of her neck.

"Your coffee's on the breakfast bar," she said as he moved away and opened a jar of honey sitting waiting for him beside two slices of wholemeal toast. "Will you be home for dinner tonight?"

"Sadly not, my love. I've a very early meeting tomorrow, so I'll be staying in town tonight."

Looking away from him, her nostrils flared in annoyance and she said, "Very well. Would you like me to make up an overnight bag?"

"No need, my love, already sorted one out." He outstretched his arm and waggled his hand towards her, beckoning her closer. She took his hand. He pulled her closer and said through a mouthful of toast, "What do you have planned for today?"

"Nothing much. I need to do some grocery shopping, but other than that, maybe curl up with a book."

"Here, treat yourself." Iain removed a fifty-pound note from his wallet and dropped it onto the table.

"Thanks." Emilia leant in and kissed the top of his head as a car horn sounded. "Your car's here."

~~~

The offices at Hart Holdings Ltd were mostly glass, tall windows that revealed the people working inside. Iain left his driver and walked into the building with the confidence that only the man in charge would have. He smiled at the blonde behind the reception desk as she welcomed him. "Morning Kerry. How was your mother's birthday?"

"It was lovely, Mr Hart. she said to thank you for the flowers."

"My pleasure." Iain knew how to keep his staff happy, especially the female ones. Who knows where a little bonus could lead?

A young man with large, round spectacles that made him look like a mole rushed to meet Iain at the top of the escalator. "Mr Hart, the contracts you requested are on your desk."

Looking at his watch "Twelve hours late. Is that a record for you, Richard?"

"I … err …" the man stammered.

"Better late than never. Now how about getting on with what we pay you for." Richard nodded; his eyes lowered submissively before he rushed away.

Iain's private office made a statement. It showcased his success. A large, dark wood desk with green leather inlay dominated the space. The modern executive ergonomic chair looked out of place with the gilt-framed pictures and walnut filing cabinet, but Iain didn't care for aesthetics. A previous injury to his back made sitting for long periods uncomfortable. A knock at the door sounded, and it opened noiselessly and stepping inside, a petite brunette brought him a coffee and set it down on the marble coaster on his desk. "Thank you, Tori," he said, rearranging his crotch area beneath the desk. He knew not to overstep the mark in the modern climate but couldn't help enjoying the vision of his assistant.

"Adrian Graham's on line one Mr Hart. I told him you were busy, but he insisted …"

"That's okay, put him through."

Iain picked up the telephone and listened to his works manager before he said, "I pay you to manage the grunts, so fucking deal with them or I'll find someone else who can." His way of speaking to the male construction workers was very different to his style with his female office workers. "So I suggest you sort out that wanker on the Forest Street job before I lose my patience."

Phone calls took up most of Iain's morning. One to book a room at the Hilton for the night, others to discuss the possibility of new projects. A knock sounded on his door and Tori entered the room. Iain watched her cross the room as he had done many times before. Tori was an excellent personal assistant, and he thought the fact that she was easy on the eye was a bonus. She was a tall, slim brunette of twenty-six with grey eyes and a blunt bob that gave her the look of a runway model. Her skirt was suitably short and her blouse just tight enough to show off her breasts. There was no doubt in Iain's mind that she was deliberately dressing for his pleasure. One day maybe we'll take our meetings further, he thought, but for now he listened as she told him he was up for a business award at a gala evening in a few months' time.

Iain grinned and said, "Keep the evening free Tori," he made sure he stayed the right side of office decorum, "Maybe I'll take a few members of the office and we can enjoy some decent champagne together… if you fancy a night out." She dipped her eyes coquettishly and left the room.

"Not done badly, have I?" he said to the faded photograph on his desk. It was him standing alongside his two brothers, the brothers who hadn't achieved much. Being the youngest, Iain always felt he had to prove himself, and he attributed his success to the desire to be the best he could be. This was a constant with everything in his life, his business, his bank balance, his love of women. He never wanted to settle for second best. No one could deny he loved Emilia; they'd built this empire together and for that he'd always be grateful, but life moves on. He had the successful business and the glamorous wife, but was it enough? Lately, he'd craved something darker, business that wasn't tied to the constraints of legality, and he found he also needed to satisfy his desire for paid, casual companionship.

~~~

After showering, Iain walked naked from the hotel bathroom into the bedroom. He dried himself off and, after a liberal dousing of expensive male cologne, surveyed himself in the mirror. Puffing out his chest, he touched himself, grinning at his arousal. The blue pill he'd taken with a measure of whisky was doing its job. He stepped into a pair of dark blue trousers, arranging himself down one leg before pulling on a Ralph Lauren polo shirt.

Iain was ready to leave when there was a knock on the door. It opened to a wiry man with a baseball cap and torn jeans; he stepped inside and exchanged a small plastic bag of white powder for some folded banknotes and left. Iain dipped a finger inside the packet and rubbed some of the powder over his gums before picking up his phone and room key and leaving the room.

Walking into the hotel bar, he saw that Chloe, the girl he'd booked for the evening was waiting for him at a table, a slender glass filled with champagne in her hand while on the table was a tumbler of whisky in readiness for his arrival. She rose from her seat and smoothed down the backless sheath dress she was wearing as he walked over and, kissing him on the cheek, she handed him his drink. His eyes rested on her cleavage and noticing this, her painted mouth opened and the tip of her tongue touched her top lip seductively.

11

~ Culture Club ~

It had been a long time since Melanie had visited a library, and the smell of floor polish and books took her back to her schooldays. She'd never been an avid reader; her literary digestion was the occasional best seller in the spa or a trashy glitz-lit novel beside a holiday swimming pool. What with shopping and her insatiable desire for designer clobber, she had little time to pick up a book.

Paul was a reader; she'd come home to find him slouched on the sofa with his head buried in a thriller. During one of her petulant moods, she'd once accused him of using reading as a way of avoiding talking to her and, as the years progressed and her feelings for him had waned, she was grateful their interaction had dwindled.

Walking between the aisles of books, she imagined avid readers would feel like they could breathe in every printed word, absorbing the stories between the covers. The romanticism of literature wasn't of interest to Melanie. She was here for one reason. Research.

For effect, she occasionally stopped and removed a book from a shelf and flicked through the pages, letting the aroma of paper and countless readers' fingers wash over her. She found the quiet of the library calming, and this helped ease the trepidation she felt about the task at hand. Remembering how hard she'd studied, learning the tendering procedure and how to converse with the local council, she would apply this method to her research on oriental antiquities.

Leaving the first floor, she headed up the stairs to the non-fiction library. There were more people here than in the fiction section. Students were sitting at tables scribbling notes into jotters, old men reading newspapers and people working at the bank of computers on the far wall. Looking up, she followed the section signs: Languages. Travel. Accountancy, until she reached the one for the antiques and collectables section.

Selecting an encyclopaedia and a book on Chinese collectables, she took a seat at the table in the centre of the section and started scouring the pages. Surprised to read that an 18th-century Imperial porcelain 'poppy' bowl had sold for $21.6 million, she assumed Andrew must be onto a money spinner. Further on, she saw prices like this were rare. She became interested in a statement about Chinese businessmen who were actively seeking to repatriate ancient artifacts. They were buying back their culture, meaning that since the mid-2000s prices had crept up. Using her phone, she took photographs of pages until a library assistant tutted at her, making her put the phone away.

"Next time I'll bring a notebook, but for now I'll check this one out," she mumbled to herself and returned the encyclopaedia to the shelf. At the self-checkout, she scanned her new membership card and, smiling, she left the library sufficiently pleased with her progress so far.

Back home, Melanie was eager to begin her research. Sitting at the kitchen island, she opened the library book, flicking through the pages as she ate her lunch. One point the author of the book mentioned stood out to her: 'the industry is populated with unscrupulous dealers, therefore anyone thinking of investing in Oriental antiquities should protect themselves by doing as much research as possible.' "That's what I'm doing," she chuckled, knowing that she'd need to do a lot more study than just glancing at pages and prices of Chinese pottery.

After her visit to the library, she had gone into town,

where she found a shop specialising in second-hand and refurbished electrical items. Melanie purchased a reconditioned smart phone before calling into a phone store to purchase a Pay as You Go SIM card. After she'd charged the battery, she switched it on and waited for it to find a signal. "Time to find what I'll need to know if I'm going to join your club," she said and typed 'Andrew Cavendish Antiques' into the browser.

The results led her to his webpage, where his smiling face beamed out from the screen. The heading read, 'Andrew Cavendish Oriental Expert.' "What qualifications do you need to call yourself an expert?" she said aloud before popping the last of her rosemary focaccia into her mouth. Chewing, she hummed as she scanned the pages of the site that were filled with pictures of elaborately decorated vases and bowls, some with prices attached.

Suffering from porcelain overload, she skipped to his bio. Andrew described himself as an ethical trader, one who was committed to helping the people in the east to regain their stolen heritage. There was a paragraph talking about his recent travels to return treasures usurped by buyers abroad.

"I don't believe you," Melanie said, remembering what she had heard from Selena. "If that's true, then why are you travelling to the Far East to buy antiques to sell in the UK? You're a fucking liar."

"Who's a fucking liar?" Looking up, Melanie saw Paul entering the kitchen. She hadn't heard him arrive home. "So, who's a liar?"

"No one, it's just something I've read in the news." She closed the screen down and palmed the phone.

"If it was a politician, then you can guarantee they're a liar. I'm certain they have to pass a dishonesty test before they're accepted into Parliament."

"Maybe you're right," she gave a nervous laugh.

She excused herself, saying she needed to wash her

hair, and in the bedroom, she found a hiding place for the new phone. When she returned to the kitchen, Paul was flicking through the library book. "What's this for?" he said without looking up.

"Just something I got from the library."

"You thinking of going into the antique business?"

"No," she laughed, slightly forced but hopefully convincing. "There was a vase on that antique show where celebrities buy pieces and then sell them on to make a profit. I was certain my mother had one similar. So, was just checking... you never know, we could have a secret fortune."

"Be nice to get a surprise pay-out, eh?"

"It would've been, but sadly I was mistaken," she laughed again. "No cash in the attic, after all."

"Oh well, it's not like we need the money, is it?" He closed the book and stood up. "Don't bother making me any dinner. I'm off to the Roebuck."

"Again?" Melanie disguised her pleasure with fake disappointment.

"I need the practice, babe." He grabbed his car keys and, without another word or a glance, he left the house.

~~~

The drinkers had gone home. Paul was standing behind the bar of The Roebuck with Ken the publican. Used, empty glasses covered the bar top and Ken was loading them into plastic dishwasher racks while Paul poured himself another pint of lager. "Do you mind if I stay for another hour to throw some arrows?"

"Not a problem, mate," Ken said, carrying a rack of glasses into the utility room behind the bar.

"We've lost two matches in a row to the team from The Fleece and there's no way we can let the bastards make it a third." Paul put his drink down and picked up his darts and moved to the board to practise his throwing.

"I'm knocking off for now. Stay as long as you need, and just one more pint. Understand."

"Okay mate."

The first hour passed quickly, with Paul's aim becoming less effective with each pint he drank. Since Ken had gone upstairs, he'd helped himself to another pint and a cheeky whisky chaser. Everyone who knew him knew that was Paul's nature; he was one of life's takers, a man who believed the world owed him a living. Most of his friends had said at some point that he was lucky to have hooked up with Melanie and her family's pot of money.

At first it was just about pulling the posh girl, he'd heard that boarding schoolgirls were gagging for it, but that hadn't been the case with Melanie, her continuous refusal meant that as a horny teenager he had to indulge in one-night stands. But somewhere along the line that all changed, and he found he was falling deeper into something he'd never experienced before and although he knew it annoyed her father, Paul became committed to his daughter. Melanie's father despised Paul's poor upbringing, being born to a single parent and living off benefits in a council flat wasn't what he saw as marriage material for his daughter. Melanie's mother, however, had been more forgiving.

Like most young couples, money wasn't as important to Melanie and Paul as their love for each other, and they set a date to marry. "How will you pay for it?" his future father-in-law had asked.

"Isn't it the bride's prerogative to have her big day paid for by her father?" Paul's off-the-cuff comment, aimed as a joke, annoyed Melanie's father and he had read more into it than intended. And over the years, realised that his suspicions about his future son-in-law were correct.

A text alert on his phone coincided with Ken's entrance into the bar. "Don't you have a home to go to?" the publican said, rubbing his eyes. "I'm ready to lock up."

Paul checked his phone and saw the text from Melanie told him she was in bed and not to disturb her when he finally came home. "The missus, saying she's off to bed."

"Shouldn't you be with her?"

"Nah, I'm okay here." He threw another three darts.

"I don't understand you," Ken said, pushing a glass under an optic. "You've a beautiful wife at home, and you choose to be here every night with a group of fat blokes playing darts." He handed Paul a glass, and they both moved to sit at a table.

"I'm still in good shape," Paul laughed, throwing his head back and patting his flat stomach. Considering he was in his thirty-seventh year and his exercise regime consisted solely of darts and a diet of junk food and beer, he'd remained lean.

"Look, you're a nice bloke. I just worry that you'll lose that cracker of a wife if you don't pay her enough attention."

"She's fine. Besides, she'll never dump me. She knows what side her bread's buttered." A smile hid the real reason behind his innocuous comment, and Ken got up to fix two more drinks.

"Last one, then off you go. I need to lock up and get to my pit.

"Not seeing Rita tonight? Paul said as Ken returned to the table.

"Not tonight. I've a delivery due first thing in the morning."

Paul downed his drink, stood up, and put his used glass on the bar before picking up his car keys.

"I'm not sure you're okay to drive?" Ken said, seeing Paul shamble over to the exit.

"I'll be fine. There are no cops around this time of night."

The door closed behind him and he made his way over to the solitary car in the car park. Illuminated by the interior light, he made a phone call and ordered a pizza for home delivery. Driving home, he passed Jez's garage and something caught his eye.

He pulled over. "Melanie can always answer the door to the pizza guy," he told himself.

12

~ Venom ~

Tori immediately addressed Emilia as she entered the office. "Mrs Hart, I didn't know you were coming in today."

"I was just passing and needed to see Iain. Is he in his office?"

"He's out at the moment. A site inspection." She looked up at the clock. "He should be back soon. Would you like a coffee?"

"No thanks, Tori. I'll just wait inside for him."

Emilia pushed open the door to Iain's office, knowing that as soon as the door closed, his assistant would be on the phone to tell him she was here.

The room didn't look any different from the last time she had been there; it changed very little. Iain was very tidy and so there was no administration detritus on his desk, the telephone and pen tray was in the same position it always is, the only thing out of place was the overnight bag, a small square aeroplane carry on case under the window, behind his chair.

Picking it up and placing it on the desk, she opened the zipper and instantly caught the aroma of perfume. "Jo Malone," she said, "At least a decent priced fragrance."

She ran her hand down the edges of the case and pulled out a hotel receipt, not sure why she needed to see it. The transaction would show up on his credit card statement at the end of the month.

Closing and replacing the case, she moved across to the sofa and sitting she waited for her husband.

"Hello darling," Iain said minutes later as he entered the office. "This is a pleasant surprise."

"I was just passing and wondered if you'd be free for lunch."

"Afraid not. Up to my eyes in it today."

"That's a pity. I missed you last night."

Iain looked at his watch. "I could do a quick drink if that'll suffice?"

"Will you be coming home for dinner tonight?"

"Sure... I'm really sorry... You should have told me you'd be coming."

"It was a spur-of-the-moment thing." She watched as Iain removed his jacket and slipped it over the back of his chair. "What's this mark?" she said, reaching over and rubbing at a lapel.

"What mark?"

"Probably just brick dust. Could you ask Tori to fetch some water?" Iain did as instructed and as he popped his head around the door, Emilia reached inside and removed his wallet and slipped it into her jacket pocket. Tori stepped inside with a cup of water from the office cooler, and Emilia went through the pretence of cleaning Iain's jacket.

"There, that's got it."

"I'm still okay with a quick drink?" Iain said.

"Not to worry. I can keep myself amused. I'll see you at home." She kissed him on the cheek and asked if Tori could watch her handbag while she used the facilities.

In the toilet cubicle, Emilia opened Iain's wallet and scoured the business cards until she found what she was looking for. She photographed it with her phone, replaced it, and made her way to collect her handbag. "It's been lovely to see you again, Tori." She dropped Iain's wallet onto the floor, where it fell noiselessly beside Tori's desk. "Iain tells me your sister's wedding went well."

"Yes, thank you, Mrs Hart. She had a lovely day." Emilia said farewell and made her way outside towards the

Tube.

Ordering a takeout cappuccino, she looked at her phone and noted the number on the business card she'd photographed. She paid for her drink and went back outside, took out her burner phone, and dialled the number. After a couple of minutes, she had the answers she'd hoped for, then made her way to the next place on her list.

~~~

The library was a grand-looking building and walking over to the enquiry desk she asked for the department she was looking for and thanking the assistant, made her way across the tiled hallway into a large room with uniformly arranged shelving. Finding the cookery section, she selected a book and took a seat, and removed a notebook from her handbag.

"Making something nice?" Emilia looked up to see a woman carrying a stack of books.

"Hopefully."

"We don't seem to get many enquiries for recipe books nowadays. I think people just find what they're looking for on the internet."

"I find a screen isn't as good as an open book beside a mixing bowl."

"Exactly. The downside for me, though, is scraping off the food fixed to the pages of returned books," she chuckled.

"I imagine so." Emilia remained polite, but internally she wished the woman would leave her in peace.

Finally alone, looking at the Indian cookery book in front of her, she noted the names of all the recipes that contained peanuts.

Looking at the ingredients, she thought that she'd rather buy a ready-made sauce than bother mixing spices. She made several more notes before returning the book and making her way to another section.

In the library's medical section, Emilia chose a book about allergies and scanned the contents page for the section on peanut allergy. Like most people, she already knew a little about anaphylaxis, information gleaned from news reports and television dramas, but she was interested to learn how the protein in peanuts reacted with a body's antibodies. Discovering that sufferers needed to be treated quickly, she copied a phrase that read, 'peanuts can contribute to shock by causing production of C3a, which stimulates macrophages, basophils, and mast cells to produce platelet-activating factor and histamine.' She didn't fully understand it, but assumed it was a serious red flag. Looking through the list of symptoms, she made more notes before putting the book back and walking towards the exit, where she made a mental note to add a bottle of peanut oil to her shopping list.

Outside the library, she walked around until she found a bake shop and made her way over. Pushing open the door, she joined the queue at the counter and waited until the girl in the hairnet asked if she needed help.

"I wonder if you can help me. I'm taking some sandwiches into work, but I know one girl has a peanut allergy. Can you recommend anything nut free?"

Emilia listened as the girl in the hairnet told her about different products, then she leant forward conspiratorially and said, "To be honest, I wouldn't take the risk. We can't really guarantee our kitchens are nut free."

"Have you ever seen anyone have a reaction?"

"Oh yes," looking up and seeing no other customers were waiting, the girl launched into a tale about a previous customer with a nut allergy. "Luckily, she had her EpiPen with her. I thought she was going to die on the shop floor." A bell rang and a new customer entered. Emilia thanked the assistant and made her way out of the shop.

"So far, today has been quite productive," she told herself as she walked away.

Looking at the three foil trays on her kitchen worktop, she found the aromas coming from them enticing, even though she couldn't distinguish any difference between the two curries she'd ordered. "I can't believe I'm forty-nine and I've never had a curry," she said. Removing cutlery from a drawer and opening a tray of pilau rice, she spooned some onto a plate. "Which to try first?"

The man at the takeaway had been helpful when she'd told him she was a curry virgin and made some suggestions. She had dismissed his suggestion of a korma, thinking the creamy almond sauce wouldn't be to her taste and so opted for the ubiquitous chicken tikka marsala and a slightly spicier palak. The tasting began gingerly, a small forkful at a time, and it wasn't long before she found she liked what she had ordered, favouring the lamb palak over the sweeter chicken one.

Hearing the front door open, she looked up as Iain walked into the kitchen. "What's that awful smell? Is it Indian food?" he said, without so much as a welcome for his wife. Emilia showed him the plate of curry. "Would you like some?"

"Why would I want that foreign muck? You know I can't abide the stuff," he said before leaving the room and going upstairs to change out of his suit.

Emilia knew her husband wasn't very experimental with food, he was in his own words a traditional meat and two veg man, his only concession being when entertaining clients he'd opt for a French or Italian restaurant, more for show than preference.

As Iain took a shower, she stepped outside and scraped the remnants of the takeaway into the garden waste before returning and liberally spraying the kitchen with air freshener.

She used to wish Iain would be more adventurous, but now she accepted that he'd never change. It was almost as if he'd been born in a time warp. Everything he did at home had a 1950s slant. Almost as if his being the sole provider gave him a feeling of male superiority. In theory, he had been a good husband thus far, and she'd turned a blind eye to his indiscretions because it was easier to go along with them than create an inharmonious home life. Does that make me weak? She had previously thought but concluded that she was happy with a simple life, as it gave her the personal freedom she required. Hearing the shower stop, she played her part in this time slip episode and removed the stopper from the decanter and poured him a tumbler of scotch.

Iain joined her in the sitting room and dropped into his chair and, handing him the glass, Emilia asked, "Good day?"

"It was okay. Started out as a normal day, chasing up lazy contractors, then after your visit I had to deal with a huge potential problem with a labourer on the Islington job."

"Why? What happened?"

"There's been a past problem with vermin on the site and the team came in to fumigate the building and a young labourer entered the downstairs and was seriously hurt. The foreman hadn't put up the restriction signs."

"Bloody hell, sounds serious."

"It was, but they got him to hospital. Hydrogen cyanide is a serious chemical, it could have been worse. Needless to say, there's a foreman out there looking for a new job."

"At least you have Tori to take over the mundane tasks for you?"

"Yes, she's worth her salary. But you know me, I prefer to be on top of things myself. That way, I know what's what. No chance of temps slacking off." Emilia nodded. "Trust isn't always a two-way street in the construction game. There's always some get-rich-quick chancer trying to crawl up your trouser leg to get at the jewels."

He drank his whisky in one gulp and added, "What's for dinner? Not bloody curry, I hope," he smiled to let her know his mood from earlier had mellowed.

"There are a couple of sirloins in the fridge if you fancy a steak?"

"Sounds good, any chance of another?" he held out the empty glass and as Emilia refilled it, he picked up the remote and the TV came to life with the latest news.

After dinner, Iain retired to his study. Emilia heard the door close as she loaded the dishwasher. He would be in there for most of the night. Working? Maybe. Who knew? Not wanting an evening sitting in front of the television, Emilia took herself off and ran a bath and as she relaxed beneath lavender scented bubbles, she thought about Paul, knowing she wanted to use the fact that he had a peanut allergy to her advantage, but knew she needed to know more about the condition. "I can't risk doing research on Google," she told herself as she lifted the wineglass from the side of the bath and took a sip. "Maybe a visit to the village library tomorrow. I could find more information there."

The thought of ending someone's life wasn't as frightening as Emilia had first thought it might be. Her relaxed attitude surprised her. It felt almost as if she was looking through the eyes of someone else, maybe a playwright or novelist.

"Didn't Shakespeare see off four characters in Hamlet to poison?" she muttered to herself, and recalled that in Ovid's *Metamorphoses*, the mighty Hercules had begged for death after being poisoned by the blood of Nessus.

She smiled and said to herself, "Paul's death needs it to be subtle. No blood and gore, nothing easily traced forensically." After taking another drink of her wine, she said, "Then, venom, to thy work!"

13

~ Andrew ~

After disconnecting the call, Andrew slipped his phone into his jacket pocket and rubbed his hands together. A wide smile formed on his face. "That's another deal in the bag," he said as he rose from his chair and left the office for his lunch appointment with Nigel.

Initially meeting at an auction, Nigel had been working with Andrew for a year now. During a bidding war for a vase Nigel had leant into Andrew and mentioned that he was looking to go into business with someone who specialised in Asian artefacts, upon hearing this Andrew had jumped at the chance to work with him. Nigel's role was to source antiques and Andrew's was to buy them at rock-bottom prices and move them on for an inflated profit. Andrew liked him and assumed the feeling was mutual. Sometimes he'd make a remark, a sideways comment that made him feel Nigel didn't trust him. Maybe he felt he would fleece him in much the same way he did the unsuspecting sellers that Nigel delivered to him.

Nigel would scour online forums and the small ads posted by people wanting to shift family treasures for a quick cash payment. He'd spend most of his time visiting small auction houses and antique shops and then pass on the information to Andrew.

Nigel's animated and charming demeanour didn't convince Andrew that he was loyal. He was everything a con man needed to be and judging by the car he drove; he must either work hard or he was also trading in tandem with other dealers to support his lifestyle. A lifestyle as a teenager Andrew had always dreamt of achieving.

He'd often thought he should be more like Nigel. It would save him the twenty per cent commission. The problem was Andrew was just too lazy and he didn't have the time or the inclination; it seemed too much like hard work to source new stock.

~~~

The bistro was busy; the room buzzing with conversation. Waiters moved efficiently from table to table, taking orders and delivering plates of food. Andrew leant on the bar and ordered two bottled beers before carrying them over to where Nigel waited for him. "Should be champers, but these will have to do," he said, as he put the bottles down.

"What are we celebrating?"

"I've had a good morning, finally shifted that bloody Jingdezhen copy for three times the price I paid for it."

"One born every minute," scoffed Nigel, before taking a slug of beer.

A waiter arrived at their table, and as Nigel requested a bottle of wine, Andrew watched him. He always looks good, Andrew thought. Nigel was wearing an immaculately pressed two piece suit and Andrew noticed the gold cufflink peeking out of the suit sleeve. He's obviously making more money than I am. As usual, he found it difficult to suppress his jealousy and picked up his beer and chugged half of the bottle in one go.

"I've been talking to an old dear who has some pieces she'd like to sell." Nigel said.

"Good prices?"

"You bet. She hasn't got a clue what they're actually worth, so should bring in a handsome profit once moved on."

The waiter was back at the table opening the wine and Andrew watched as Nigel tasted it before he confirmed it was good enough. Once again, jealousy surfaced, but Andrew quickly quelled it as he watched the waiter pour the wine and Nigel lifted his glass in a toast, and said, "Here's to making money."

"To partners in crime," joked Andrew.

"Partners."

The lunch was pleasant; they chatted about future appointments, and Andrew talked about his recent disastrous trip to China.

"That's a real bummer," Nigel said, "but this might cheer you up. I'm looking at a pair of Kutani bowls later. The seller says his grandfather bought them back from Japan in 1918. More than likely, he smuggled them out during the postwar confusion."

Across the room, a police officer in uniform approached the bar, and Andrew's mind wandered away from Nigel's story. The officer was speaking with the barman and this reminded Andrew of his dream as a teenager to join the force. "What do you want to become a pig for?" his father had said. "More trouble than it's worth, dealing with drunks and criminals."

"Brandy?" Nigel's request cut through Andrew's thoughts and he politely declined, said he had a long drive ahead of him. "You're probably right. I'd better get going, actually." He stood up and, after throwing enough notes onto the table to cover the bill, said, "I'll send the details about the Kutani over to you later."

"Sure, looking forward to it."

Andrew didn't watch Nigel leave; his eyes were back on the police officer.

His mind slipped back over thirty years to an untidy kitchen where his father was arguing with a policeman. The police were regular visitors to his family home, dealing with his father's drunkenness and his mother's black eyes.

Maybe he wouldn't make it into the force, but Andrew had vowed to show his father he was better than him.

"Am I though?" he muttered to himself as a waitress cleared the table. She looked at him, but he ignored her. The anxiety he felt swirled in the pit of his stomach. He'd become fearful lately that he was becoming the man he had grown up hating.

The wine with lunch had dulled his senses, and he took the rest of the day off. Driving away from the bistro, he took a detour to visit Gordon, the man responsible for turning his life around.

Pulling up outside the modern, faux-Tudor property with its gravelled front garden and cottage garden layout, it looked, as Andrew knew, at odds with its rich, antique filled interior. Gordon was outside dead heading roses. Hearing his name called, he looked up and after wiping his hands down the front of his jeans, he and Andrew shook hands.

"What are you doing around these parts?"

"I was in the area and thought I'd drop in."

"Always good to see you. Drink?"

"Coffee would be great." Andrew followed Gordon around the side of the house and took a seat in the shade overlooking a verdant manicured lawn surrounded by borders of colourful perennials. "The garden's looking good," he called. "Retirement must suit you."

"Need to keep busy," Gordon said, standing inside the open patio doors, "Stops the joints seizing up. I'll put the kettle on." He disappeared inside for a few minutes before reemerging with a tray. "How's business?"

"Oh, you know. Up and down."

"Talk is that you're making quite a name for yourself in the Asian market." Gordon lifted the coffeepot and poured the dark brown liquid into matching ornately decorated coffee cups, which made Andrew think his old master hadn't lost his appreciation for beautiful things. "I'm glad things are going well for you."

"I'd be happier with a higher turnover."

"Show me an antique dealer who doesn't want more." Gordon joked. "I remember when you first came to work for me. Right tyke you were, thought you knew it all."

"You soon put me straight. Weeks of dusting, polishing and making tea before you showed me how to catalogue things. I loved it, though."

"You were an attentive student, always asking questions, always eager to learn."

"A marked change from university. I was lucky to scrape through with a third."

"Aye, when you first started working for me, we sold everything from tat to genuine antiques, and you quickly absorbed the training. You seemed to enjoy the interaction with both customers and staff alike and early on it became apparent the job suited you. I recall the first time I let you loose on the auction block."

"I was as nervous as…" Andrew stopped himself from swearing. Gordon wasn't a fan of coarse language.

"It didn't take long for you to gain the confidence to coax bidders to dig deeper into their pockets, and you were soon handling the gavel with ease."

"I'm so grateful you supported me, especially when I set up on my own."

"Taught you everything I could and as they say, once a bird has fledged, it must fly away to make its own way in the world."

"I wouldn't be where I am now if it hadn't been for you."

"Come on, stop gushing lad," Gordon said with good humour. "Sun's moved position. Do you fancy a cold drink?"

With Gordon inside the house arranging drinks, Andrew thought back to how he'd cheated him. He'd met Bridget, and she had been the perfect stooge. Attractive, but not so much as to raise suspicion. When he was at the block, she would bid on the items he asked her to and then manipulate the sale. This went on for a year, and while Bridget was happy with her seven per cent Andrew was accumulating enough stock to leave Gordon and venture out alone.

Gordon reappeared with two glasses of cold lemonade. "Get this down your neck, lad."

"Thanks, Gord. I'll have to be making tracks soon."

"Deals to close?"

"Always Gordon. Always."

Driving home, Andrew thought about Gordon. In the past, he'd often wished he'd been honest with him and not, as his age advanced, taken advantage of his good nature. He took a detour to drive past the old shop where he had first set up; it was now selling cheap household items. He recalled the day he'd signed the short-term lease on it and began selling stock at a meagre profit, using Gordon's premise of keeping the till open regularly, rather than occasionally, for a larger sale. "Remember the daft old biddy?" he asked himself as he drove away. A woman had called into his shop with a ginger jar. He'd recognised it was quality but convinced her it was worthless, buying it for a quarter of its worth. He'd made a handsome profit on its resale and his interest in oriental artifacts became aroused. Later, he moved his business to the small warehouse where it remained.

14

~ FX ~

Looking at the photograph she had taken in Iain's offices, Emilia checked the address again before she pushed open the door and stepped inside the modern reception area. The young man behind the desk checked her name and confirmed her appointment. "Mr Johal will see you in a few minutes." He pointed to the sofa under the window, signalling she should wait there, and went back to his computer screen. Emilia noticed he looked up and glanced across at her several times and she smiled back, thinking, I'd eat you alive sonny. A door to the right opened and a slim man with skin the colour of honey and soft, dark eyes beneath long lashes stepped into the room. Now, that's more like it, she thought as she watched him proffer his hand.

"Ms Lewis?" he said, his voice hanging onto a hint of his family heritage.

Standing and taking his hand, Emilia said, "Yes. Pleased to meet you."

Mr Johal held the door open for her and after he'd asked the receptionist to deliver coffee, he followed Emilia inside and gestured towards a chrome tubular chair. She removed her jacket, folded it and placed it over the back of the chair before sitting down making sure she showed just a little too much leg.

She observed him as he walked around his desk. He was trim, with a tiny waist and small, round buttocks. She took in his hair, so black it shone like oil. It touched the top of his shirt collar and as he leant forward, she caught a tantalising glimpse of the back of his neck. "It's quite warm today," he said. "Do you mind if I remove my jacket?"

"Not at all," she replied and watched as he slipped it from his body and hung it over the back of his chair. He unbuttoned his shirt sleeves, and she watched as he folded back the cuffs to reveal slim wrists and arms covered with dark hair.

"We're trying to do our bit for the planet by not switching on the air-conditioning unless absolutely necessary." He sat down and formed a steeple with his fingers and she noticed there was no wedding ring, but a very expensive-looking watch. "You said in your call you have some money to transfer and wanted to –"

The door opened, and the receptionist entered with a tray. "I'll deal with that," Johal said, and once they were alone again, he continued. "Obviously, we cannot be a party to money laundering, but you say you have substantial funds that you want to keep away from your bank's prying eyes."

"I have an amount that I'd like to move out of the country for a proposed purchase abroad," she said as Johal depressed the plunger on the cafetiere and poured two cups of coffee.

"When you say an amount, what are we talking about?" He moved a cup towards her and pushed forward the cream jug.

"Initially around three hundred thousand GBP."

"And this is to purchase property?" he asked.

"Yes, but you'll think me foolish."

"I doubt that," he said, stirring a sachet of sugar into his coffee.

"I haven't yet decided where I want to buy. It was a friend who introduced your company to me. Recommended you as being discrete."

She watched as he looked up and his eyes widened.

She'd caught his attention. "It's always good to hear when clients recommend us."

"Obviously I need to be discrete too, but she told me her husband at Hart Holdings was using you to move funds abroad for a new business venture." Emilia paused, faking alarm… "I'm sorry I promised not to mention his name."

Johal looked at her, studied her face and said, "The Spanish market is remarkably stable since Brexit." He stopped as if he'd realised his mistake and said, "Seems we've both been a tad indiscrete." He smiled, and she returned it, thinking, he knows he's playing a game.

Thankful that Johal had taken the bait and, relying upon his greed, she asked him about the process of transferring money. Occasionally, she mentioned France as a place of interest, but kept returning to Spain, citing the better climate.

Their meeting ended cordially and, leaving with a glossy brochure, Emilia shook Johal's hand again and gave the receptionist a smile.

A metre along the pavement, she dropped the brochure into a litter bin. She had got the information she had wanted and now all she needed to do was to search her husband's online history for all references relating to Spain.

15

~ Sunglasses ~

Melanie was sitting in the hotel lobby, an empty coffee cup in front of her. She watched a woman in an aquamarine trouser suit walk past. She had a silver-grey bob with a heavy fringe and eyes hidden behind oversized sunglasses. Melanie thought the woman looked elegant and to herself, she muttered, "I wish I was tall enough to carry that look off."

The lift doors opened, and the stranger stepped inside just as Melanie's phone vibrated, rattling against the coffee saucer. Picking it up, she read the text message which simply said, Room 216.

After gathering up her things, Melanie walked over and summoned a lift. The doors opened silently, and she stepped inside and selected the second floor. Within seconds, she'd stepped out into the corridor, reading the room numbers. Melanie counted backwards until she reached 216 and tapped on the door. It opened to reveal the silver-haired woman from the lobby, who said, "Hello Melanie."

"Emilia?"

"That's right, come inside." The door closed behind her, and Emilia removed her sunglasses and smiled. "I'm guessing you didn't recognise me?"

"Not at all."

"Excellent," said Emilia.

Another knock sounded on the door and she opened it and with her hair tucked up beneath a wide-brimmed sunhat and her green eyes shaded by sunglasses, Selena walked into the room. She was wearing a sage-coloured jacket that hid her shape beneath boxy shoulders and wide lapels and cream canvas trousers.

"I'd never have recognised you," Selena told Emilia, and she removed her hat and shook her hair loose. She paused before removing her sunglasses and, as she did, she waited for the others to gasp. Behind the sunglasses, she had hidden a black eye.

"What the –"

"Andrew," Selena said, cutting Emilia's question in half.

Melanie, reached into her bag and removed a bottle of red liquid, breaking the tension in the room, "Look what I brought with me, voddy and cranberry. I've pre-mixed it." A ripple of laughter fluttered around the room.

"I've brought provisions," Emilia said, picking up an M&S carrier bag and placing it on the dressing table. She removed pre-packed sandwiches, crisps, and a box of chocolate truffles and laid them out. "I've also packed a large flask of coffee; we don't want to be disturbed."

"What's in the other bag?" Melanie said, pointing to the large one on top of the bed.

"You'll see." Emilia laid out plastic cups and poured drinks. "So, Selena, are you going to tell us what happened?"

Melanie dropped into a tub chair and Selena perched on the edge of the bed before she spoke. "Andrew found my birth control pills." She looked into the other's faces, but no comments came. "I'm normally very careful with things I don't want him to see. I go to a great effort to keep him away from stuff I want to remain private, like my phone. He added a GPS tracking device once."

"Are you saying he tracks everywhere you go?" Emilia asked.

"Not any longer. I purchased a second phone and when I go out, I leave my old one on show at home. As he installed it without my permission, he's never mentioned it."

"So, how did all of this happen?" Melanie took the cup she was being offered.

"I had a headache one morning. It was a real humdinger, so I went back to bed. Andrew was supposed to be out all day, but he came back at lunchtime and he found the pills in the boot of my car. I've always hidden them under the spare wheel."

"What was he doing in your car?"

"He said he was looking for a jack, but I knew he was lying, as his car has one. He was raging, calling me a cheat and a liar. His anger rose to volcanic, and he began accusing me of taking the pills so I could sleep around and when I denied it, he punched me."

"Bastard," Melanie hissed.

"He's never hit me in the face before. My bruises were previously in places where I could hide them."

"Have you thought about leaving him?" Emilia leant forward and squeezed her hand.

"It's not that simple. He controls everything, my bank account, credit cards etc. I'm not even allowed to open my mail. He monitors my emails and checks the computer history daily. It's like being in prison, constantly being monitored. Once I came very close to bashing his brains out with a meat tenderiser, but I'm not prepared to go to prison for him."

"And you won't. That's why we're all here today. We need to discuss our plan in a little more detail. But before that, I think Melanie should pour us all a small vodka and cranberry and we can have some lunch."

Emilia steered the conversation over lunch away from their husbands and they chatted about their week, the places they'd been and, of course, Melanie told them what new designer clothes she'd bought herself.

After lunch, Selena and Emilia refused a second vodka as they were driving, but Melanie poured herself another. "I'm okay," she said. "I've come on the train."

"How did you pay for your ticket?" Emilia asked her.

"On the app on my phone."

"That means it's traceable. You need to be smarter from now on. We can't afford to have anything that connects us to a place or each other."

"Oh well, looks like I'll have to go back into town and do some shopping," she chuckled and placed the flat of her hand on her forehead and in the manner of a 1950s Hollywood starlet and said, "Oh the hardship of more credit card bashing."

"Okay," Emilia said bringing her back in line, "If you remember Melanie had the idea that we should all use disguises, hence what I'm wearing today and judging by your remarks, I suggest you both think about how best to disguise yourselves too. It will be nigh on impossible not to appear on some CCTV, so if we can change our appearances, we're at least doing our best to protect ourselves."

"You walked right past me in the lobby and I didn't twig at all." Melanie said, "Mind you, as you know, I'm not the sharpest chisel in the toolbox."

Emilia smiled and said, "It's not about how sharp people are, they'll see what we show them and that's all we need to do, portray a different persona."

"Like we're acting?"

"Yes, Mel, but no amateur dramatics. Whatever you choose, it must be consistent. No changing styles, wigs and suchlike. We need to be savvy if we want to stay one step ahead of the authorities."

"What about..." Melanie started, then said, "Selena, will you be okay hiding a disguise at home?"

"I can rent a locker at the gym and people will just see me come and go with a sports bag."

Emilia refreshed everyone's coffee cups. "I've printed out Iain's schedule for the next few weeks. Melanie, can you do the same for Paul?"

"I'm afraid it'll be tricky for me," Selena said. "Andrew is so secretive and doesn't really use a diary."

"Don't worry," Melanie said, "I've already made a plan, and once I've made contact, I'll get to know his movements."

"How?"

Emilia held up a hand to stop the exchange. "I don't think it's a good idea for us to talk over the how's and why's of what we're going to do. It makes sense to be unaware of what each of us is planning. There'll be no chance of a slip of the tongue if we're ever questioned."

"Do you think there's a chance of us being questioned?" Selena asked, worry etched on her face.

"We have to be ready for it if we are, but if we get everything right, then I doubt there'll be anything to connect us together." She rose and picked up the large bag and, pulling out a desktop shredder, she continued, "Once, we have performed our tasks. We must each dispose of the phones, destroy everything, parking receipts, everything. And as soon as we are all ready to begin, we can only contact each other if it's absolutely necessary. Once it's all over and it's safe to do so, we'll meet up again."

Melanie and Selena nodded in agreement.

"Did you bring the original paperwork as I asked?"

Selena removed her envelope from her bag, and Melanie nodded towards the plastic wallet on the bed. Emilia collected the sheets they'd shared and fed them through the shredder.

16

~ Astley House ~

Iain had arrived home in a good mood and, standing in the hallway, he put his arm around Emilia's waist, pulling her into him and kissed her cheek. "What plans do you have for tomorrow, darling?"

"Nothing. Why?" she replied.

Earlier, he had placed his briefcase on the console table and now he clicked the latches. "There's something I'd like you to see," he said, removing a glossy brochure and handing it to her.

Emilia flicked through the pages and walked into the sitting room as he removed his jacket. "Astley House," she called over her shoulder, "Where's this?"

"Near Banbury. It's been empty for a few years. It'll be a sound investment."

She was looking at the estate agent's details for the impressive country residence when he joined her and started fixing two drinks at the cocktail cabinet.

"Looks impressive," she said, scanning the images of high ceilings, plaster cornices, and windows that would need many bolts of fabric to curtain them.

"I think the property would easily convert into apartments." Iain said, handing her a drink.

"But it's a long way from London."

"London is choking on rental properties, seems every man with a cement mixer is climbing onto the rental bandwagon."

He moved to his chair and dropped into it with an end of the day sigh. "Besides, I'm thinking of making this a solo project, something separate from the existing business. I've an appointment with the agents tomorrow and I'd like you to come with me to give it the once over. You know I always value your opinion."

When it suits you, she thought.

~~~

The August sunshine made the drive to Oxfordshire enjoyable; the roads had been fairly quiet and meandering along a leafy lane with hedgerows filled with wildflowers, gave Emilia a feeling of well-being. Iain's request for her input still puzzled her. For the past few years, he had done everything alone, rarely sharing his business endeavours, let alone asking for her opinion.

Sandwiched between rows of limes that cast long shadows onto a gravelled driveway Iain drove at a gentle pace allowing Emilia to take in the woodland plants that had become established over years. Red campion flowers held on delicate stems popped with colour, surrounded by the white umbels of wild angelica that looked like it had self-seeded around.

They came around a bend and the house displayed its magnificence, and Iain slowed the car further to allow Emilia to take in the sight.

Built in red brick with a black slate roof, it stood out against the verdant countryside beyond. A pair of columns dominated the front elevation, flanking an enormous olive-green door, the paintwork sun-bleached and rain washed over time.

Emilia counted three rows of eight windows, each with frames in the same olive colour. There appeared to be four attic rooms perched on the roof with round windows, giving each one a cycloptic appearance. As the car pulled up, she noticed the side of the building was identical to the front but minus the attic rooms and with a side door that was smaller and without pillars. Between the ground and first-floor windows grew what looked like an ancient wisteria, the weight of which was pulling mortar from the walls and in need of serious attention.

A young woman stepped from a car parked out front and she made her way towards them. Iain slid out of the driver's seat, and Emilia watched as he shook hands with the woman she presumed to be the agent. They walked towards his car and Emilia got out and waited for them to reach her.

Proffering her hand, the woman said, "Pheobe Dent. Whickham and Dent Properties. Pleased to meet you." Emilia introduced herself and followed as the agent led them over to the main door. She held up a large key that wouldn't easily fit inside a lady's handbag and tried to open the door. The lock appeared frozen, and with a practiced eyelash flutter, she allowed Iain to take over.

Emilia noticed the heavily perfumed air around the house and wondered where the smell was coming from. She was about to ask when Iain opened the door to reveal the hallway. It was vast. A wide staircase curved upwards, putting Emilia in mind of the old Hollywood musicals where a leading lady would drift silently down to meet her guests. The floor's blue and white tiles complemented the pale cream walls and the plaster cornices and ceiling roses appeared to be undamaged.

"As mentioned in the catalogue, the ground floor of the property is in excellent condition," Pheobe said beginning her sales patter, "Until six-months ago the owner employed a caretaker who lived in a small self-contained flat to the left," She pointed out a door off the hallway.

"The house has been empty for twelve years, a protracted probate and family wrangling. But I'm led to believe that's now all settled."

"I'm surprised a hotel chain hasn't snapped it up,"

Emilia said.

"It's had interest," Pheobe replied, "But as it's currently being sold off market, there's been no firm offers as yet."

"I'm assuming the vendor is open to offers," Iain said, Emilia noticed his eyes resting on Pheobe's décolletage. Maybe the plunge neck, lantern sleeved blouse had been a considered choice that morning.

Emilia opened the door and walked into the caretaker's sitting room. A window took up most of the opposite wall and sunshine poured in, illuminating the space with warmth. There was a dusty but not unpleasant smell coming from the covered furniture and nicotine stained ceiling. The leftover smell of a cigarette smoker oddly gave the room a lived-in feel.

Another door led into a small kitchen opposite a large bedroom, including an en-suite shower room. "I think these rooms would make good offices for an estate manager, maybe even a live-in space," she called to Iain.

Iain entered, followed by Pheobe, who was talking about utilities and possible commercial ratings. "The property has residential status, but at Whickham and Dent we don't envisage any problems getting a change of use."

"What could you see a buyer doing with the house?" Emilia asked.

"As you intimated, it will interest hoteliers. Pheobe turned her attention to Iain. "It would make an excellent spa or wedding venue." Iain nodded as he listened.

"It would also be perfect for residential apartments, with a service charge to cover the gardens and maintenance."

After viewing the downstairs rooms, which included a large open space that was once used for banqueting and an orangery on the south side, they returned to the hall and, looking at a door recessed beneath the staircase, Emilia asked where it led. Before Pheobe could reply, she had opened it and stepped outside to discover where the airborne perfume had originated. A central bed filled with old-fashioned roses, the blooms releasing their scent into the air. "What a beautiful quadrangle," Emilia said as Iain joined her. "I guess the agent details call it a courtyard," she said to Pheobe. She knew she was being petty, but didn't care. It wasn't the woman's fault Iain was more interested in her cleavage than the room dimensions.

"The owners currently employ a landscaping company to care for the gardens and the grounds. There's a suggestion that a student who worked alongside Gertrude Jekyll designed and planted the rose bed."

"Looking at the exterior, you'd never know this was here," Iain said.

Emilia removed her phone and took some photos of the roses before they returned to look inside. The second floor was in varying stages of decay. Walls needed re-plastering, and some windows needed to be replaced. Pheobe pointed out that the roof was sound. "The owners made repairs two years ago to protect the property's integrity. They repaired the old plumbing, and it is now sound. As you can appreciate, with a property of this age, there is the need for some electrical rewiring." She explained that the wooden stairs up to two of the attic rooms were unsafe and needed to be replaced, but on the whole, it looked like the bulk of the work was modernising and cosmetic.

"Do you mind if I go back downstairs?" Emilia said.

"Everything okay?" Iain asked.

"Yes, one room looks much like another after a while. I want to look around outside. If that's okay Ms Dent?"

Pheobe nodded and directed Iain to another open door, while Emilia set off downstairs and out into the courtyard. "This place is amazing... was amazing," Emilia told herself. "I can see this working as a communal space." She walked around the rose bed that was awash with colour, hybrid teas and floribundas ranging from yellow to red and white to orange. The poorly clipped box hedges needed reshaping, and the overgrown jasmine and old woody lavender plants needed to be removed and replaced. Sitting on a paint peeling bench, she put on her sunglasses and lifted her face towards the sun, letting her mind drift away. She thought, why can't things always be like this? Why can't… Iain and Pheobe's return interrupted her thoughts.

"I'll let you both look around at your leisure," Pheobe said and looking at her watch said, "I've an hour before I need to be at my next appointment." Emilia watched as Iain shook the agent's hand, his hold on hers lasting a little longer than she considered necessary.

Walking around the house alone, Emilia watched as Iain took endless photographs and talked non-stop about what he saw. "I'm guessing it could house ten two-bedroom apartments and eight one beds and, with space permitting, the attic rooms could become studios."

~~~

Waiting for lunch to be delivered to their table, Emilia looked through the agent's brochure again while Iain checked the images on his phone. "If the price is right, it would be a sound investment."

"It needs a lot of work; the rooms need more than just a daub of plaster and a lick of paint. It will be costly and time consuming."

"We could bolster the financing by selling off-plan, and maybe for a fee customise some of the larger spaces for the client."

"That's good and well if you were to build apartments." Emilia stopped speaking as the drinks arrived.

"What else could I do with it? I know nothing about the hospitality industry?"

"I can see that Oxford is an ideal investment. Properties here are at a premium but think about the disposable income of the population. Pheobe mentioned a wedding venue. Imagine people on their big day being photographed in the quadrangle with the roses behind them. The banqueting suite would make an excellent venue for the wedding breakfast and the rooms mean you could have the wedding party on-site, meaning you can charge higher bar and food prices."

"Again. I know nothing about running a wedding venue."

"You don't need to. You could get professionals in to run the place."

"That would be expensive."

"Weddings are expensive. Besides, it could double as a conference centre and at a later date you can add a spa. Run properly, it could be a licence to print money."

Iain was quiet during their lunch; she could see he was mulling things over and as the waiter served coffee, he said. "Would you be interested in a project?"

"What sort of project?"

"Looking after the design and décor?"

"Why do you want to involve me now after so long? You've not asked for my advice or sought my input in the business for years. What's changed?"

"This is a new venture, something different from building office suites and buy to let properties. It needs a woman's touch."

"Don't you think that's an outdated phrase?"

"Maybe, but you know me. Old school and hopeless when it comes to the finer things. I just thought it would give you something to sink your creative teeth into. You might even enjoy it."

"Okay, it's pleasing to know you value my input on this, but how could I run the works if I'm in Essex?"

"You could stay on site. Like you said, the caretaker's rooms would make good living quarters, or if you prefer, a hotel nearby."

"If you turned it into a conference and wedding venue, those rooms would have to house the administration offices."

"The attic rooms would make offices."

"I agree, but you would need ground floor points of contact for guests." Iain let his lower lip jut out like a child and she smiled, "Okay, I'll dress the rooms and choose the paint and wallpaper, but don't expect me to be in dungarees all day ordering decorators about."

Iain laughed and lifted his glass and, holding it out, Emilia chinked hers against it and they sealed the deal.

On the drive home, Emilia was considering Iain's request for her involvement. Pushed out of managing the day to day running of the business for so long caused her concern. Was the project Iain's way of keeping her out of harm's way? To prevent her from finding out about his deal with Mr Johal and the Spanish connection?

"What are you thinking about?" Iain asked her as they pulled up outside their home.

"Just thinking about today. The house is magnificent and I think it could be a winner. But the decision is yours to make. You need to do the figures and speak to the accountants."

"Let's have a drink and we can talk some more inside."

Iain walked around the car, opened her door, and walking into the hall, Emilia thought about how much time this new project would take up. Even if it was only the décor she dealt with, it'd still keep her out of the way for prolonged periods of time.

Emilia was suspicious and going on recent track records, she had good cause to be.

17

~ Oakham ~

Emilia's text had said,

come in disguise

Melanie looked at herself in the mirror and chuckled. The combats and khaki jacket looked strange after her usual designer clothes, but she quite liked the image she was portraying. She had fastened the black Dr Marten boots with yellow laces and she made sure they shone like new. Her skin was fresh, almost devoid of any make-up, just a dusting of powder to take away any shine. "I look like a tomboy. I could even pass for a boy," she told herself.

Melanie was lucky to look much younger than her forty-one years.

It was a two-hour drive to Oakham, a town she'd never been to before and to assuage her desire for shopping she'd filled her purse with cash and for a safety net had left her credit card at home. Avoiding the council's phone app parking machines, she left her car at a Tesco superstore and walked to the coffee shop that Emilia had chosen for their meeting. She was the first to arrive and ordered herself a cappuccino. She chose a seat against a wall facing the door just as Emilia entered, dressed as she'd been at the hotel. Without drawing attention to herself, Melanie sat in silence as Emilia ordered her drink and, after looking around, she walked to Melanie's table. "You look good," she said, sitting down opposite.

"Could you tell it was me?" Melanie asked.

"No, but as you're the only single person in here, I took an educated guess."

The bell above the door rang again, and they both turned to see a woman with long blonde plaits enter, she was wearing a floral maxi dress with a floppy sunhat and wedge-heeled sandals enter. She walked over to their table and placed a straw shopping bag on a chair before saying hello, then Selena walked over to the counter and ordered a drink.

Once the three of them were sitting together, Melanie asked Emilia, "What made you choose this place?"

"It's a small town and one that's probably not covered with too many cameras like a city centre. Chances are the crime figures are low, so we'll just look like tourists or locals on any CCTV."

"It's always the sleepy town where murders take place in cosy mysteries, like Midsomer."

"Good job we're not in Midsomer then," Selena said.

Melanie noticed Selena's voice had a little more light in it than at the previous meeting. "You look fabulous," she said. "I'm loving the 1970s vibe."

"Does it look natural?"

"I think so," added Emilia. "And you look very different too, Melanie."

"I got this lot for a few quid at the army surplus store and thought because of my build and small tits, at a distance, I'd maybe pass as a boy."

"Well, I think you both look convincing."

"Now all we need is a false name," joked Melanie.

"Funny you should say that." Emilia reached inside her handbag and removed two envelopes and placed them on the table. "I've got these for you."

"What's inside?" Selena said, picking an envelope up.

"Pre-paid debit cards. No credit checks needed, so I got these for each of you. There's a balance of £20 already added to them."

"How do they work?" asked Melanie, taking the remaining envelope.

"You can top them up with cash at a bureau de change and some banks, and because I have registered them to an assumed name, they will protect your identity. You can destroy them once this is over."

Selena opened her envelope and removed the card and a plain post card where Emilia had written the name that she had assigned to it. "They're all registered to addresses in London that are scheduled for demolition next week."

"I'm Heather Fox," said Selena, looking at her card.

"Charlotte Allen? I'm not sure I'm a Charlotte," said Melanie.

"The name's irrelevant. Just remember it if asked when you top up the card."

"Should we use these names when we communicate with our —"

"Yes, I think it's safer to use these pseudonyms when and if we contact the men."

"So, what's your..." Melanie giggled, "undercover name?"

"I'll be Ruth Lewis." Before anyone could respond, Emilia's phone rang, and she mouthed, "It's Iain." The table fell silent. "Hello... That's good news... When?"

Melanie watched as Emilia spoke with her husband. She thought the conversation was quite warm, not how she'd have spoken to Paul if he'd called her: there was always a hint of irritation in their conversations. "Okay, no problem. I'll see you in a couple of days." She disconnected the call and looked at the two expectant faces before her. "Nothing to worry about. We've had an offer accepted on a property we've looked at."

"Are you moving house?"

"No, it's a business property. An old manor house in Oxfordshire. Iain's planning a renovation. Now back to us."

She took a sip of her coffee and, lowering her voice, she asked if anything had changed and if the others had any questions. The reply to both was, no, and so she wrapped up the meeting. Emilia put her sunglasses back on and said, "Charlotte, if you can text me details of Paul's upcoming calendar, that'll be a great help."

It took Melanie a while to recognise that she was being spoken too, and after a nervous giggle, said, "Very well, Ruth. I'll do that."

"Right, I think we're all sorted now, so I'll be off." Emilia rose and before she walked away leant into the table and whispered, "Good luck, ladies."

Selena and Melanie watched as she left the coffee shop, and Melanie thought, this has now become real.

18

~ Chop Shop ~

Paul had been watching the garage for many days and sitting in his car, he watched as Jez slid open the door to allow a skinny youth to drive in. The car was a new Mercedes CLA Coupé, a vehicle the teenage driver obviously couldn't have afforded. The youth left minutes later, counting banknotes, a sure sign that something illegal had taken place.

Paul and Jez had dreamed of setting up their own car mechanic business, but his marriage to Melanie had put paid to that idea, that and his mistrust of his long-time friend.

Sixteen years earlier, Jez had come looking for financial help and Paul had helped him to secure the garage he still traded from and had loaned him a lump sum to get the business off the ground.

Jez repaid the loan in full but Paul's name was still on the garage lease and he received a nine per cent dividend each year from the profits.

He put his car in gear and headed home, wondering how he'd approach Jez about what he'd seen.

As he drove away, his mind churned. It was obvious by what he'd seen that Jez was up to no good. He couldn't afford for whatever he was up to come back on him. Besides, Paul thought, what if I can benefit from whatever he's up to?

When he arrived home, the house was empty; he assumed Melanie would be out shopping.

He reheated some of yesterday's lasagne in the microwave and poured himself an orange juice from the fridge and took his meal into the conservatory.

The garden was immaculate, the envy of his neighbours. Although Paul occasionally got outside with a trowel, the result was down to the gardener that they employed, but this would never stop Paul from taking credit whenever anyone complimented it.

As he ate, he ran through what he had seen that day and on his subsequent visits to watch the garage. Top of the range motors being delivered to a backstreet mechanic didn't ring true. Executive cars continually delivered by young men dressed in black, their faces hidden by hooded sweatshirts.

"It doesn't take a genius to know something criminal is going on. But what?" He told himself as he carried his plate and glass back to the kitchen. He was pouring a second glass of orange when he heard the front door open.

Melanie walked in and placed some carrier bags down on the counter. "I got a Chloé blouse at a bargain price."

The name meant nothing to Paul as he watched her remove the silk crepe de chine blouse from a carrier; it was a pastel pink with ruffles over the shoulders and he thought it wouldn't have looked out of place in an Adam and the Ants 80s music video.

"Should have been over four hundred pounds. I got it for a steal at one hundred and thirty."

"Hundred and thirty quid for that. Has someone replaced your brains with shit?"

"You've no class, Paul Rothman," Melanie said.

"And you've got more money than sense."

"Anyway, I'll wear it tonight when I go out with the girls."

"Where are you going?"

"Bloody hell, don't you ever listen? We're having an overnight stay at a spa."

"Well, you're always prattling on. Sometimes it's difficult to filter out what's important." He gave her a wide smile to show he was only joking and she, in turn, gave him a fake hard stare.

"We're celebrating Rosalind's engagement."

"Well, have fun."

"We will." Melanie gathered up her shopping and breezed out of the kitchen and headed upstairs.

~~~

Melanie had left in a flurry of excitement, overnight bags and a bottle of prosecco in hand as she clambered into Rosalind's car.

Now the house was empty. Paul was glad of the opportunity to be out in the early hours.

He'd spent the evening trying to watch the television, but the lack of beer and constant clock watching disrupted his attention. When the clock read 02:00 a.m. he changed into dark clothing and collected the spare set of garage keys from the junk drawer in the kitchen and went out to his car.

The streets were empty, the only cars on the road, taxis taking late night revellers home. Approaching the garage, he pulled up a distance away and killed his headlights and watched; he had to be sure he was going to be alone.

There was no activity and no lights on inside, so he walked over, turning the keys in his hand, hoping the alarm code would be the same as it had been for years.

He knew the only cameras on the business were at the rear that backed on to open land. There were none at the front, and he'd never seen evidence of any inside.

He undid the padlock and turned his key in the lock. It clicked open, but no alarm sounded as he slid the door open and pulled it closed behind him.

He took out his iPhone and switched on the torch setting. The workshop was messy, with tools strewn over the workstations. There was no semblance of order, but this didn't surprise him. Organisation had never been one of Jez's strong points.

Paul noticed the small hatchback minus its exhaust on the scissor lift waiting for a new one to be fitted and recalled seeing it there the last time he'd visited. Shrugging, he made his way through the second set of doors into the rear and what he found there interested him.

The Mercedes from earlier was there, minus its front wings and bonnet. In the room were the remains of another car. Nothing more than a frame, its brand unrecognisable.

Looking at the workbenches, he saw a multitude of smaller engine parts, most of them had been cleaned, looking virtually new.

"So that's Jez's game," he said as he took a few photographs on his phone. "Looks like there's a side hustle here that I can become a part of."

He closed the door and made his way back through the workshop and left as quietly as he'd arrived.

19

~ You Snooze, You Lose ~

Andrew pulled up outside a Victorian semi-detached house, with a manicured front lawn and rows of regimented, red salvias like soldiers in borders either side of a path. The house maintained a lot of the original features, a storm porch and sash windows, there was even a stained glass insert in the original front door. This, Andrew thought, bode well for what he might find inside.

Frank, a man of advanced years, opened the front door. He smiled as Andrew introduced himself and stood aside to allow him inside. Andrew was told to make himself comfortable while Frank went to make a pot of tea. In the sitting room, Andrew's eyes skimmed the pictures and porcelain on display, taking in everything that he thought could be of any value. The paintings looked original, but knowing little about artworks, he took out his phone and started taking photographs. He'd ask around later. A dresser was full of Royal Worcester china, hand-painted game birds and fruit designs. Andrew knew there was a market for the decorative china, albeit a small one as it had fallen out of favour of late. He picked up a vase and turned it over to read the maker's mark as Frank came into the room. "This is a lovely piece."

"Belonged to my late wife," Frank said, resting the tray on a corner table. "It's Aynsley. The wife liked Staffordshire ceramics."

"Yes, it's Pembroke design," Andrew said, placing it back down. "Very popular in the late 1980s."

"That's right. Ten-a-penny now, but I'd not sell any of them."

"That's okay. It's not what I deal in."

Silence pushed its way into the room, making the atmosphere heavy as Andrew felt Frank had been making a point rather than just idle conversation. He took his tea; a china cup and saucer in a traditional pattern, but he didn't know the manufacturer. Frank pointed to a pair of sugar tongs and said, "Help yourself."

"You don't see these very often," Andrew replied, picking up a cube of sugar from a bowl. "My father used to say, 'only posh folks had cubed sugar'."

"It's what we've always had, saw no need to change it when my wife passed."

Feeling the atmosphere turning frosty, Andrew chatted about the traffic and the weather. Frank listened and replied when required as his guest babbled on until he called a halt to the inane chat and said, "Shall I show you the pieces I have for sale?" Andrew nodded and followed the old man out of the sitting room and up the stairs. Opening a bedroom door, Frank said, "These have been in my family for many years. I hope they'll be worth something to you."

"I hope they'll be worth something to you too," Andrew said. He knew his remark was patronising, but he had never mastered the wherewithal to camouflage his comments with sincerity.

Frank led him over to wardrobe and opened it to reveal shoeboxes stacked on shelves where shirts would ordinarily be. He selected one and carried it over to a chest of drawers and removed the lid. Unwrapping the newspaper, he revealed a small blue jar about four inches tall and handed it to Andrew. He was silent as the dealer turned it over in his hands, umming and ahhing and giving small sighs as he checked for any damage. "It's Ming, I believe."

"It is," Andrew said, "16th century. Ming dynasty, blue porcelain with a lion motif."

"Is it valuable?"

"Well, sadly not as valuable as people assume when they hear the term, Ming. I have seen lots of these, some with lids and some like this one."

"Oh, it's never had a lid, should it have?"

"They do come with lids as it's referred to as a jarlet not a vase." His mind was whirring, he knew the jar was worth around £450 to a collector but said, "Sadly, this reduces its value." Frank's face fell and inside Andrew smiled, thinking he'd got the old man on the ropes. "You said on the phone that you had two pieces to show me."

Frank removed a taller vase and handed it to Andrew. He tried not to let the surprise show on his face. This one was a treasure he hadn't expected to see, and just holding it made his hands tremble. He repeated the same procedure as before, looking closely at the apple-green vase decorated with cranes and famille roses standing on an enamelled base. "Qing dynasty," he said. Knowing the value to be around two thousand pounds and thinking he could sell it for £3,000 plus. He took a breath and said to Frank, "Shame it's green. Collectors are mostly seeking the rare blue ones."

"In your opinion," Frank said, "how much can I expect to get for them?"

"First, the small blue jar. I think a price of ninety pounds would be sufficient."

"Really," Frank fidgeted, obviously uncomfortable, "as little as that?"

"I could… maybe… go to a hundred."

"And the vase?"

"This one is more valuable, but as I've said, collectors are seeking the blue ones. So I think we'd be looking at around four hundred pounds…"

Andrew gave a long pause and looked out of the window, feigning disinterest, before he was ready to play to play his trump card that never failed.

"Look, I like you Frank, and I'm feeling generous. I'll

go to four fifty. How do you feel about five hundred and fifty for the two? It will strip back my margins, but as I've said, I like you, Frank, and you can spend that bit extra on something to remember your wife."

"Maybe I should wait for the other guy who was interested in them. He might give me a better price."

"Other guy?"

"Yes, a dealer name Nigel."

"Yes. Nigel works for me. He asked me to come along to give you a valuation. He's less experienced in Chinese porcelain."

"Oh... I see."

Andrew could feel Frank beginning to falter and so pressed ahead, "So do we have a deal?" Pausing for a few seconds, Frank nodded his head, then held out his hand and Andrew shook it.

As Frank re-wrapped the china, Andrew removed his phone and went through the motions of making a call. "Hi Nigel... Yes, I'm with Frank now... Okay, I will." After pretending to disconnect from the fake call, he said, "Nigel sends his best wishes." He counted out the agreed amount in cash and shook Frank's hand again before leaving.

The car's ignition fired, and Frank called out. "Shall I expect a receipt in the post?"

Andrew nodded, "Certainly, I'll do it today." And as he pulled away from the kerb, he muttered to himself, "I wouldn't hold your breath, old man."

~~~

The sign read simply, Andrew Cavendish, but his company base wasn't a shop or an auction house, but a 1930s building. Little more than a scruffy warehouse. A simple storage space with no real showroom to speak of.

The floor and walls were bare, and the lighting came from fluorescent tubes that buzzed and flickered high in the rafters. This suited Andrew, as he purchased the bulk of his wares to order and sold them on quickly. Only his mistakes hung around gathering dust on shelving.

Andrew parked his car at the side, just off the road that led down to the canal at the rear of the warehouse and walked around to open up. The main door was old wood, solid but pock marked after years of use with a single mortice lock. Andrew hadn't bothered to fit an alarm or cameras. He preferred to save rather than spend, and his attitude was that because he kept little of any great value inside, it wouldn't pay anyone to break in to steal from him.

He placed Frank's box on top of a filing cabinet and walked around the battered desk to pull out an office chair that had seen better days. Everything in his private office looked tired. Even the computer was an old desktop PC. He waited for it to reboot while he switched on the kettle beside the sink under the window. He rinsed a mug and dropped in a tea bag and then fell into his chair and checked his emails.

There was one from a dealer in China who had several pieces he thought he'd be interested in, another from someone enquiring about a vase for sale on his website. After deleting the usual spam, he came to the email he'd received from Nigel the day before. With a snigger, he re-read it.

> Forgot to mention I'm away for 10 days, taking the girlfriend to Corfu.
> I've a seller named Frank who has a couple of pieces to sell.
> I'll text his number. Can you check it out for me?

Andrew smiled, remembering a telephone conversation when Nigel had joked about him not forgetting his commission. Something he'd done quite a lot lately.

Was he joking?

He poured hot water over the tea bag, grabbed a packet of biscuits from the worktop, and fired up a reply to Nigel.

Hope you're enjoying your jolly mate. Went to see Frank today. Sadly, not much of any interest, lots of Staffordshire ceramics. So a wasted trip, but that's the game. See you later.

Andrew dunked a digestive into his mug and said, "You snooze, you lose."

He spent the rest of his afternoon contacting previous buyers on his mailing list and looking around the forums for anyone who had asked after pieces similar to those he'd picked up from Frank.

Luck was on his side. There was a listing from a buyer looking for any porcelain from the Qing Dynasty. Andrew introduced himself by email and, after pressing send with a self-satisfied smile, he congratulated himself.

20

~ Wedding Plans ~

Selena spotted Emilia's car as the house came into view. She turned off the engine and got out and walked around the parking area, looking up at the impressive frontage. Row upon row of windows looked down at her and she shivered, recalling a painting depicting the slaying of Argus Panoptes, the giant with a hundred eyes. The memory made her feel like she was being watched until the sound of wheels on gravel shook her from her thoughts. Turning around, she saw Melanie's car approaching.

"Very impressive," Melanie said, joining Selena at the front door.

"It certainly is."

The door opened and Emilia, minus her silver wig, invited them inside. "I hope you both had a pleasant drive down." The women nodded as she ushered them through into the caretaker's rooms that were now stripped of the old furniture and with a desk and a couple of small sofas installed. "Take a seat, ladies. I've put the coffee machine on," she said, running her fingers through her hair.

"I love your hair," Melanie said, dropping onto a sofa. "is it dyed? I mean... Do you have the white streak put in specially?"

"It's poliosis. I've had it all my life. My mother used to call it my Mallen streak." Unconsciously, she ran her fingers through her hair again.

"Talking of hair, I thought this was a good place to meet

as there's no one here to observe us, so you can remove your wigs if it'll make you more comfortable."

The ladies did as requested and Melanie said, "What's a Mallen streak?"

"It's a book by Catherine Cookson about a family where children born to the landowner all have the genetic white streak." Selena watched as Melanie's eyes crossed a little. She was processing the information. "I wanted to know more, so read the book as a teenager. The themes were too adult for me at my age, but I loved the story."

"Was it lusty landowners taking advantage of young local wenches?"

"Something like that," Emilia said.

Changing the subject, Selena said, "This house is impressive. Any chance we could have a look around?"

"Yes please," Melanie added, "I love looking around old houses."

"Certainly, and after we'll have something to eat. I've prepared us a picnic lunch."

Emilia picked up the architect's preliminary plans from her desk and, using it, she showed them around the ground floor, explained what they were going to do with each of the spaces. Melanie couldn't resist shouting in the banqueting hall, listening to her voice echo around the room. Outside, Selena leaned in and sampled the fragrance from each bloom in the rose garden. The quadrangle impressed her more than the actual building.

"This floor," Emilia said on the second, "Will be the rooms for wedding guests, or delegates for business conventions."

"Will there be a bridal suite?"

"Of course Melanie, you can't have a wedding venue without one."

"Are you employing specialist designers?" asked Selena.

"No, I'll be doing most of the work myself. Iain has

asked me to do the décor. He seems to think I'll make a good job of it." She delivered a self-deprecating smile, but Selena didn't imagine the work was beyond Emilia's capabilities. "It was all a little strange a few weeks ago when Iain asked me, and it was nice to be here with him, feeling my input was valid. I even found I was getting a little jealous of his flirting with the agent."

"Were you?"

"Thinking about it, no, I was angry that he did it in my presence, but I wasn't jealous."

They returned to the office and dropped onto a sofa each as Emilia made three coffees. "I thought we should meet to see how we're all progressing; we last met in early August and now September is upon us."

"Is everything okay with you, since the jealous, not jealous, issue?"

Emilia tossed a frown Melanie's way and replied, "Everything is okay with me, no changes here."

"Non here either," Selena said, butting in. "Sorry to interrupt… but… I wish it was over already."

"Are you okay?" Melanie gave her a comforting smile.

"Yes… No, I don't know…" Selena's shoulders shook and her voice failed mid-sentence as incipient tears pricked at her eyes. She scrabbled in her pocket for a tissue.

The three women sat in silence. Selena looked down at the floor, while Melanie and Emilia exchanged confused glances. "Who fancies a drink?" Melanie said, her voice full of false jollity. "I did my weekly shop before coming here and so there's a bottle of voddy in the boot of my car."

"Why don't we have lunch now?" Emilia added. "We'll need some food to soak up the drink. You fetch the vodka and I'll lay out the plates."

The atmosphere remained uncomfortable as they tucked into smoked salmon sandwiches and an heirloom tomato salad.

The conversation was stilted and stale. Emilia spoke a

little more about the plans to turn Astley House into a wedding venue and the others gave simple, monosyllabic replies and sipped at their vodka and cranberry. Pulling a mock-up of a brochure from her bag, Emilia handed it to the others. "This is a sample brochure that Iain's having printed. Although he calls it a catalogue. He thinks brochure sounds too common, like those flyers you get through the door with special offers on pizza."

"I quite like pizza," Melanie said, breaking the tension, and their laughter carved up the flat air. "Sorry, you know I have no filter."

"Feeling better now?" Emilia asked Selena.

"Yes, thank you."

"If you want to talk, we're happy to listen." Melanie nodded her head in agreement while Selena sipped at her drink.

"I really shouldn't burden you with my troubles. But I'm glad you arranged a catch up. I've needed to talk to someone and … well… There's only you two that I trust."

"A trouble shared, as they say," Melanie said.

"The last thing you need is to be stressed about something else on top of what we're planning to do."

Selena smiled. "I know you're right, but I've been carrying this shit around for so long I don't know where to start."

"Start where you want to and we'll just listen." Emilia reached over and took a box of tissues from the desk and handed them to her.

Selena took a sip and placed her glass down and looked at her friends. She was nervous, worried she wouldn't be able to speak, let alone say what she wanted to say.

"A few days ago, Andrew came home in a good mood." She took a deep breath as if to push her reluctance to speak down inside her. "Andrew came home. He was in a good mood, almost bouncing off the walls with happiness. He told me he'd got a good price for some porcelain and he didn't have to pay commission to Nigel."

"Nigel?" Emilia asked.

"He's a freelancer who sources antiques for him. He works with many dealers and charges a finder's fee. Andrew had deliberately taken Nigel's lead and had cut him out of the deal."

"What a twat." Emilia tossed a disapproving look at Melanie's comment, giving Selena a chance to take another sip of her drink.

"The evening was going well. Andrew ordered a takeaway, and I opened a bottle of wine. It made a change for us to be together without my feeling afraid. Some evenings I feel like I'm perched on razor blades. We watched some TV, doing what normal couples do. Andrew opened another bottle of wine and I could see he was becoming tipsy. He leant into kiss me but I wasn't in the mood and pulled away. I saw his face change, the smile turned to a sneer, and he pushed me down on the sofa and just… He took advantage of me."

Silence crashed around the room until Melanie whispered, "Bastard."

"Have you done anything about it?" Emilia asked, reaching out to take Selena's hand, which she moved away out of reach.

"What can I do?"

"You should report him to the police." Melanie said, her face fixed with irritation.

"And what do I tell them when they ask about the time before?"

"Are you saying he's…" Melanie stopped talking and then said, "let's get this straight, he raped you?" The others watched as Selena winced at hearing the word. "And he's done this before?"

"It's my fault."

The collective intake of breath sounded loud in the stillness of the room. Emilia shook her head and Melanie took a large gulp of her vodka.

"Your fault?" Melanie's voice was high with anger.

"I knew it could happen again." This time, she allowed Emilia to take her hand. "At university, he used to whine when I refused to have sex. He used to say childish things like, 'you would if you loved me' and, 'It's normal for couples like us to do it.'"

"Men can be such–" Emilia's look stopped Melanie, talking.

"One night at university, I told him I wanted to end our relationship. He was angry. Angrier than I'd seen him before. He called me names – I'd expected that – horrible names. Said I was ungrateful and frigid and before I could push him off, he'd pushed me down saying he'd show me what was wrong with me... and... it happened. It's been like that ever since, at night when we're in bed, he just takes what he wants, then falls asleep."

"You poor thing," Emilia said.

Selena's head snapped up, her eyes were wide, "Poor thing... poor thing... that's how people must see me. Well, I'm sick of being Andrew's poor thing. Sick of hearing his snivelling apologies, sick of his attitude, sick of his controlling, sick of being, Mrs fucking Cavendish."

Selena downed her drink and handed the empty glass over for a refill.

Everyone watched as Melanie unscrewed the cap from the bottle and poured the spirit into the glass.

Selena sat back and accepted the top up and said, her voice calm now but her face a flinty picture of anger. "So you can see why he has to die."

Emilia remained still, but Melanie nodded.

"Thank you for not going on about consent in marriage and all the bollocks people hand out in this situation. Thank you for just listening and understanding. Without you two, I don't think I'd have ever been able to admit this." She held her glass aloft and continued, "I want it over and done with as soon as possible."

21

~ Three Telephone Calls ~

"Hello, is this Andrew Cavendish Antiques?" the voice at the end of the line said.

"Yes, Andrew Cavendish speaking. Can I help you?"

"I hope so," Melanie said. "My name is Charlotte Allen and I've been looking at your website. I see you specialise in oriental artefacts."

"That's right."

"I have some pieces of porcelain that I'm looking to sell and I wondered—"

"What sort of pieces?" Andrew interrupted. "Do you know much about them?"

"They belonged to my great-aunt. One is what she called a Rouleau vase. She told me it was… I think… Kangxi period. Does that make sense?"

"That's fourth emperor, Qing Dynasty." Andrew's fingers clicked on his keyboard as he searched an online resource and, seeing an estimated value of forty thousand pounds, a smile as wide as a saucer opened up on his face. "You said you had several pieces."

"Another is a small lotus flower bowl from the same period, but I'm not sure it'll be worth much." Knowing what she was talking about, Andrew thought the bowl could make at least a thousand at auction. "And there's a Famille-Verte dragon box."

"Is it complete?" Andrew said, entering the details online and seeing the estimate come up at thirty-six thousand. He could hardly contain himself.

"Yes, it has its cover."

"I can't give you a valuation over the telephone. I'll need to see the items before I can do that. If you're happy, we can either sell them at auction, that will incur auction fees, or we could save you the costs by buying them ourselves."

Melanie told him she'd need to think about it. She gave him the number of her burner phone and said she'd call him again soon with her decision.

~~~

Ken walked from the bar to the door, the keys jangling in his hand; he knew that there'd already be three old gents waiting outside for him to open. The telephone behind the bar rang, and he called out to the barmaid, buffing glasses to answer it. The three stalwarts who couldn't let a day pass without their early pints of pale ale entered as the phone stopped ringing and the barmaid said, "Roebuck pub." As Ken poured three pints, he listened into the one-sided conversation. Ken's three regulars took up position at the table where they'd sit for the next three or four hours, and the phone call ended. "Who was that?"

"Some woman asking about the darts match."

"What did she want to know?"

"She asked me for the date."

"Probably a wife checking up on her husband's whereabouts."

"Yeah." she replied, picking up a cloth.

~~~

Iain was happy with the catalogue. He flicked through the pages as his driver drove him to his lunch date.

Emilia had given him some input into the layout and there was no doubting she had an eye for design.

She'd had two bedrooms decorated in advance and dressed them for the photographer.

The Astley House website had gone live a few days before and was already seeing some traffic. There had even been a tentative request for further information, which made him think his new venture looked promising.

The trades were cracking on with re-wiring, plastering and decorating, as per Emilia's instructions, and Iain had hired extra labourers for the job.

At lunchtime, Iain spotted his wife as soon as he entered the bistro. He leant in and kissed her on the cheek as he joined her at the table. "Good day?" he said before raising his hand to summon a waiter. "Did you get much done?"

"Yes, I've found some wallpaper that will be ideal." She held out her phone to show him the photographs. "This sofa is oversized and will look good against the wall opposite the window in the bridal suite." They ordered lunch and just as the waiter arrived with a bottle of wine, Iain's mobile rang.

Emilia sipped her wine as her husband took the call. She saw his face light up and a smile formed on his lips. "Good news?" she asked as the call ended and he punched some details into its electronic notebook.

"Another enquiry," he said, putting his phone down on the table. "A woman named Heather Fox. Says she's interested in a viewing." He raised his hand and asked the waiter for a bottle of champagne. "We need to celebrate with something better than Pino Noir."

Their glasses chinked, and Emilia smiled. Selena had made contact.

22

~ Paul ~

Jez looked up as Paul's car pulled up outside and wiping his hands on an oily rag, he walked out of the door towards him. "Hello mate. Long time no seen your ugly mug."

Paul noticed Jez give the rear of the workshop a backwards glance. He's checking the doors are locked, he thought. "It's been a while since we've seen each other."

"Nothing wrong, is there?"

"Not sure, is there?" Paul smiled and hoped Jez would open up.

Jez grinned like he always did, cocky as ever. "So what's brought you here? No problem with your payments?"

"No, everything's fine on that score. I wanted to talk to you about something else. Shall we go inside?"

Jez looked concerned as he backed up to allow Paul to enter and walk into the small, partitioned space that pretended to be an office.

The room had a dirty window and an equally dirty desk. Chocolate wrappers fought for space with plastic sandwich containers and empty crisp packets.

"Fancy a coffee?" Jez said.

"Don't think so. My jabs aren't up to date," Paul said, picking up a dirty mug and showing Jez the inside.

"Funny," Jez said, "Look, if this is just a social call, I'm sorry, but I'm up to my ears with work."

"You sound nervous."

"Not at all. I just need to get on."

"I bet you do."

"Okay, Paul, what's with the attitude?"

"No attitude mate, just dropping by to say hello."

"Okay, but as I said, I'm rushed off my feet. What do you say we go out one night for a few jars?"

"How long have you been running a chop shop?"

Paul's question stopped Jez in his tracks, and he blustered through a fake laugh. "Not sure what you're on about, mate?"

"Shall we go through to the back?"

"What for?"

"Come on Jez. I'm not stupid. You're using the garage as a front."

"A front? For what?"

"Don't insult my intelligence. You're stripping down cars and selling on the parts. I've been watching you for ages now. I even paid a visit one night and saw the cars in the back workshop."

The bravado fell away from Jez's face and at a lower volume, he said, "It's nothing you should worry about."

"But I do worry. My name's on the lease, not to mention the business account, so whatever you do implicates me."

"I… It's a…"

"Don't say it's a one off. You forget I know you Jez, we grew up together."

"So, what do you want?"

"I haven't decided yet. I just wanted to give you something to think about. I'll be in touch."

Paul walked away and as he opened the office door, Jez pushed it shut and with his face close to Paul's said, "Look, there's people involved here that won't be happy if this gets out."

"Who said anything about it getting out? Just take some time to think about my recompense."

"Blackmail?"

"Blackmail, compensation. Call it what you will. See you around, Jez."

As Paul's car pulled away from the kerb, he saw Jez remove his phone from his overall pocket.

***

Grabbing a clean T-shirt, Paul left the bedroom and made his way downstairs and walked into the conservatory, where Melanie was flicking through a magazine. "You off then?"

"Yes, we're going to thrash The Fleece tonight. Fancy coming?"

"No, watching fat blokes throw darts isn't my idea of fun," Melanie said, turning her attention back to her book.

Paul looked at his reflection in the conservatory glass and patted his flat stomach. "You could just watch me if you want to look at a toned bloke."

"No thanks, seen it all before."

Paul looked at his wife and then back at his reflection. We make a good couple, he thought. Mel is still stunning and I'm on the right side of going to seed.

Over the years, people had told him he was handsome. From his mid-teens, women had made it obvious they found him attractive and even Ken had once said he was a jammy bugger to be blessed with good looks. He had unruly blond hair with no style; it curled around his ears and touched his collar, giving him a Nordic appearance. His eyes were pale blue and his slim pink lips only added to the appeal.

He pulled the t-shirt over his head and strolled into the hall, looking at himself in the mirror positioned above the console table where he always dropped his car keys. He gave himself a smile and called to Melanie, saying he'd be back late, and walked outside.

Driving to the pub, he thought about Melanie. He'd been faithful to his wife since their wedding day, even when his resistance was weak and an attractive woman made herself available to him. "I might be many things," he said to himself, "But I'm not a cheat."

Eighteen years he'd been married and, in that time, had remained faithful to his vows. In the past, he had wondered if Melanie knew, but now he didn't care. He knew, and that was all that mattered.

Honesty in a relationship was important to Paul and although he still loved Melanie, his respect for her had faded when he'd discovered the deception, she had been a part of alongside her father. He knew his blackmail made him a hypocrite, but he would never have shopped them to the police. Although he was grateful, they relented, and the tidy sum of money he had in his bank account and the monthly bonus he received made him happy. But, it was cold comfort, and sometimes he wished he could turn the clock back.

The Roebuck was busy, along with the regulars there were many who had come especially to see the darts match. As Paul walked in, someone called his name and he spotted the darts team. He nodded when one of them told him there was a drink already waiting for him.

"Don't drink too much, save it until after," Ken said. "We need to win this one."

"Don't worry, I'll just have the one then when we're celebrating, it'll be up to you to supply the drinks for free."

"Don't get ahead of yourself," Ken laughed.

The door opened, and a rowdy gang of men entered. The darts team from The Fleece had arrived with their publican in tow. "Line them up Ken," the man with the red face and nose the colour and shape of an over-ripe plum shouted across the bar. "Ready for defeat?"

The two teams congregated around the dart board, where banter and jokes flowed like water between them as they all took practice throws. Paul stuck to his promise and had just one pint, moving on to cola after.

Walking towards the board to retrieve his darts, Paul spotted the woman walk in. She looked out of place. Dressed in a cream two-piece with silver-blonde hair and wearing sunglasses, she certainly wasn't the pub's usual clientele. He watched her order a drink and take a seat at the rear of the room.

"Come on. Get a shift on."

"Sorry," Paul said, pulling his darts out of the board and moving to the back of the line of men waiting for their turn to throw.

The volume in the room increased as regulars from the rival pub arrived to support their team and soon there wasn't a free table or stool in the place. Ken rang the bell to get everyone's attention and declared that the match would get underway in ten-minutes, his announcement caused a flurry of fresh orders as the bar became swamped by people keeping Ken and the barmaid on their toes, while others turned their seats around to face the dartboard.

The match started, and the Roebuck's fans were more vocal than the visitors' supporters. There was an air of friendly rivalry in the room. Everyone took the match seriously; however, it didn't generate a tense atmosphere; the room had a good-natured, easy friendliness. Between throws.

Paul looked across at the woman at the rear. She appeared to be taking notes, and he assumed she must be a reporter from the local newspaper. He gave her a small nod when she smiled at him. Maybe she'd want an interview if they won.

At the end of the match, the bar erupted with cheers as the home team were triumphant finally beating The Fleece. Paul had thrown the winning dart and the rivals and their supporters quickly departed, leaving the bar filled with people ordering drinks to celebrate.

Ken walked over and patted Paul on the back before handing him a measure of whisky, which he placed on the table that was already overflowing with full pint glasses.

The woman stood up and Paul watched her put the notebook into her handbag. She placed her empty glass on the bar and sauntered towards him.

"Call me," she said, pressing a business card into his hand, and he watched as she left the pub.

~~~

Driving home, Emilia thought that seeing Paul in the flesh had taken her plans for him from fantasy to reality. He was handsome, she conceded, the odd one out in the team made up of balding men with beer bellies. She was happy that he had noticed her. That would make any interaction with him easier.

Returning to the Moto services she'd visited earlier to design and print off her fake business cards, she ordered a coffee and felt the burner phone buzz in her pocket. She carried her drink over to a table and looked at the text that Paul had sent.

> I will call you next week

With a smile, she switched off the phone and said, "Perfect, he's taken the bait."

23

~ Bed Linen ~

It had been late when Cyndi woke up; the space beside her in the bed was empty. Vinnie had already left the flat. She knew where he'd be. Nothing ever changed.

She slid from under the duvet, the smell of unwashed bedding was unpleasant. Every surface had clothing sprawled across it, sweatshirts and t-shirts that looked like they'd hauled themselves there and collapsed. The floor was littered with socks and underpants and poking out from beneath the bed were unwashed mugs and bowls.

"I can't live like this anymore," she said, making her way to the bathroom. "Now I'm with the agency, I'll have more money, and I can make changes."

Showered and wrapped in a bathrobe, she pulled the laptop she shared with Vinnie from beneath a pile of dirty washing in the kitchen and, after picking off the dried Rice Crispies from the keyboard, she opened up a shopping browser.

Shopping online was a luxury for Cyndi. Delivery drivers didn't like coming onto the estate, with most companies leaving items for collection at secure sites and drop boxes.

She looked at the bed linen on offer. A cool green set of Teddy fleece would look lovely, she thought, and keep them warm too. Vinnie needed the warmth. He felt the cold more than most people, especially when he was shaking and in need of a fresh fix.

"Maybe I could save some money towards getting him some extra help," she said.

Vinnie had had help before; he had registered with the local health authority and three times a week visited the local pharmacy for a prescription of methadone.

Cyndi added the bedding to her online basket and got dressed before opening up her banking app. She'd need to add funds before she could make a purchase. All she had to do was retrieve the cash she'd hidden and deposit it at the bank so later she could go back online and buy the fleecy duvet set.

She scanned the area outside their flat; the window looking out onto the square of tarmac and messy grass verges. No sign of Vinnie, and after putting the chain on the door, she pulled the bath panel away and slipped her hand inside and took out the takeaway carton. The cash was gone. Vinnie had found her hiding place and taken it.

She rushed into the bedroom, tossed Vinnie's clothes from the stool and climbed up to feel across the top hem of the curtains. The card was still there, slid inside the gap she'd unpicked between the fabric and the heading tape.

Standing looking down at the mess of the room, she felt her heart slide further down, as it seemed to do each day lately. She wanted to cry, but her anger wouldn't allow it.

~~~

Joining the agency had excited Cyndi. No more working on the street and the dangers it brought. She imagined being an escort would be different. No more chapped legs from short skirts in winter, no more climbing into cars that were parked up behind the estate where varying degrees of lowlife hung out with the rats.

The reality of the work differed from her fantasy. It wasn't accompanying men to functions as a dinner date. It was very much like before, with cars being replaced by hotel rooms.

The men were mostly of a better quality, washed and with manners. She'd gained through her new clients a taste for prosecco, and the extra money had enabled her to buy some less slutty clothes befitting her dates.

The agency kept the fee from her first job to pay for the photographs that advertised her services on the website. Ever since then, she had built up a small client base and, with her fees being paid directly into a bank account, she had saved the little that Vinnie wasn't aware of.

She had another client that evening and thought about buying a new outfit. Probably not a good idea. With the cash gone, Vinnie would have questions.

Vinnie's key sounded in the lock, and the door opened as wide as the chain would allow.

"Cyndi, why's the chain on? You got company?"

She rushed into the hallway and as he banged his fists against the door; she took off the chain, and he barged inside. "What have I said about working from home?"

"I'm not. I'm here on my own."

Vinnie looked inside the bedroom and bathroom before he relaxed. "Sorry babe. You know I don't like strangers coming here."

Cyndi knew that the rubbish he pumped into his veins made him paranoid. She always forgave him, knowing she shouldn't. But she loved him.

Didn't she?

Vinnie sloped off to the bedroom, pulled off his hoody and strapped up his arm before flicking the air out of a syringe. Cyndi knew where her cash had gone. It was pointless talking to him about it. In a few seconds, with eyes rolling, he'd leave her for oblivion.

The days moved along slowly, always did. With Vinnie flaked out, she watched daytime television; she had to be on hand, in case he needed her. Or an ambulance.

As she got ready for her evening appointment, Vinnie sat on the sofa in his boxer shorts, eating breakfast cereal from the box.

"Who's this fella tonight?"

"I don't know. He's a new booking."

"Don't forget, take a blade in your bag."

"I can't. You know the agency doesn't allow it."

"You gotta be safe, Cyn. Lots of nutters out there."

"They vet everyone, so don't worry."

Because the agency took its payment in advance for bookings, their clients were mostly considerate. There was the occasional one who got too free with his fists. Though rare, the agency banned those responsible when any violence occurred.

Because of this rule, all bookings had to go through their office. When any of their girls or guys booked an agency client direct, it often led to dismissal.

"You look sexy, Cyn," Vinnie said. "Save a little for me later when you get home."

She smiled, knowing that when she returned, he'd be asleep, either after another dose or from the cans of larger he'd carried home earlier.

Pulling the door closed behind her, the sound of her heels on the uncarpeted staircase sounded as hollow as she felt.

She prayed tonight's client would be pleasant. Not like last night, a nice enough man, kind but overweight and sweaty when he was out of his expensive suit. Still, the tip had been generous. This thought reminded her of earlier and how Vinnie had spent it on the garbage he had pumped into himself.

The bad mood that had walked with her faded away as she saw the Bentley waiting where the agency had said it would be. Beaming as a rear door opened, she climbed inside and the handsome man asked his driver to head to the hotel.

Iain was charming. The conversation during the journey was pleasant. He asked her about her day and, being adept at lying, she conjured up a tale of shopping and meeting friends for lunch.

She found him relaxed; he kept his hands to himself and complimented her on her dress. It made a change from the men who saw finding themselves alone, an opportunity to paw at her.

The driver opened the door for Cyndi before Iain released him for the night. "I'll cover your taxi fare home," he said, offering his hand.

Cyndi allowed herself to be escorted into the hotel, the soft lighting and discreet conversation very different to her life in the flat with Vinnie. This was the life she had aspired to but never achieved. Still, Once Vinnie was clean, and with savings tucked away in the bank, one day this could be her reality.

"Shall we have drinks in the bar?" Iain asked her.

"That would be lovely."

He ordered himself a measure of scotch and she felt special watching the barman open a bottle of prosecco just to pour one glass for her.

She usually declined when a client asked if she'd like anything from the menu, but this evening was so pleasant that she wanted it to continue. She didn't need to worry about the time; the agency charged a flat fee, rather than by the hour, so there was no rush.

The hotel room was generic and lying back on the bed, Cyndi ran her hands over the linen, enjoying the feel of the freshly pressed cotton sheets that were cool against her skin. Iain had undressed her slowly, taking his time. He had appeared to enjoy the act of revealing her body without urgency, and now she watched as he undressed, folding his clothes as she gazed at him.

Cyndi smiled. He was in good shape and she knew she'd enjoy the time spent with him and if all went well; she hoped he'd become a regular.

The lovemaking was unhurried and attentive and afterwards he allowed her time to relax, ordering another glass of prosecco delivered by room service as she took a shower.

"I've ordered you a taxi," Iain said as she sipped her drink. "They'll wait out front until you're ready. I'm sorry I can't have my driver take you home. He has a family to get back to."

"That's okay," she replied, knowing she couldn't let him see where she lived. Litter strewn streets and gangs hanging out in the shadows would spoil the illusion she hoped she had created.

"I hope you've enjoyed yourself," he said as she picked up her handbag. "I know I did." He reached over to a bedside table, opened the drawer, and removed an envelope.

"I hope this won't offend you."

Cyndi opened the flap and saw a clutch of notes inside. She tucked it inside her bag and said, "Thank you, that's very kind."

As she opened the door to leave, Iain said, "I hope we see each other again."

"Yes, that would be nice."

24

~ Hyena ~

"Looks like you've caught the sun," Andrew said as Nigel entered the office.

"Fell asleep by the pool and woke up looking like a beetroot." Nigel laughed as he dropped into the chair opposite Andrew and told him about his holiday. He ended by asking about the lead he'd given him before he'd left for the break in Corfu. "So, what happened with Frank?"

"I went to see him, but it turned out the items he wanted to sell were all cheap copies and worthless. Shame, really, he was a nice old chap."

"Oh well, can't win them all." Nigel took his notebook out of his jacket pocket. "I've some more leads to follow up." He flicked through the pages and told Andrew that later he was off to look at some pieces of furniture for a dealer in York and he'd had a call from a woman with some pieces of Chinese porcelain she wants to sell.

"What's her name?" Andrew asked, remembering the call from Charlotte Allen. He hoped the lead wasn't the same person.

"It's…" he checked with his notebook before he continued, "Doreen, an old dear in Brighton. Bit of a distance to travel if her treasures turn out to be tat. I've also got a lead you might be interested in from a retired dealer in Skegness." Nigel had caught Andrew's attention but said nothing more. He tapped the side of his nose, giving him a knowing stare, and the secrecy annoyed Andrew.

Minutes later Nigel's phone rang and, leaving his notebook on the desk, he excused and himself and left the room.

Andrew snatched at the opportunity. Taking out his phone, he turned the open notebook over and began photographing the pages. He disregarded the woman in Brighton. That would be too far to travel if it was a wasted journey. Nigel can put the mileage on his car, he thought. Hearing the phone conversation being wound up, he replaced the book and slipped his phone back inside his jacket pocket.

"I'd better get off," Nigel said as he picked up his notebook. "I'll let you know how these leads pan out," he patted the book in his pocket. "Until then, I've got an old bookcase and some chairs to look at." The two men shook hands and Andrew followed Nigel outside to his car and watched as he drove away.

Returning to his desk, he took out his phone and looked at the images he'd taken; he copied the phone number from the photographs onto a desk blotter and dialled it. A man's voice answered. "Am I speaking with Lionel?"

"Yes," the man replied, and Andrew launched into his rehearsed patter. "A colleague has asked me to call you. Is it convenient to talk?"

"Yes. To whom am I speaking?"

"Cavendish. Andrew. My colleague says you have some items you want to sell."

"That's right," Lionel said, "I retired a couple of months ago but still have a few items that I need to move on. Are you a collector or a dealer?"

"A bit of both." Knowing that a dealer would be more open to negotiation with a collector rather than another dealer, Andrew lied, "I deal in artworks, paintings and such, but personally, I'm a keen collector of oriental artefacts."

"I may have a few pieces of interest if you're prepared to travel to view them."

"That's not an issue. You're in Skegness, is that right?"

"Yes, I am, but I don't have a business premises any longer." Hearing this pleased Andrew more, as he assumed the seller would be even more amenable to negotiation in his own home. "I've already had a chap who is interested call me, but there's no guarantee he'll call back. What's the earliest you could come over?"

"I'll check my diary," Andrew paused. He was free for the rest of the day so could take a trip to Skegness and on the way home drop in to see a friend in Wragby, who owed him a favour. "I can be there this afternoon if that's convenient for you. If I am interested, would cash be okay?"

"Cash is fine. I'll be home all day." The man gave Andrew his address and, with a metaphorical pat on the back, Andrew disconnected the call.

Two-hours later, Andrew pulled up outside a neat bungalow. His car's central locking clicked as he turned towards the open front door, where a friendly-looking man waited for him, his hand already outstretched. "Lionel," the man said as they shook hands.

~~~

Bridget opened the door and, seeing Andrew, she smiled. "Long time no see," she said, moving aside to let him inside. "Your call earlier surprised me," Bridget said.

"Had a little business in Skegness and thought I'd drop in and say hello."

"You never drop into anywhere to say hello. I know you too well, Andrew. There's got to be an ulterior motive." Bridget nodded towards the sofa and asked if he'd like a drink. "There's some wine in the fridge, or if you'd prefer, there are some bottled beers in the garage."

"Wine will be fine," he said as she left the sitting room for the kitchen. "Just the one as I'm driving," He called to her before sitting down on the sofa. "You've got it nice in here."

"Thanks," Bridget said. She returned with two glasses. "You should have seen it when I first bought the place. It was stuck in the 1970s. The wallpaper and carpet patterns alone could give you a migraine if you looked at them for too long."

"I like the layout, and just a few interesting artworks dotted around to attract attention."

"I knew an antique dealer back in the day. He gave me a few lessons in buying the right pieces." She gave a forced laugh before she took a sip of her wine.

They chatted openly for several minutes, Andrew talking about business and Bridget telling him about how much she enjoyed being retired. "Retired, you're too young to retire."

"Thank you," Bridget said, thinking flattery will get you nowhere. She placed her glass on a coaster on the coffee table and said, "When Michael died, he left me well provided for."

"I was sorry to hear that. Sadly, I was abroad. Otherwise I'd have paid my respects."

You wouldn't, you lying bastard; she thought, you hated Michael. Mind you, the feeling was mutual. What was it he used to say? ... oh yes... Andrew Cavendish is as trustworthy as a hyena.

"Have you eaten?" she asked, rising from her seat and smoothing down her skirt.

"I missed lunch, as usual."

"I guessed. Perhaps you should have something to soak up the wine before you leave."

"I don't want to trouble you."

"It's no trouble. Will a chicken salad sandwich be okay?" Andrew nodded and said yes, and Bridget went back into the kitchen.

"I wondered if you could do me a favour." Andrew called.

Here we go, thought Bridget, "Depends," she shouted

back.

"Nothing dodgy," he said, entering the kitchen. "Could you look after a couple of pieces of porcelain for me until I'm ready to sell them on?"

"Why?"

"I have a buyer lined up and don't want any other clients seeing them and making an offer. You know how sniffy these collectors can be. They all think they have a special connection with the dealer and get jealous easily."

"Sure," she said, handing him his sandwich. "But I'll want a small fee for looking after them."

"That's fine. We can discuss it after I've eaten this." Andrew walked back into the sitting room and took a bite out of his sandwich while Bridget poured herself another glass of wine.

25

~ Taking the Bait ~

Emilia's burner phone rang and, looking at the screen, she saw it was Paul calling.

"Ruth Lewis."

"Err... Hi ... This is Paul ... Paul Rothman."

"Hello Paul. I've been waiting for your call." Emilia poured herself another coffee from the cafetiere. "I guess you're wondering why I gave you my card?"

"To be honest, yes. Why were you at the darts match? Are you a reporter?"

"No, not a reporter. I originally went to observe another player, but I saw something special in your technique." The line went silent, the only sound being Paul's breathing. "Is everything okay?"

"Yes," he replied. "I'm just a little confused."

"There's no need to be. Let me give you a potted history. I used to be a features writer for Darts World before I became a sports agent. I'm DRA registered and now solely represent darts players."

"DRA?"

"Darts Regulation Authority. I was hoping we could meet and I could explain myself further."

"Sure..." Paul faltered, "when, where?"

"You're Worcester based?" She heard Paul grunt, yes, and continued, "I'm going to be in Birmingham tomorrow, so why don't we meet for lunch?"

"Yes, we can do."

"It'll be on expenses, so no worries about the bill."

"That's not a worry," he said.

I bet it isn't, Emilia thought, half hoping she hadn't said it out loud. "I'll text you the time and place later."

~~~

Emilia adjusted her wig and washed her hands before returning to the mirror where she applied a fresh coat of red lipstick.

Leaving the facilities, she walked through the bistro allowing any interested parties to observe her; she believed that in the event of any police enquiries all people would remember is the silver-haired woman in sunglasses.

Returning to the bar, she gave Paul a smile; he'd dressed smartly, aubergine coloured chinos showed off his trim waist and gained him appreciative looks from women sitting in the dining area.

Emilia slid a bowl of peanuts across the bar towards him.

"I can't have those," he said, moving them away. "I'm allergic to peanuts."

"Is it a serious allergy?"

"It is. Just a small amount could kill me."

"Well, we had better move and take a table away from any potential peanut fatality." Emilia chuckled, and Paul joined her in an uneasy, abrupt laugh. "You'd never think that death could lurk in an innocent ceramic bowl."

She stopped at a table and pulled out a chair and sat down before taking a sip of her white wine spritzer, leaving a red lipstick imprint on the chilled glass that was beaded with condensation. "Did you drive into the city?" Emilia asked, keeping the conversation simple until the waiter had taken their orders.

"I took the train. Parking can be a pain in Brum."

"Tell me about it," she said, taking a roll from the breadbasket and tearing it in two. She could see Paul was watching her intently as she smothered the inside with butter. "I'm assuming I'm not the first agent to approach you regarding representation."

"Representation? No, I'm not even sure why I'm here."

"I asked you here to talk about you being represented by my agency and working towards your becoming a professional darts player."

"Professional?"

"Yes. I believe you have talent."

"Really…"

"Why so surprised? You could be the next Luke Littler. Since he took the darts industry by storm, every agent is looking for the next big thing."

"Is that what I am?"

"Not yet, but with guidance, you could be. Although nothing can be guaranteed."

"What would I need to do? How–"

Emilia put up her hand to silence him as their lunch arrived at the table, she thanked the waiter and flicked a napkin open and laid it in her lap then said, "I understand this can be a daunting prospect coming out of the blue, but all you'll need to do at the start is get in as much practice as you can while I arrange for you to take part in some matches."

Paul nodded, and she saw an eagerness appear on his face.

"It'll be a long road. We're not talking about overnight success, but you're still young enough to do a year on the circuit before taking on pro matches."

"Will I get paid?"

"Initially, just expenses. It's up to you to show willing and practice until I can secure matches for you. You will, of course, if successful, win the purse."

She paused and took another sip of her drink. "Subject to my agency's eleven-per cent commission."

The lunch continued, with Paul asking questions and Emilia feeding him tempting morsels of impending celebrity status and wealth to come.

With the table cleared, Paul ordered another pint, while Emilia had a sparkling water with lime.

The first time he called her Ruth, she missed it and he spoke again to get her attention. "Sorry Paul, I was miles away then thinking about how we can proceed." He nodded and smiled. She would have to be on the ball, make sure she didn't make that mistake again. "Where will you practise?" she asked.

"I can use the Roebuck. Ken usually lets me stay over."

"That will be good for a start. Can I ask, is there a Mrs Rothman at home, and will she be upset with more late nights?"

"She'll be okay with it. She has her own interests to keep her entertained."

"Very well." She sat up straighter, giving off, she hoped, an air of professionalism. "You will need to get a set of professional darts. They don't come cheap, but if you're serious about this you'll need a set, maybe two. The purse winnings from a couple of matches will more than cover the cost." Knowing she had said all the right things and fed him the lines he wanted to hear, she picked up her sunglasses and stood up; she covered her eyes before she shook his hand. "If you have questions, you have my number. Sorry to rush, but I need to get to my second appointment. It's been lovely, Paul."

She turned and with a toss of the head, her silver hair caught the light and she walked away, knowing he had taken the bait.

26

~ Fillet Steak ~

Andrew left the house early, he'd told Selena he had clients to meet and would be out for the day. Before closing the front door, he shouted upstairs to say he'd like a fillet steak for dinner when he returned.

Listening for the sound of his car to grow quieter as he drove away, Selena threw back the duvet and slid out of bed and made her way downstairs.

In the kitchen, Andrew had left the lid off the butter dish and a knife covered in toast crumbs. Smears of jam were on the counter beside his empty coffee mug and Selena picked up the lid and screwed it back on the jar before placing it back inside a cupboard. She flicked the switch on the kettle and as the water heated, she wiped up the mess left behind by her husband and put his dishes into the dishwasher; she had done this so often that she didn't even think about it; it was as if she was on autopilot.

After making her coffee, she removed the burner phone from its hiding place behind the fridge and switched it on. Instantly, it buzzed with a text from Iain that told her he was already booking viewing appointments for the wedding venue.

Sitting at the breakfast bar, she considered what she was going to say. She rehearsed a scenario in her head several times and wanted to sound professional and self-assured when she spoke with him. Nothing must raise his suspicion that she wasn't an experienced wedding planner.

"I wish I was as confident as Melanie," she said as she stepped into the shower after breakfast. "She appears the most eager of the three of us."

The warm water relaxed her and helped her to prepare her thoughts, and after dressing, she was ready to call Iain.

A second mug of coffee sat on the counter in front of her as she dialled Iain's number. He answered in three rings and cheerfully said, "Good morning, Heather."

"You remembered my name," she said, hoping she hadn't sounded like he'd caught her off guard.

"Good business practice," he replied. "To know your prospective clients' names, it instils confidence."

Thank you for that patronising lesson in business, she thought before she said. "Thank you for the message. I'd be happy to visit the venue at a time convenient with yourself. And explain more about myself and my operation."

"So you're not looking for a venue for yourself?"

He sounds a little put out, slightly annoyed, she thought. Maybe he thinks I'm trying to sell him something or muscle in on his business. Selena gave a small laugh and said, "Heaven's no, not me. I'm a bespoke planner. I recommend venues to my clients and organise their event with the owners." She paused, letting it sink in. "If that's not your thing, I'll understand, but I can bring a lot of business to your door."

He sounded flustered. "I... err... no, that's fine. I... think we can be of service."

"Superb. I have a client meeting in ten minutes, so if you can message me with the dates you have available, I'll get back to you later."

Iain said he'd let her know, and as she disconnected the call, she let out a deep breath and congratulated herself on a winning performance.

~~~

Andrew picked up his coffee and grimaced as he took a mouthful. He'd been catching up with paperwork all morning and it had gone cold.

He found admin tedious, and the pile of receipts that needed to be logged into his online ledger never seemed to get any smaller.

His eyes were heavy with boredom and his head rolled forward as sleep tried to take him, only to be thwarted by a loud knock at the door.

He scooped up the receipts and tipped them into a desk drawer before rising and walking across the office. He opened the door and standing on the threshold was a woman dressed in pseudo army fatigues with a baseball cap pulled down over her eyes.

"Hi," Melanie said, holding out her hand. "We spoke on the phone, Charlotte Allen, but people call me Charlie."

"Pleased to meet you Charlie," Andrew said, shaking her hand and inviting her inside. "What can I do for you?"

"I was passing and thought I'd drop in and check you out." She gave a good-humoured laugh. "See if you're a bona fide dealer."

She allowed him to lead her through the display area into his office as he said, "And what have you deduced thus far?"

"I'll reserve judgement until I've discovered the quality of your coffee." She plonked herself in the chair opposite Andrew's desk, and he walked into the small kitchen and switched on the kettle. As he spooned instant coffee into mugs, he watched her as she spun in the chair from side to side. She looked younger than she had sounded on the telephone and had a cute tomboyish look about her. "How do you like your coffee?"

"Black, one sugar," she replied.

Andrew returned with two mugs and retreated behind his desk and took his seat. He watched as she took a sip and asked in a manner that he hoped sounded light-hearted what her decision regarding the coffee was.

"It's passable." She shrugged and gave him a wink. "You're not how I imagined you to be."

"Really? How did you imagine me?"

"Well," she said, knitting her fingers together and resting her chin on them, giving him direct eye contact that made him feel a little uneasy. "I expected an older guy in a stuffy suit and tie. You know, like the auctioneers you see on TV."

"I'm sorry if you're disappointed."

"Hardly." there was that laugh again. "I was hoping for someone I could relate to. Someone nearer my age, rather than some dusty old man."

"Thank you, but I'm sure I'm quite a few years away from your age."

"Ooh, you're smooth," she giggled, and he smiled, a little perturbed by her confidence. He was never good around confident women.

"Did you bring the items you wish to sell with you?" he asked and Melanie shook her head. "That's a shame."

"I have some photos you could look at." Reaching into a jacket pocket, she removed her new, second-hand phone and clicked a few buttons and held it out to him. "Sorry, they're a bit shit."

Andrew looked at the images, unaware that Melanie had taken snaps of the objects she'd told him about from the encyclopaedia. She'd blurred them slightly and pasted them into a collage frame to disguise the background. He said nothing and after scrolling through; he handed back her phone.

"You're right. The photos are shit."

She returned his smile. "But they look like the items you told me about on the phone. However, I will need to see them to establish they're authentic, and only then can I give you an approximation of value."

"I understand. But now you've sort of seen them, do you think they're worth much?"

"I can't make an educated decision based on a blurred image. But everything is worth something." He shifted uneasily in his seat; afraid he'd lose control of the situation. "Sorry, I can't be more positive. I hope you understand, in the current climate, it's best to reserve judgement."

"I can assure you I'm genuine." Melanie said. "Not a scammer."

Andrew watched her finish her coffee. He hoped he hadn't offended her and lost what he knew could be a lucrative purchase.

"I don't think for one minute you're disingenuous. I'm just cautious. It's best to be that way for the both of us." He tried out a good-humoured laugh, but it sounded flat to his ears.

Melanie rose from her seat, making ready to leave, and taking a chance Andrew said, "When do you think you could bring the pieces? Or I could always travel to you, whatever is easiest?"

Melanie held out her hand and shaking his, she said, "I'll check my diary and when I've made my decision, I'll call you. Nice to meet you, Andrew."

As the door closed behind her, he said under his breath, "Bollocks."

~~~

Selena stood at the bus stop; her blonde plaited wig covered by the floppy sun hat. A warm breeze lifted the hem of the maxi dress and she repositioned the tote bag on her shoulder before she held out her hand to stop the bus. She paid her fare and walked up the aisle, trying to work out if people were watching her.

Happy that she had passed the test, no one had stared at her and even a lady she knew hadn't rumbled her disguise. This was one of her worries put to bed.

The town centre would be another test. The last thing she needed was someone to recognise her and report back to Andrew.

She purchased his fillet steak from the butcher and a wedding magazine from a newsagent before making her way back to the gym to get changed.

Back home, she looked out an old Filofax that had been Andrew's and the used pages and Post-It notes gave the impression of an industrious owner – Iain wouldn't need to see the notes scribbled inside; it was just a prop. She cut out images from the wedding magazine and stuffed them inside, hoping one or two would slip out at their meeting.

She placed everything in her hiding space behind the fridge and took Andrew's steak out of the fridge to come to room temperature. Selena resisted the temptation to drop it on the floor or stamp on it. Pettiness wasn't in her nature.

27

~ Steady Tiger ~

After the labourers and other trades had gone home for the evening and Emilia confirmed that there were no workers hanging around, she double checked that every external door was secure. She walked down the corridor to the room the project manager used as an office and unlocked the door and stepped inside.

It didn't take long to locate what she was looking for and, sliding the metal case open, she removed a single glass vial and slipped it inside her pocket before locking up and heading back to the reception area.

Looking up as she heard Iain's car arrive outside, she opened the flowers she'd bought earlier and smiled at him as he stepped inside.

He walked over to her and kissed her gently on the cheek, and she placed the vase of fresh flowers on the modern console table that resembled a plank of scaffolding board on metal legs. The reception area at Astley House was now decorated. The walls were a pale green with cream coloured woodwork. He smiled thinking, Emilia would die rather than paint anything magnolia. "It's looking good," he said.

The main desk was a central island with two cream sofas facing the stairs. Sheer voile hung at the windows, a darker green, the only pop of colour in the space that was designed intentionally to be relaxing.

The caretaker's rooms were now a fully equipped administration hub, with desks, computers and printers just waiting for staff to power them up.

"I'm hoping it gives a good impression," Emilia said. "Bride's must get sick of seeing pink and gold."

"I knew I could rely on your impeccable taste to make this work."

"When will the function room be ready for dressing?"

"The sparks and chippies are going in after we've fumigated it."

"Is there a problem?"

"Nothing serious, just insects and mice. It's expected after years of neglect. Once the wiring's in and the plastering is complete, it'll be all yours."

"Perfect. Once it's dressed for a wedding breakfast, it'll be perfect for prospective brides and grooms to visualise their special day. Have you seen the bridal suite?"

Iain shook his head, and after rearranging the flowers again, Emilia led him upstairs.

Iain opened the door and stepped inside, immediately pleased with what he saw. A super king bed dominated the space that was painted in subtle tones of yellow and gold. The polished floorboards shone in the lemon-coloured haze from the wall lights and moonlight filtered through the voile curtains at the windows. A sofa with sumptuous cushions backed onto the bottom of the bed and placed either side of a small circular dining table were two chairs. Emilia had dressed the table with a champagne bucket and flutes and two place settings in anticipation of a room service breakfast.

"This is perfect," Iain said, giving his wife a hug. "You're a bloody genius."

"Glad you like it. I think it beats the usual Tiffany-style lamps and chrome bedsides. I wanted it to be sensual rather than virginal."

Iain slipped an arm across Emilia's shoulder and blew gently into her ear before nodding towards the made up bed.

"Steady tiger," she said. "We've work to be getting on with."

After putting on hard hats, they walked down the corridor to look at progress with the guest bedrooms and the bathrooms. Some were still empty shells. Channels cut into the walls for wiring, bags of plaster on the floor and doors stacked under windows. Iain had told her the attic room stairs were now reinstated and that he'd opted to use them for staff accommodation when the spa was up and running.

"Makes sense," Emilia said with a nod of her head as they walked back to the reception area.

Iain's phone rang. He removed it from his pocket and looked at the screen. "I need to take this," he said.

"I'll powder my nose," she said, picking up her handbag and disappearing into the admin suite, where she removed the vial from her pocket and placed it inside her handbag.

Back in the corridor, she heard Iain ending his telephone and as she joined him, she said, "So, where are you taking me for dinner?"

As the waiter delivered a chilled bottle of Torrontés to their table, Iain once again thanked Emilia for the work she'd put into the project so far. "I had an interesting telephone call today," he said as he tasted the wine and nodded his acceptance to the waiter. "The woman who made contact before. Heather Fox. Turns out she's a wedding organiser and books venues for clients. Could be a money spinner getting into bed with a wedding planner."

"Just as long as it's not the one in my bridal suite," she laughed. "I don't want those Egyptian cotton sheets creased."

Iain chinked his glass with hers and joined in, laughing at her joke.

28

~ Mr Chan ~

Bridget handed Andrew a mug of coffee and sat down opposite him as he said, "I'm really grateful you could look after my latest acquisition for me. I've already found a buyer for these." He tapped the box that contained the items he'd purchased from Lionel.

"It was a pleasure," Bridget said as she smiled, a gesture that Andrew thought was insincere, but didn't care.

He'd got his hands on the items behind Nigel's back, and that meant he kept one hundred per cent of the sale price, minus a paltry holding fee for Bridget.

"Have you any other deals in the offing?" Bridget asked.

Guarded, as usual. Andrew just shrugged and told her, "A few in the pipeline. To be honest, I'm getting a little tired of jetting backwards and forwards to the Far East. It cuts into profits, especially when the margins are as tight as they are at the moment."

"You need to find someone on the ground out there to do the searching and shipping for you."

"I tried that once, but the guy I hired ended up double crossing me on a deal." Bridget smiled again and nodded.

"What I could do with is moving on to more lucrative artifacts rather than run-of-the-mill Chinese porcelain."

"Have you thought of introducing yourself to Mr Chan?"

"I've heard his name, but that's about all I know, apart from, he's a guy who deals in top drawer cultural relics."

"Some say he also trades in looted pieces."

"I had heard something along those lines, but Mr Chan is a paradox. Some dealers even say he doesn't exist."

"Maybe he doesn't, but there was talk of him shifting books from the Tang Dynasty through an auction house in Tokyo. Obviously, no one has provided proof of the rumour."

"Exactly. Looks like I'm destined for long-haul flights for the foreseeable." He gave a shrug and after he'd said goodbye, he left Bridget and headed off for a lunch appointment.

~~~

"Thanks for helping," Nigel said as he spotted Andrew enter the bistro. "I'll get back to you later with an update." Nigel put his phone down on the table as Andrew arrived at his side. "I've ordered drinks," he said, as the waiter delivered two pints of amber liquid. "Lager, okay?"

"Sure," Andrew replied, pulling out a chair and sitting at the table. "I've not been here before." Looking around, Andrew liked the open aspect of the bistro. A place to see and to be seen, he thought as Nigel passed him a copy of the menu. "Is the food good?"

"Your normal run of mill gastro pub fare but decent sized portions." They sat in silence, choosing their lunch and after giving their order to the waiter, Nigel said, "I've a client wanting to sell a Chinese tapestry. I know it's not your usual thing, but I think it'll move quickly."

"It's worth considering," Andrew said before taking a glug of his drink. "Silk?"

"Yes, a famille rose design with cranes."

"What do you think I'll fetch?"

"Five hundred easily at auction, a grand in a private sale."

"Let me have a photo and more details and I'll put the feelers out. I'm sure one of my previous clients would be interested."

As they ate their lunch, they exchanged pleasantries, mostly mundane observations, and didn't talk about business again until the table was clear and they had coffee. "I was telling a friend this morning how I'd like to sell more profitable pieces. The flights back and forth to China are becoming a real ball-ache."

"When you say 'profitable', what exactly do you mean?"

"Don't get me wrong, I'm ticking over nicely and I appreciate the clients you send me…"

Andrew paused, and Nigel assumed he was trying to find the right words. "I think I'm ready to handle more prestige pieces rather than the endless vases and pots that come my way."

"When you say 'prestige' I'm guessing you're talking about…" Nigel lowered his voice, "… items that private collectors would go for. Irrespective of provenance and procurement?"

"Spot on."

Nigel allowed a smile to stretch across his face and signalled the waiter asked him to for two brandies.

"Can you help in any way?"

Warming the bowl of the brandy glass in his hand, Nigel leant forward and said, "What you need is an expert at finding and selling on cultural artifacts without them being linked to you."

"How would that work?" Despite the tabletop between them, Nigel thought Andrew had moved closer.

"It's complicated. You have put up the capital and take responsibility for documenting the transaction." Nigel made discreet air quotes, "… how you see fit."

"Falsifying the records?" Andrew whispered, and Nigel nodded.

"You'd certainly be playing with the big boys. Ensuring you get the right goods, so to speak, you could earn enough in a year or two to retire comfortably."

Nigel enjoyed seeing the greed written across Andrew's face. "But as I said earlier. You'll need someone with experience."

Andrew swallowed his brandy in one mouthful and asked the waiter to deliver two more and, after looking left and right, said, "Someone like Mr Chan?"

"What do you know about Mr Chan?"

"Not much. Some dealers I've spoken to say he doesn't exist."

"He exists all right. It's his name that's fictional." Nigel noticed Andrew's brow furrow in confusion and continued, "I could tell you more. But you'd have to promise me you'll keep what I say to yourself. You mess with Mr Chan at your peril."

"You know me Nigel, my word is my bond."

With a bland expression, Nigel picked up his drink and let the brandy warm his throat as he thought, Yes, I know you, Andrew Cavendish. I know you better than you realise. He put the brandy glass down and with a fixed stare said, "The first thing you need to know is that Mr Chan is an alias. Mr Chan is, in fact, the art dealer Hugh Milton-Cole."

"Milton-Cole, he's sourced antiques for heads of state, international royalty and wealthy celebrities."

"Exactly. That's why everything is pseudonymous. One thing you have to understand once you're accepted inside his circle, there's no way out. It can be very lucrative. Mr Chan protects his loyal associates. But in equal measure, it's dangerous if anyone cheats him or attempts to reveal his identity."

Inwardly, Nigel was smiling. He had gambled that Andrew's greed would gloss over the realisation that he was being told that he was being warned against getting involved. It was a bet Nigel had placed and won.

"Don't share this information." Nigel looked around.

"Last year he sold a single statuette looted from Tuyugou Grottos in Xinjiang to an American businessman for 2.5

million dollars." Andrew let out a whistle and Nigel held a finger to his lips to silence him.

Nigel's phone buzzed. He picked it up and read the text message before he said, "I need to be getting off, but before I do, I'd better visit the loo. You can guarantee as soon as I'm on the M1 I'll get the urge to pee." He rose from the table and walked over towards the facilities and before entering he secreted himself behind an artificial palm and watched as Andrew picked up the phone from the table, guessing he was scrolling through the contacts list.

"I've paid the bill," he said when he returned to the table and picked up his phone. "What we've been discussing. Remember not a word and we were never here today."

29

~ Tragedy In Three Acts ~

Emilia was sitting at the breakfast bar looking at the empty syringe and the bottle of peanut oil. Beside it was the vial of hydrogen cyanide she'd taken from Astley House. She had worried that the manager there would have alerted Iain that it was missing, but he'd been careless and not reported it. She had spent days considering which of the liquids to use, worried that it might be too much of a risk, too dangerous to change her original plan at this late juncture. "Should I stick with the peanut?" she asked herself as she picked up the cyanide and turned it over in her hand. "What if he has his EpiPen? What if I don't administer enough to kill him? What if... Enough of the what ifs," she told herself. "The cyanide is fast acting and more reliable." She had made her choice and so rose from the breakfast stool and put the peanut oil inside a kitchen cupboard and went to have a shower.

She was meeting Paul that evening after the Roebuck had closed for the day, and had told Iain that she was sourcing some fabrics for the wedding venue bedrooms and he could reach on her mobile if he needed to call her—she knew he wouldn't. He'd be with his *'entertainment'* for the evening.

Emilia was certain she'd register on ANPR cameras, so she had booked two appointments, one with a curtain and blind maker in Solihull and the other with a bespoke furniture maker.

"I'll be tired so will stay overnight and drive home the following morning," she had said to Iain after he'd told her it would be okay as he was staying in town.

With her overnight bag packed and ready in the hallway, she called Paul's mobile.

"Hey Ruth, how's things?"

"Just double checking you'll be free tonight to go over a few things. I've an exciting prospect for you," Emilia said.

"I'm intrigued. What is it?"

"You'll have to wait. Did you check with Ken about the CCTV?"

"Yes, there's none at the pub. The skinflint is too tight to pay for it."

"That's a good thing. The last thing we want is people watching you as you practise and taking notes."

"Does that really happen?" he asked.

"The underhand tricks some managers employ would surprise you. Some will do anything to get one over on a competitor. I should be with you around 11:00 pm, meetings all day. Will it be okay to come over at that hour? If not, we could arrange a lunch date, but that'll have to be a few weeks away, and we could miss the opportunity I've found for you."

"No, it'll be fine. I'll be practicing, anyway."

Before disconnecting the call, she told Paul she'd see him later and then arranged some paint charts and fabric swatches on the breakfast bar to give the illusion she'd been working, should Iain by chance come home early. She picked up the glass vial and secured it inside a Ziploc bag and with her jacket over her arm; she carried her overnight bag out to the car and thought, here we go Emilia, no turning back now.

Pressing play on the car stereo, Alison Moyet's voice filled the car, and Emilia pulled out of the driveway and put her task to the back of her mind as she sang along.

The man behind the reception desk looked up from his

phone screen as Emilia entered the Premier Inn. "Welcome to Rugby North," he said, putting his phone down on the desktop. Emilia apologised for being early, adding for colour that an appointment had been rescheduled. She opened her handbag and fumbled inside, looking for something when it tipped up, spilling its contents all over the reception desk. "Sorry," she said, and the assistant gave her his practised smile that really said he didn't care for her apology, and after helping her to collect up her belongings he handed her a key card and directed her to the stairs before turning back to his phone.

In the room, Emilia congratulated herself on the fuss she'd engineered at reception. "That little performance should be enough to make my check-in memorable," she told herself in the mirror.

During her appointments, she asked lots of questions and took away brochures and swatches and after she'd said, "They'll be perfect for a quiet area in the bar," she left an order for ten stools with the furniture maker.

She paid a visit to the Touchwood Shopping Centre in Solihull, making herself available to the CCTV cameras as she purchased some items for the bedrooms. Stopping off for lunch at an independent coffee shop. While eating her sandwich, she scoured the room for cameras, and seeing none, she paid the bill and slipped into the toilets to change her clothes before driving the three miles to Knowle; the road bordered by agricultural land was quiet. Parking in a layby using black electrician's tape, she changed the letters L and F on her numberplate to E and donned her wig and sunglasses and continued on her journey.

~~~

Paul thought about Ruth's phone call all day, wondering what the exciting prospect could be.

Because he'd spent many hours dreaming about fame

and fortune, he'd put in serious hours of practice and found his game had improved, so much so he had thought about talking to Ken about inviting other local pub teams to play a tournament at the pub, but he'd need to ask Ruth's advice first.

Thinking it best he put in some extra practice, he showered and changed and headed off to the Roebuck where, after a couple of pints, he began throwing darts.

"Your game has really come on," Ken said, putting his third pint down on the table.

"Thanks, and I appreciate the help you've given me."

"Help. What help?"

"Letting me come over and train out of hours."

"If you're here, I know the place is safe. Saves me worrying about the place being turned over while I'm away pumping Rita."

"You're all heart," Paul laughed.

For the rest of the day, Paul passed the time with friends playing darts. Despite several beers, his game was still on point and he was happy to beat each of his friends, rewarding them all with a round of shots.

"Looking sharp," a man in a British flag t-shirt said, while another said his game had been flawless. The men banged their glasses down on the table after swallowing the spirit in one mouthful, and Paul asked the barmaid to refresh their glasses. He was enjoying this period of being a pseudo-celebrity and hoped this was a suggestion of the lifestyle to come.

Paul returned to the Roebuck just before 9:00, tossed his jacket over a chair and joined some friends. Later, Ken sidled over to ask the lads to leave. Grumpily they left the pub and Ken said, "There's not much doing, so I'm knocking off. Closing up early."

"What time is it?"

"10:20. If you're staying on to throw some more darts,

try to stay off the booze. You've had a skinful already today."

"Sure," Paul replied, "I'll even load the glass washer for you."

"Thanks and take note of what I've said."

"I'll be fine."

"No doubt, but don't leave my door unlocked." Ken walked away whistling, and Paul knew the old man was off to spend the night in Rita's bed.

~~~

Jez killed the car's engine. Despite his car having cloned plates, he parked in the darkest part of the Roebuck's car park and waited, watching until he saw Ken drive away. He assumed if the bar lights were on inside that Paul would be there.

He tossed his cigarette butt into the undergrowth, then picked up the takeaway bag from the passenger seat and strolled across to the entrance. The doors were unlocked and noiseless as he pushed one open.

Paul was throwing darts, and Jez stood silently watching him until he turned from the dartboard and saw him.

"Shit. You scared me, man. What are you doing creeping about?"

"Didn't want to put you off your throw. I've brought food." Jez held up the paper bag.

"Curry?"

"Of course, your favourite."

"Is it…?"

"Yes, man, no peanuts. Told your mates at the Indian it was for you. Thought we could sit down, eat some food and talk."

"I've a meeting at 11:00."

Raising an eyebrow, Jez said, "Oh yeah, late night meeting. Isn't your missus doing it for you anymore?"

"It's nothing like that. You know me, I'd never cheat on Mel."

Paul got up and walked behind the bar. He was pouring two pints as Jez leant over and removed something from Paul's jacket pocket.

"So," Paul said, putting the drinks down on the table, "have you thought about what I said?"

"Sure. I've given it a lot of thought." Jez tore off a piece of naan bread and dipped it into the sauce. "It's difficult."

"What's difficult? You cut me in or I'll speak to the law."

"I thought we were mates. We go way back."

"Did you think of that when you used a business that I'm part of to run a chop shop?"

"There are others involved. They supply the tech to disable the trackers and central locking systems."

"And I'm guessing the car on the scissor lift's a decoy, if anyone comes sniffing around?"

"Yeah. Look these guys I'm working with, they're not keen on outsiders. They want me to front exports abroad. It could be good for me."

"Or see you doing a stretch inside." Paul stabbed a piece of chicken with a fork. As he chewed, he pulled off some bread and scooped up some sauce and rice.

The two friends sat in companionable silence eating until Jez said, "Why would you want a cut? You've got a flash house and your wife's family's bank balances. Come on mate, you're minted."

Jez watched as Paul shook his head and licked his lips. "You, okay?"

"This pasanda, it has peanuts, hasn't it?"

"Sorry, did I forget to mention your allergy to the guys at the takeaway?"

Jez could see Paul was becoming dizzy as his speech became slurred.

Paul got up from his seat. "You bastard," he said, and

made his way shakily to the chair where his jacket was. He rummaged through the pockets, his balance compromised, knees giving way.

"Looking for this?" Jez said, holding up Paul's EpiPen.

"Give it me," Paul demanded. He needed a shot of epinephrine and shook his head as his heartbeat increased and his breathing became laboured.

"I guess your tongue is swelling now. That should stop you blabbing about my business."

"Jez," Paul implored. "I'll keep schtum."

"Can't take the risk, mate."

Paul took a step towards Jez, an abdominal cramp winded him and he collapsed. The last thing he saw was his old schoolfriend standing over him; looking at his wristwatch, watching and waiting for him to die.

Jez tossed the EpiPen across the room, picked up Paul's darts and threw them at the dartboard before he grabbed a piece of naan bread, dipped it into Paul's pasanda and walked out of the pub.

~~~

Emilia endured a traffic delay and arrived ten minutes later than she'd arranged with Paul. She looked and saw the downstairs light was still on and parked up.

She checked her wig in the rear-view mirror before stepping out of the car and putting on her sunglasses.

The air inside the bar was old, with the stale smell of beer clinging to the walls and furnishings. She spotted three darts impaled in the dartboard and at first wondered where Paul was.

Then she saw him, lying where he had fallen, between two tables.

From behind her shades his skin looked a blueish colour, and raising her sunglasses, she could see he wasn't breathing.

She calmly walked over to him and touched his

forehead; he was warm but when she felt for a pulse in his neck and then his wrist, she couldn't find one.

She stayed looking at him for several minutes before checking again, noting that his skin was cooling. "No pulse," she muttered under her breath. "He's dead." Taking out a handkerchief, she wiped his neck and wrist where she'd touched him and calmly stood up and walked out of the pub and drove away.

After briefly stopping in a country lane to remove the wig and place it, with the sunglasses and her suit inside a plastic carrier bag. She removed the electricians' tape from her registration plate and smashed the glass vial, using her foot to sweep the glass into a patch of weeds. The air outside would disperse the fumes. She straightened up, smoothed down her skirt, and made her way back to the Premier Inn.

Thoughts were racing inside her head and at the main doors. Seeing that the desk was unattended, she used her key card and made her way up to her room.

In the shower, she replayed the evening's events and couldn't remember seeing anything that could tell her why Paul was lying dead on the floor. She knew she couldn't call Melanie; they had already agreed to no immediate contact after the act and so she'd have to abide by the rules.

After drying her hair, she went to bed and lay between crisp white sheets, and with a head filled with questions, sleep stayed away.

30

~ No Way Back ~

Seeing the police car pull into the drive, Melanie shivered and pulled her dressing gown tighter around herself. Paul hadn't come home last night, and she wondered if he'd spent a night in the cells on a drunk and disorderly. She soon realised, as she looked into the face of the young female police officer on her doorstep, that it was more serious. "May we come in?" Melanie held open the door and stood aside as the two police officers stepped inside. She offered to make coffee, but they both declined, asking her to sit down. "This is the home of Paul Rothman?" the male officer asked, consulting his notebook as the female officer removed a pack of travel tissues from her jacket pocket.

"Yes, I'm his wife."

"I'm afraid we have some bad news." The officer removed a tissue and hovered, waiting to hand it to Melanie. "We discovered the body of a man at the Roebuck Inn this morning. The publican..." he looked down at his notes, "Kenneth Swift called us. He identified the body, but we will need you to do the formal identification."

"When?"

"Possibly later, maybe tomorrow."

"Where is he?"

"He's been taken to the mortuary," the male officer said. "We'll let you know when you can see him."

"What happened?" Melanie sniffed, and the other officer saw her opportunity to pass her the tissue.

"We're not entirely sure at present," she said, "But there are no injuries, so we can hypothetically rule out the possibility of an attack. Kenneth says he left him alone in the pub last night. Is that normal?"

"Yes. Paul and Ken are good friends..." she paused as the police officers' eyes dipped, "...were good friends. Paul often stayed behind to practise his darts playing. He was captain of the pub's team." There followed a few more mundane questions about her husband's lifestyle before the officers bade her farewell and drove away.

Melanie sat in silence for a while, thoughts filtering down from shock to apprehension: Had Emilia fulfilled her side of the pact or could it be something else had happened? She shook the thoughts from her head as another slid into her consciousness. He's gone. We're free. She felt a lump form in her throat and as it rose upwards wondered if she'd need the tissue she was still holding, but the upset she thought was rising turned into a chuckle, developing into a sinister laugh. She balled the tissue and tossed it onto the side table and pulled herself together and did the one thing Melanie thought was situation appropriate; she made her way upstairs and, opening her wardrobe, she prepared a couple of suitable grief-stricken outfits.

~~~

Emilia folded the tissue and blotted her lipstick before dropping it into the wastebin. She'd slept sporadically, her mind racing and questioning what had happened; would she have done the deed or had fate stepped in to deal the fatal blow? She chastised herself for her theatrical notion as the quote, *Sleep that knits up the ravelled sleeve of care*, slid into her thoughts; now she understood how an anxious mind can be repaired by sleep, as knitting repairs a frayed sleeve, but as she had rolled and revolved beneath the duvet, the racetrack of thoughts kept her from slumber.

The shower had done little to energise her. Dressed and with no appetite, she climbed into her car and pulled out of the car park and headed home.

~~~

Sitting in the car park outside the public mortuary, Melanie pulled down the sun visor and checked herself in the mirror, eye shadow and blusher discrete enough to look respectful. That morning, she'd chosen a Karen Millen dress in Maroon and teamed it with matching shoes and handbag. She'd packed tissues partly for subterfuge, but also because she wasn't sure how she'd react when she saw Paul.

After she gave her name to the disembodied voice on the door's entrance system, the electronic door opened with a click and Melanie stepped inside. A woman in a sombre suit met her and, after an introduction and condolences, she allowed herself to be led along the corridor. She was directed to a room with a curtained window and a low table on which sat a box of tissues and a vase of flowers; Melanie noticed they were fake and remembered her mother had called silk flowers 'dust collectors'. Following a knock at the door, it opened and the female officer from the previous day entered, along with a man she'd not met before. "This is DS Toft," said the officer, introducing her colleague. They shook hands, and he explained the procedure, telling Melanie that after the formal identification because of Paul's relatively young age, the coroner had requested an autopsy. Melanie nodded, and putting a tissue to her nose, she gave a forced sniffle.

The procedure was over quickly; she confirmed what the police already knew and found herself surprised by the pang of sadness that twisted in her chest as she looked at her husband's pale face and whispered the confirmation to the DS.

With the curtain once more drawn across the viewing

window, an assistant offered coffee, which she declined and asked, "When will the autopsy take place?"

"It's scheduled for this afternoon."

"As soon as that?"

"Yes, sometimes it's best to get these things sorted out as quickly as possible. Luckily the pathologist has a free window."

Luckily? An odd choice of word, Melanie thought before she said, "When will I know what happened?"

"If it's straightforward, we could have an answer for you within 48 hours."

Later, sitting in her kitchen with a glass of red wine in front of her, Melanie stared into space for many minutes. Her mind was blank apart from one thought. It's started, there's no going back now.

31

~ The Appointment ~

Selena was nervous. Iain's telephone call had surprised her. His jovial manner had caught her off guard; she'd expected him to be more businesslike, maybe a little hard, rather than friendly. Perhaps this was his sales persona. "Good morning, Heather," he'd said – on first-name terms already she had thought – "We've finished most of the main rooms at Astley House and I have a free appointment slot available if you'd be interested in taking it."

"That sounds good," Selena said.

"I'll be there all day tomorrow and I could give you a tour of the property and answer any questions you have. I've had some interest from other wedding planners, so it would be good to have you on board too, if you like what you see."

Selena had agreed to an appointment but was still undecided about how she'd take care of Iain. She thought it would be a good excuse to check both him and the house out. Maybe she'd get an idea while she was there.

~~~

Selena could see her hands shake as she buttoned up her blouse, and she hoped the drive south would calm her nerves.

Andrew was away for a couple of days and she had hoped this would give her time to think, but trying to piece together any ideas hadn't been easy and she wondered if the others were wrestling with their thoughts, too.

She wasn't concerned with the morality of the pact it was the details regarding the act of killing she was worried about. "Stop it," she chastised herself, and picking up her keys, stomped defiantly out to her car.

The drive had calmed her and as she parked outside Astley House; she looked up at the rows of windows again, wondering if she was being watched. The electronic beep as her car automatically locked sounded loud in the stillness, and a chill raced up her spine. She didn't have time to worry about being alone as the main door opened and Iain stepped outside, his hand outstretched in welcome. "Heather, lovely to meet you." Selena slid her hand inside his, noting the size compared to her own. "Coffee?" he asked, and she told him that would be very nice. "Have you travelled far today?" he said as he closed the front door behind them.

"Just from Buckingham, thirty minutes away," she surprised herself at how easily the lie slipped from her mouth.

Iain led her into the office, which had once been the caretaker's rooms. He motioned to a sofa beneath a framed photograph of an aerial shot of the property.

Iain was filling a cafetiere and telling her about his plans for the business when the door opened and Selena's heart leapt into her throat as Emilia walked into the room. "Heather, let me introduce you to my wife, Emilia." Standing up and smoothing down her skirt, Selena's pulse raced as she shook Emilia's hand. "Pleased to meet you, Heather."

"Likewise," she replied.

"Has my husband offered you a coffee yet?"

"I was just making it," he said as the kettle clicked.

"Let me," Emilia said as she took over and poured the hot water over the ground coffee. Selena returned to her seat and clasped her hands between her knees to hide the trembling.

She was in awe of how detached Emilia was. There was no inkling of recognition, not even a twitch of a smile or a sideways glance. After placing a tray with two cups and the cafetiere onto a table, Emilia made her excuses and left the room. "My wife's hosting a publicity shoot today for Hello Magazine." Iain said, pushing the plunger down into the coffee.

After refreshments, Iain gave Selena a tour of the rooms that were completed and asked her questions that she had already rehearsed answers to.

Opening the door to the bridal suite, Iain stepped aside, allowing Selena to look around alone. Emilia's styling impressed her.

She was looking out of the window, and hoped her performance was convincing when Iain asked, "What do you think?"

"It's lovely. The view is perfect and what a good idea to have a dining area in here."

"So, Heather, could you see yourself working with us?"

Selena nodded and, thinking on her feet, said, "I like everything you've shown me so far. If we can agree on some costings and I can have some images to deliver to clients, we could begin working together in a matter of weeks. Obviously, people book weddings months, sometimes years, in advance, so the completion of the property renovations isn't a concern to me."

Iain escorted Selena back to the office and was organising a press pack for her when his phone rang. "Excuse me," he said and asked the caller to wait. He handed the folder to Selina and excused himself and stepped outside.

Minutes later, he returned and apologised for his absence, as the door opened again and Emilia walked in.

"The photographer would like a word, Iain," she said and, giving Selena a businesslike smile, added, "I apologise for interrupting your meeting. Have you enjoyed the tour?"

"Yes, thank you," Selena replied as once again Iain apologised and stepped outside.

The room fell silent, Emilia scribbled something in a notebook, and Selena read the press pack. The atmosphere felt leaden, and Selena wanted to leave, but couldn't until Iain returned.

The minutes ticked by, and she breathed a sigh of relief when Iain returned. "Sorry again."

"That's okay, I understand. I must be going as I've another appointment later today."

"I'll see you out," Emilia said and opened the door for Selena.

"It was lovely meeting you today and thank you for showing me around. I'll be in touch soon." Selena shook hands with Iain and followed Emilia outside.

At her car, Emilia offered her hand and as they shook, Selena felt something being pressed into her palm.

After climbing into her car, she looked up and saw Iain at the office window watching and despite the distance, gave him a smile before she turned on the ignition and drove away.

She drove for several miles before she stopped the car and after removing the wig that had been irritating her scalp; she opened the scrunched up ball of paper.

Part one is complete.

At first, she thought Emilia was referring to Astley House, but with a shudder, she realised what the message meant. Emilia was telling her the first part of their plan had come to fruition.

It must mean Paul is dead, she thought, knowing both Andrew and Iain were still alive. Suddenly, she felt woozy and her mouth dried. She tried to swallow, but it was impossible. "Don't panic," she said aloud as she rifled through her bag for a bottle of water.

Back at her gym with her disguise secured away in her locker she was worried that if she went home, she'd just fret and the last thing she'd need if Andrew arrived home was to be out of sorts, one never knew how he'd react.

Selena walked into the café, ordered a drink and a sandwich and, watching people work out through the viewing window, her anxiety faded and with it, she pieced together her plan to deal with Iain.

Screwing up Emilia's note, she placed it inside the empty sandwich wrapper and, before she left, dropped it into the waste bin.

32

~ Change ~

Cyndi looked around the sitting room of her flat with its second-hand furniture and tired carpet. On the sofa her boyfriend, Vinnie, was lying motionless, his eyes rolled back inside head as his body succumbed to the chemicals coursing through his veins. He'd be out of it for hours.
She'd received a call from the agency and was happy to hear the receptionist tell her that there had been a request for her services that evening.

"Iain, does it ring a bell? Say's he'll pick you up in the same place."

"Yes, I know who you mean." She remembered his Bentley and the envelope of cash he'd given her before.

"We'll give him a callback to confirm."

"I'll be there," Cyndi said and, after ending the call, made her way to the bathroom. She'd probably be back before Vinnie came around from wherever the drugs took him.

~~~

After Selena had left, Iain told Emilia he had back-to-back meetings all afternoon and they could run late, so he wouldn't be home until the next day. "Boozy meetings. You know how they can be." He smiled as he said it and she just nodded in agreement. Said she'd see him the following day.

As she drove away, she thought about the unexpected

appearance of Selena and how the two of them had played their parts so well, each pretending never to have met before. Emilia also hoped Selena would dispose of the note sensibly.

One hour into her journey, she felt hungry. She'd been so busy that she'd forgotten to break for lunch, so, parked in the car park outside a supermarket and went inside to purchase a bottle of water and a sandwich. She took a swig of the carbonated water, enjoying the bubbles on her tongue, and tore open the sandwich wrapper.

As she ate, her attention turned to Melanie. How was she feeling? She wanted to know but knew she couldn't call. She'd seen enough episodes of *Vera* to understand how telephone masts and tracking worked.

Removing her burner phone, she turned it over in her hands, wondering if she should, but common sense took hold and she realised that initially if the police suspected foul play, then Melanie would be one of their persons of interest.

You never could tell how a sudden death could pan out in a detective's mind.

"Maybe I can check online?" she said to herself, "after all, even if my car's registered on APNR, it's not an offence to stop and purchase a sandwich."

Opening a web browser, she typed Worcester news. At the top of the search was the local newspaper, and she scrolled through, finding nothing. She chose a date a few days before and found a report stating that the publican of a local pub had found a customer dead in the bar. It mentioned Paul's name, but nothing more.

Emilia closed down the page and erased her browsing history. She decided for now, as far as the others knew; she had completed her part in the plot.

Leaving the car, she walked to a litter bin and pushed the empty bottle and sandwich wrapper inside. Instinct told her to dispose of the burner phone but without a thought she slid it inside her jacket pocket, returned to the car and drove away.

~~~

The Bentley pulled alongside the kerb, a door opened and Cyndi slid inside.

The car moved silently through the dark lanes, the purr of the engine comforted her and combined with the smell of the leather and mixed with Iain's musky aftershave it made Cyndi think of wealth. Pushing aside her own situation, allowing her to imagine she was someone else.

At Astley House, she allowed Iain to take her by the arm and direct her to the main door. Her eyes widened at the size of the hallway and she wanted to whistle at the splendour. Instead, she kept tight-lipped and let him take her by the hand upstairs to the honeymoon suite.

He poured her a glass of champagne and she watched him remove his jacket and shirt; he was very different to Vinnie, who was rangy and covered in spots. Iain had a body that was cared for, hard and unyielding. The body of a successful businessman, one that said, alpha. Surprisingly, with the gentleness of a kitten, he undressed her and carried her over to the bed.

A pencil shaded sky implied morning was approaching and watching the Bentley drive away, Cyndi removed the cash from the envelope and walked home, her heels clacking on the pavement and a sense that something had changed, washed over her.

33

~ Milton-Cole ~

Hugh Milton-Cole smiled. He looked pleased with himself. As expected, Andrew; his mouth running away with him had dropped Nigel's name into the mix. Honestly, the man was a jerk, a liability. But he'd pacified him. He'd told him not to worry. "This conversation is confidential Andrew, no one needs to know."

"Thank you, I appreciate that," Andrew replied before the call disconnected.

Milton-Cole walked over to the window and looked outside before he scrolled through his contacts and pressed the green button.

"Nigel, I have news."

~~~

Andrew was in a good mood; he wore a self-satisfied grin that hadn't faded since his call earlier that morning and even the tedious job of cataloguing hadn't dampened his spirits. "Maybe I'll take Selena out for dinner tonight," he told himself as he wrote a description for a silver and lapis the ivory trinket box he'd recently purchased. His phone vibrated on the desk and looking at the screen, he saw Nigel's name. Taking the call, he found it difficult to disguise his happiness. "Hiya mate, how's things?"

"All is good here. Someone sounds cheerful," Nigel said. "I was just wondering if you were free tomorrow?"

"Sadly no. I've a bit of business to see to."

"Anything I can get involved with?"

"Nothing that'd interest you. Just some old guy I've bought a few bits and pieces from in the past."

"Oh well, can't blame me for trying. We must catch up soon." Andrew agreed but thought if everything went well with Milton-Cole tomorrow, he wouldn't need Nigel's help anymore.

His day continued to pass without interruption and the fact that he hadn't any customer footfall didn't worry him. Soon he'd be moving up in the antique world and wouldn't need his backstreet dealership.

Arriving home, he was still in a good mood and found Selena in the kitchen, "You're home early," she said, "Coffee?" He nodded and walked towards her, she switched on the kettle and he placed a kiss on her neck. "What was that for?"

"Can't I kiss my beautiful wife?" he said, his voice light and charming. "I was thinking we might go out tonight, maybe try that new Japanese place."

"You know I'm not keen on sushi."

"There's bound to be other things to eat. What about sashimi?"

"Isn't that just sushi without the rice?"

Although he didn't know the difference between the two fish dishes, a tremor of annoyance developed. What's Selena doing? he thought. Is she deliberately trying to make me sound stupid?

"If you want to go out for dinner, I'm sure we could find something you'd like."

"No. Not now, you've spoiled the moment."

"I'm sorry."

"You're always sorry." He turned and left the kitchen as the click of the kettle turning off filled the quiet space.

Later, Andrew was sulking on the bench in the garden when Selena stepped through the open patio doors and delivered him a cold bottle of beer. Barely looking at her, he said nothing as he took it from her and she turned and walked back towards the house. Just before she stepped back inside, he spoke. "So, what are we having for dinner?"

"There's a moussaka in the fridge, or I can cook you a steak."

"I don't want steak."

"What about…"

"Or a bloody moussaka."

"We could have a takeaway."

"What do you fancy?"

"I don't mind whatever you're having."

"But you must have a preference. Just tell me."

"Indian, maybe Chinese."

"English rubbish. I'm used to traditional Chinese cuisine."

"Sorry, I didn't think."

"You never do." He looked across at her frozen on the step and with hardly any motion, shook his head. "Looks like it'll be steak then. Do we have mushrooms?"

"I can nip to the shop to get some."

"You do that."

Andrew was sitting drinking whisky in the sitting room when his wife returned and popping her head around the door. Selena said, "I stopped off to buy a bag of chips from Meryl's. I know how much you like them. You always say she makes the best chips in the county."

"Yes, I do always say that."

Selena sliced the mushrooms as the chips stayed warm in the oven, and she put the steaks into a pan.

Andrew could hear the steaks sizzling and like his mood the heat was building up within them.

Checking it was to Andrew's liking; Selena plated up the chips and mushrooms as it rested before placing his dinner down on the table. "It's ready," she called, and he entered the dining room. "So you couldn't bother to cook me any chips," he said, placing the empty glass down.

"I just thought –"

"You just thought, did you?" He closed into her; his self-satisfied smile replaced by a sneer. Taking her arm, he marched her over to the cooker. "Maybe I should do the cooking from now on." He felt her struggle, but his grip tightened on her arm. He pulled her towards the hob. As punishment, he'd held her hand over the hot frying pan.

Selena found the strength to break free and this caused his rage to increase. He reached for the pan and lifted it above his head, and she screamed, the shock of which stopped Andrew in his tracks. He threw the pan across the room and stalked out of the kitchen.

As he drove away, the shock of hearing his wife scream punched into his head. She usually took her punishment silently. She's changing; he thought, but knew she'd pay for the evening's outcome at a later date.

~~~

The following morning, Andrew thought the house, which was initially hidden from the road behind a row of trees was impressive. Built in sandstone with mullioned windows it looked every inch a grand property. A low yew hedge flanked the driveway up to the pillared entrance and the front door painted in a pale lemon paint. "Must be Milton-Cole's taste," Andrew said, also noticing that his was the only car in the driveway. "Milton-Cole's will be garaged," he told himself as he rang the bell.

The door opened and invited inside; he lifted his head to view the galleried landing reached by the wide staircase leading down to the traditionally tiled Minton tiled hallway.

"We've been expecting you," the man in the velvet jacket said as he showed Andrew into the drawing room. "Help yourself to a drink. Mr Milton-Cole will be with you shortly." Andrew did a three-sixty looking around the room.

He liked the wooden panelling and the dark furniture. The pieces of porcelain looked expensive, as did the portraits in gilt frames, and the high-backed chairs looked like quality. "Of course it's quality," he said aloud. "This is Milton-Cole's home."

"Andrew." Milton-Cole said, entering the room, hand outstretched. "Pleased to meet you."

"Likewise, Mr Milton-Cole."

"Please call me Hugh. Did you help yourself to a drink?"

"Sorry, no Mr… Hugh."

"What's your poison?"

"I'm a whisky drinker, but as I'm driving, I'll just take a tonic and lime, if that's possible?"

"Of course," Milton-Cole walked over to the drinks trolly and the shush of the tonic water being opened filled the awkward silence. "You will join me for a bite to eat, won't you?"

Milton-Cole nodded to the two chairs in the bay window and Andrew sat down.

The door opened and the man in velvet looked in and asked, "Mr Cavendish, will you be taking lunch?"

"Please," Andrew replied. He liked the formality of being addressed as Mr Cavendish.

"So, I understand you specialise in oriental antiquities?" Hugh said, handing him his drink.

"That's right."

"And what brings you to my door?" Andrew thought the question odd, as he'd already explained during their phone call that he'd like to work alongside Milton-Cole.

He'd exaggerated how well his business was doing, claiming his turnover to be higher, but was looking to expand into a more prestigious marketplace. "You may recall I said I was growing tired with the constant travelling to China."

"But a move into a more influential market will still require travel to East Asia."

The fact Milton-Cole referred to it as East Asia impressed Andrew. Shows class, he thought.

"I understand that future travel will still be required, but the gains hopefully will outweigh the hardship."

Milton-Cole gave a small laugh and Andrew aped it.

"So, I'm guessing you'd like me to put some of my contacts your way?"

"I'd prefer to be honest and say, I would appreciate that."

"I'm sure you would, Mr Cavendish."

Was there a hint of malice in his response?

"In return, I will require your help."

"I'll do everything in my power."

"The clientele, I have require total discretion."

"I understand."

"This game's not known for its integrity. We are antique dealers, after all." This time, Andrew didn't mimic Hugh's laughter.

The door re-opened and Velvet Jacket announced lunch. "There's a facility here," he said to Andrew, pointing to a door to his right. "If you'd like to freshen up. The dining room is over there. No need to knock."

Andrew closed the door and short of hugging himself, he felt he'd made it. Hugh had been friendly and suggested that they could work together. Andrew felt he was on the way up.

He checked himself in the mirror and ran his fingers through his hair, before leaving and walking along the corridor with its deep plum carpet and portraits on the wall.

He stood outside the dining-room door and composed himself before he stepped inside, and his face followed his heart as it plummeted towards his shoes.

Andrew froze. His eyes registered the scene, but his mind found itself unable to process what was before him.

A table laid for lunch dominated the room. Velvet Jacket stood at the head, holding a wine carafe, a tight smile on his face. Three men were sitting looking at him. Milton-Cole,

Nigel and an old guy whose face he couldn't place.

Andrew opened his mouth, but no words came, so Velvet Jacket spoke first. "Here's a seat reserved for you, Andrew."

Slowly and without purpose, Andrew walked towards the chair. Silence pushed down upon him like a weight crushing him from above as he watched each of the guests' wine glasses being filled.

Milton-Cole took a sip before he spoke. "Surprised?" Andrew knew he couldn't bluff his way out of this situation and so gave a lethargic nod. What's going on? He thought and hoped it was to talk about a lucrative deal, but somehow, he knew this wasn't the reason for the ambush. Velvet Jacket slid open a small door on the wall and removed plates from the dumbwaiter. "Is beef, okay Andrew?" he said, placing the last plate in front of him.

"I hope you like it rare," Milton-Cole said. "There's something pleasurable about seeing some blood as you enjoy a meal, don't you think?"

Andrew didn't respond. The question unnerved him. He followed the lead of the other guests and as they ate their lunch with relish; he devoured his slowly, cutting the meat into small pieces and chewing until there was no flavour left. Swallowing was difficult, and even a mouthful of wine didn't help. The meal was awkward, oppressive, the four men ate in silence, the only comments puncturing the quiet came from Milton-Cole and were directed to Velvet Jacket.

After clearing the table and pouring four brandies, Velvet Jacket left the room and Milton-Cole spoke directly to Andrew. "You're wondering, no doubt, why I have assembled the following company to meet you for lunch."

"I... I," stammered Andrew.

"It was a statement not a question. Here's a question for you. Did you think you'd got away with it?"

"With what?"

"Double crossing us," Nigel said. "Did you honestly

think you could fool us?"

"I don't know what you're talking about."

"You remember Lionel?" Andrew glanced across at the remaining man and his memory kicked in, Skegness he thought, followed by, oh shit.

Nigel tossed a handful of photographs onto the table, Andrew didn't need to pick them up, he could see the images of him meeting Lionel at his door shaking hands.

"Look, it was just…"

"No, you look," Milton-Cole said. "We can tolerate half-arsed, amateur dealers like you poaching small pieces, but when someone deliberately fleeces you, it's hard to not take it personally."

"I didn't know you were –"

"But you knew my colleague here," Milton-Cole looked across at Nigel.

"I thought Nigel was…" Andrew's voice trailed off.

"Was what?" Nigel asked, "Stupid."

"No… I meant to say I didn't know he was working with you, Mr Milton-Cole."

"I've already told you. Call me Hugh."

"If I'd have known that Nigel was working with you, then…"

"So you assuming he was… let's say an independent dealer made him fair game?"

"You said yourself earlier, the industry isn't known for its integrity."

"Touché. Still, it doesn't excuse the fact that by stealing from us, you've disrupted our business dealings."

"We've been watching you for months," Nigel said. "I gave you leads that we thought you could siphon through the system for us without raising suspicion, but you got greedy."

"So, we had to set you up," Lionel said.

"Set me up?"

"First with Frank when I was in Corfu, then in case it had been a one off, we did again with Lionel."

"Not that we were ever in any doubt," Lionel added.

"Even Bridget knew about our ruse."

"Bridget? I don't know…"

"Come on, don't insult us with lies. What do they say on TV cop shows?" Nigel paused, "Oh yes, that's it. We've caught you, bang to rights."

"Or, as Agatha Christie would say, we've caught you, red-handed," said Milton-Cole.

Turning, Andrew saw that Velvet Jacket had re-entered the room and this time in his hand he held a gun.

Andrew felt beads of sweat prickling in his hairline. The atmosphere in the room had changed from uncomfortable to toxic. Lionel rose from his seat and walked over to take the gun and he closed in on Andrew. Placing the gun's barrel against Andrew's temple, he leant in and half-spoke and half-whispered, "I knew from the moment I met you that you were vermin."

"And you know how to deal with vermin," Nigel said. Andrew's eyes, wide with fear, flicked his way, catching a disturbing smile. "Lionel – if that's his real name," a small laugh, "is very adept with a revolver, one benefit of working for the intelligence services."

"I… I can repay the money," Andrew's voice was shaky, his fear unmistakable. "If that's what you want."

"It's not about the money. In fact, what we allowed you to get away with was peanuts."

Milton-Cole moved away from the table and walked over to the wall to ceiling windows and pulled a cord, closing the curtains.

Velvet Jacket flicked a switch and a subdued light inched its way into the room. The gloom ramped up Andrew's anxiety, and he started begging.

"What can I do?" he squeaked; conscious he was close

to tears. "I'll do anything. What do you need me to do?"

Milton-Cole lit a cigar and watched a curl of smoke float upwards before he continued, his voice measured and clear, "You see, Mr Cavendish. As I said, it's not always about the money, in this game reputation is everything, and... well you've made me look like a fool."

"How can I make things better?"

Milton-Cole's flat palm silenced Andrew and, walking over, he blew out a stream of smoke. Bringing himself down level with Andrew's face, he said, "I'm not sure you can make things better. What do you suggest, Nigel?" Andrew glanced across as Nigel shrugged and helped himself to another glass of wine. "Lionel?"

"I think you know my opinion. Some damage is beyond reparation."

Andrew shifted in his seat as Lionel moved the gun from his temple to beneath his jaw. "Quicker this way, less chance of dying slowly."

Milton-Cole nodded and Lionel took a breath. Andrew closed his eyes, ready to accept his fate, when in the silence he heard a click followed by sniggering, and he suffered the ultimate indignity of wetting himself.

"Now that's a pity. I'll need to have the carpet cleaned. Take him into the utility."

Velvet Jacket yanked Andrew out of his seat and, with his hand in his armpit, marched out of the dining room, through a kitchen into a room housing a double sink, washing machines and an industrial sized dryer. Velvet Jacket kicked a chair into the middle of the room, its scraping feet echoing around the tiled walls. "Trousers off."

Andrew did as instructed and winced as he was told to remove his underwear, too. He followed instructions and loaded them into the tumble dryer, and as the machine rumbled, he was told to sit. Milton-Cole and Nigel walked into the room and, suddenly conscious of his nakedness, Andrew crossed his legs.

"You didn't think we'd shoot you in the dining room," Milton-Cole said. Andrew didn't know if he should nod or not. "The help wouldn't be happy clearing up the mess. But tell me, how are we going to clear up the mess you've left behind…" Andrew looked at his trousers and boxers bouncing in the dryer and dipped his eyelids. "I'm not referring to the piss on the carpet. I mean the mess we were discussing before your… um, unfortunate accident."

"I've got a contact wanting to shift some porcelain. One is the Qing Dynasty and two others, similar periods. I'd estimate the three at around eighty thousand, more in a specialised auction. I'd be prepared to share the sale with you."

"Share?" Nigel said.

"Yes, you can't expect…"

"I don't think you quite understand the seriousness of this issue," Milton-Cole said.

"I could receive the pieces and –"

"Donate them to us for the sales. I feel that's what you're implying?"

"Yes, exactly that."

"Jolly good. So let's shake on it and you can leave." Milton-Cole offered his hand and Andrew rose and took it, ignoring the crushing handshake. "You will organise the collection of the porcelain with Nigel and after we've sold it, we can discuss any further action we need to take."

"But –"

"No buts Mr Cavendish. Now put on your pants and fuck off out of my house."

34

~ Red Dress ~

Melanie had been upset at Paul's funeral, not because she was saying goodbye to her husband, but because the October sun had refused to shine. The temperature in the graveyard had been a chilly seven degrees and as dense grey clouds scudded across a charcoal sky, she muttered to herself, "Was it too much to ask for, a sunny day?"

Standing around the hole in the ground where Paul's coffin was lying were members of his family and pub regulars, including Ken and Rita. There were people she hardly knew – mostly out of choice – and her father, who held her hand, giving it an occasional comforting squeeze.

The service had been short. Paul hadn't been a fan of organised religion, and so the service was lacking in hymns and readings. Melanie had sniffed and sobbed at suitable moments. A handkerchief pressed to her eyes beneath the dark glasses.

The wake had taken place at the Roebuck. "It's the least we could do," Ken had said.

Sandwiches cut into triangles rested on plates alongside pastry based snacks with just a small bowl of green leaves representing the salad option. The darts team told her they'd organised a tribute. "It's going to be a twenty-four-hour marathon to raise money for an allergy charity."

"Thank you, that's very kind," Melanie replied to the man wearing a Birmingham City FC shirt beneath his black jacket.

Twenty-four hours of darts, she thought, how tedious, much like this party. She clutched her throat as she explained to Ken that she needed to leave. "I think it's because it was here that he –"

"I understand," Ken had replied as he escorted her out to her car.

"Sorry Ken," she said as she tossed her sunglasses on the passenger seat and pulled out of the car park.

Looking in the bedroom mirror, she removed the navy two-piece suit to reveal cerise lingerie and reaching into the wardrobe; she took out the red Valentino mini dress that she'd purchased especially for the day and stepped into it.

She admired herself and said, "That's better. Now I need a drink," and walking from the bedroom to the kitchen, she fixed herself a large vodka and cranberry juice.

35

~ Spanner ~

Vinnie had been shaking and sweating since waking. Cyndi had made him a cup of tea and no sooner had it gone down than it was back up and splashing over the duvet until he dry heaved.

"You gotta help me, Cyn," he said, clutching his stomach and bringing his knees up to his chest.

"We're skint. Can't Spanner give you something to tide you over?"

"As he's fond of saying, 'no cash, no stash.' Spanner don't care."

"I could speak to him."

"No. You'll make me look flaky if you do that."

Cyndi picked up the empty mug and left the room, making her way over to the meagre collection of cupboards and a sink in the corner of the sitting room that was masquerading as a kitchen. Picking up her purse and looking inside, she saw a paltry collection of coins, hardly enough for a carton of milk, let alone a fix for Vinnie. Striking a match, she lit the grill on the gas cooker and, after scraping the mould off a slice of bread, slid it under the blue flames. "Do you want something to eat?" she called.

Walking back into the bedroom holding the toast with its scraping of margarine, she asked Vinnie if he'd like some and he groaned, his eyes looking into hers for help. "You might feel better if you eat something," she said, knowing it to be untrue. What he needed; she couldn't pay for.

"How long before we get paid?"

"Not until the end of the month."

"Can't you ask for a crisis loan?" Vinnie pleaded.

"It won't help you. You know it takes a day to organise and after the last loan, we were told we were stretching the limit."

"I thought Universal Credit was supposed to help?"

Cyndi shook her head; she'd had this conversation many times with Vinnie, and he still couldn't grasp the fact that the DWP clawed back the loans from their benefits.

Rolling over, he coughed and began dry heaving again, and Cyndi sat down beside him and rubbed his back. He shrugged her off and started coughing again, his sickly skin turning red. Groaning, he rolled over before pulling the duvet up to his chin; he was visibly shaking. "Please Cyn," he said, his voice taking on a pleading tone. "Can't you go out and earn some money?"

"Vinnie, you know I can't work on the street. If the agency finds out, they'll drop me from their list."

"Please, if you loved me."

"Don't start playing those games." Cyndi got up from the bed to walk out of the bedroom.

"You must have some numbers. Men who've passed them on to you."

"Yes. But if the agency finds out."

"You'd do it Cyn, if you cared."

"I do care Vinnie."

"Well then, prove it. What about the bloke who gave you a big tip?"

"He hasn't booked again." Vinnie reached out to her and she looked away from the track marks on his arm. "You said he'd given you his card."

"He did but…"

Despite Vinnie's weakened state, she felt his hand squeeze hers and he began mewling, his tears sitting in sunken lids. "Call him. There's a reason he gave out his card." Cyndi said nothing in reply. She slid her hand out of his and silently left the room.

Holding the card in her hand, she tapped the numbers into her phone and waited for the call to connect. "What if he ignores it? People often do with unknown numbers."

A voice interrupted and said, "Iain Hart."

"Hello. Err… sorry to call I…" Cyndi faltered.

"Who is this?"

"Cyndi. Remember me?"

"Yes, I remember. What can I do for you?"

"I… err…was wondering if you wanted to meet… sorry… hire me again."

"If I do, I'll call the agency."

"Yes. I was thinking maybe you'd like to book direct. I could do you a better rate."

"The money's not an issue."

"Sorry, I didn't mean…"

"Okay, look," he sounded irritated, "I'll have a couple of hours free this evening. Book a taxi and get here for seven."

"I can't –"

"Don't worry about the fare, I'll cover it. Don't be late." He hung up before Cyndi could confirm she'd be there.

She held the phone to her breast for a few seconds before she dialled another number, left a message, and waited.

Spanner leered at her as she opened the door. His lank hair hung across his eyes and she noticed the tide mark around his shirt collar. He stepped inside, and Cyndi recoiled at the stench of male body spray mixed with stale sweat. "Thanks for coming," she said.

"No worries, doll."

Doll thought Cyndi, where does he think he is? This is Banbury, not the Bronx. "I'm glad you said you'd help Vinnie."

"You know my motto."

"Yes, no cash, no stash. Look, I've some money coming my way tonight and I can pay you later. Or tomorrow, if that's okay. Vinnie really needs your help."

"As I always say, no cash, no…" Spanner paused, then adjusting the front of his jogging bottoms said. "There is a way you could put a deposit down." Cyndi felt her insides knot but stood aside as Spanner went into the bedroom to sort out Vinnie's needs first.

Standing in the shower, the water barely warm, Cyndi washed away every trace of Spanner.

Will life ever get better than this? A thought she'd had many times before but couldn't answer. Turning off the shower, she wrapped herself in a towel and looked in on Vinnie. He was away, in his blurred world, one she couldn't and wouldn't want to share. She dried herself and dressed, selecting a short red skirt and sequined boob tube. She shrugged on a black bolero jacket as the beep of a car horn sounded outside. Pulling back the net curtain, she saw the taxi outside waiting for her and checked on her boyfriend again before slipping out of the flat and with heels clicking on the concrete; she walked towards the waiting car.

The silver moon appeared to be hanging directly above Astley House. Its light contrasting with the tin-coloured sky, giving the grounds a ghostly, almost foreboding feel. The headlights from the taxi lit up the trees, black and silhouetted against the emptiness above, giving them a sinister form.

Cyndi left the car and walked to the front door and rang the bell. The driveway became bathed in saffron-coloured light as Iain opened the door. "Punctual. I like that," he said, stepping aside, allowing her to step inside.

"Thank you," Cyndi replied.

"We'll go to one of the guest bedrooms. The beds are new and unused." His smile was friendly, not at all leering as Spanner's had been earlier. "Drink?"

"Please," she said, looking around. "It's changed since I was last here."

"It's getting there. I'll show you the banqueting space."

He poured her a glass of prosecco, and after she took it,

He escorted her into the vast open space. "Maybe, when we're open for business, you could apply for a job waitressing."

Iain's arm slid across her shoulder, and his hand moved down and slipped between her skin and the boob tube fabric. He smiled again, and she allowed him to lead her back into the hall and up the main staircase.

~~~

Cyndi had gone to the supermarket the following morning when Vinnie stirred. He rolled the duvet back and scratched himself before reaching down and picking up his jogging bottoms from the floor. Bare-chested, he shuffled to the kitchen area and opened a cupboard. Taking down an opened box of Pop Tarts, he removed one and ate it, enjoying its sweetness.

He sniffed the armpits of a T-shirt that had been lying on the sofa and, happy with it, slipped it over his head. He opened a trinket box that lay beside the television and saw the bundle of ten-pound notes Cyndi had earned the night before and taking three from the elastic band that secured them, stuffed them into his joggers and leaving the flat he went in search of Spanner.

His dealer was sitting on a bench in the local park when Vinnie saw him. He sauntered over and Spanner gave a subtle tip of the head and made his way into the public conveniences. The smell was eye watering as Vinnie completed his transaction and after bumping knuckles, the two men separated and Vinnie called a taxi to help ferry home the beers he planned on buying.

After pulling up outside the flat, the taxi driver handed Vinnie his change and said. "I picked your lady up last night."

"Yeah, she was off out."

"She looked good," the taxi driver said.

"Always does my Cyn." Vinnie opened the car's rear door and was about to get out when he said, "She was out on a girls' thing. Can you remember where you dropped her off?"

"Sure. That big old place on the Tadmarton Road. Astley House, I think it's called."

"Cool man," Vinnie said and closed the door and walked towards his flat's entrance.

36

~ Little Monsters ~

Two weeks had passed since Paul's funeral and Melanie was becoming used to living alone. Actually, she had thought, I now prefer being on my own. She didn't miss her husband, and her father was glad that he was, in his words, 'out of the bloody way'. She did, however, have a strange feeling of loss for her friendship with Emilia and Selena. You know the rules, she told herself whenever the desire to contact them came over her and knowing she needed to knuckle down and plan her part of the pact, she began compiling a list.

~~~

Selena read the text again; it had arrived the day before from Iain's office, sent by someone named Tori informing her that the guest bedrooms were now completed and that Astley House was planning a grand opening, with publicity covered by the biggest players of the press. She was eager to get her part of the deal over and done with, but looking at the calendar, she could see that Andrew had nothing booked for the foreseeable future.

"Why can't he be flying to China," she said, dropping a slice of bread into the toaster, "or at least going for an overnight somewhere to look at dusty old relics?"

He hadn't been into work for a few days and his mood had been more irascible than normal.

While emptying the washing basket she'd come across his trousers, they looked stained and held a stale smell that she thought was urine and after asking him if everything was okay, his reply was monosyllabic and terse.

Yesterday he had made himself busy in the garden, only coming inside to eat and today he'd taken himself away at first light without telling her where he was going.

Before showering, Selena opened her knicker draw and removed the piece of paper she'd taped to the underside and unfolded it. It was a list of things seen on a builder's merchant website that she could use when the time came.

She ruled out an over-elaborate plot she'd conjured up to electrocute him in favour of bludgeoning. He was a large man, and she knew that her success would rely upon an element of brute force and surprise. Looking at the list, she ticked off the axe, hammer and scaffold pole in her head while mentally crossing out chisels and screwdrivers; too messy, she had decided, and no guarantee of a quick clean exit.

~~~

Andrew sat in his car looking out of the windscreen at the scrubby patch of trees with a well-trodden path leading through them. He turned on the radio, but after a couple of minutes of chatter, he turned it off and sat in silence.

Minutes later, he turned the radio on and music filled his car, but nothing pleased him, so he turned it off again.

He picked up the rope on the passenger seat, climbed out of the car and shut the door with more force than was required and set off towards a wooded area.

He'd only walked a handful of paces before he turned around and returned to his car. He couldn't settle. His mind was racing and had been ever since the confrontation with Milton-Cole and Nigel.

"If I ever see that old git again," he muttered, thinking back to Lionel putting the gun under his chin, "or that pompous bastard in velvet

Being made to strip had bothered him more than he realised at first, and the anger he should have felt became outweighed by humiliation. "I'll make you pay... In fact, I'll make all of you pay."

He threw the rope into the car boot and took out his phone and called Melanie. The call went to voicemail, and he left a message saying he would call her again the following day to discuss meeting up and looking at the pieces she had for sale.

Next, he took out his diary and first listed the names. Nigel, Lionel and Hugh Milton-Cole, Velvet Jacket he just abbreviated to VJ. He marked a cross beside three of the names, but beside Nigel's he put a question mark. Putting his diary away, he turned the key in the car's ignition and, with a squeal of tyres, did a U turn and headed home.

~~~

Selena showered and dressed and after making herself a coffee, she lit the gas hob and set fire to the list she had been reading, watching as the charred paper rose in the air current given off by the blue flame.

The sound of Andrew's car pulling into the drive caught her attention and, using her hand, she wafted away the smell of burning.

She took down a mug and as Andrew stepped inside; she told him she'd fix him a coffee.

"Don't bother," he replied and marched out of the patio doors opposite the dining table and made his way towards the shed in the garden. Minutes later, he returned with a cardboard box in his hands. "What's that smell?" he said, placing the box on the table.

"I caught a piece of kitchen roll in the gas earlier. You sure you don't want a coffee?"

"Go on then. I have to go away again for a day or so."

Selena switched the kettle to boil again and unscrewed the lid from the instant coffee. "

"A day or so?"

"Just a couple of nights. Not a problem, is it?"

"Not at all." She handed him his drink.

"Do you have anything planned?" Andrew blew across the surface of his coffee and then smiled at her. Selena hated it when Andrew was being reasonable but seized at the opportunity. "There's a Grayson Perry exhibition touring at the moment. I'd quite like to see it."

Andrew grunted.

He's already lost interest, Selena thought. "Would you like me to pack a few things for you?"

"Please, my blue suit, a couple of shirts and a pair of jeans will do."

Selena watched as Andrew tossed his overnight bag onto the back seat of the car and, without so much as a glance in her direction, he drove away. Walking outside, she looked down the road, making sure he'd gone before returning to the kitchen and reaching behind the fridge for the hidden phone. She scrolled through the few contacts it held and selected a number and waited for the call to connect.

~~~

Melanie pressed the button and waited for the voicemail to kick in. She listened to Andrew's message as she accepted her drink from the barista.

Sitting at a vacant table looking out of the window, she watched as a small girl dressed in a Halloween costume walked past holding her mother's hand while at their side the father carried an orange pumpkin.

"I must get some sweets," she told herself. "No doubt the little monsters will come knocking at my door tomorrow evening."

As she stirred a sachet of sugar into her coffee, a thought crossed her mind. The thought of the trick or treaters had delivered an idea to her.

37

~ Trick or Treat ~

Andrew woke up in his office chair feeling stiff and hungover. The empty whisky bottle on his desk had tipped up, and the remnants of the amber liquid had soaked into the pile of paperwork on which it rested. He rubbed his eyes before sliding his hands down his face over several days of stubble before he got up and staggered over to the sink. Pushing aside the dirty mugs, plates, and empty noodle pots, he ran the tap and swilled his face before returning.

Since leaving home, he'd been scouring his diary for potential leads for new acquisitions. He'd made an abundance of calls, but thus far, none had been fruitful. It felt as if every one of his contacts had suddenly nothing to offer him. Was it paranoia or had Milton-Cole put the word out to give him a wide berth?

Yesterday, he'd selected items from his showroom that he thought could sell quickly. "God knows I need the money," he'd said to himself as he waited for a call to a previous client to connect. Auction houses he had worked with suddenly didn't have any slots available for his antiques and in desperation he's searched the local papers and online forums for car boot sales and want ads, anywhere he could offload some stock and raise money to pay back Milton-Cole.

He knew he'd never raise much from his stock but hoped a down payment would buy him some time.

He picked up his phone and checked the screen. "No

calls. Why isn't Charlotte Allen getting back to me?" He contemplated calling her again. "I've left her two messages; her pieces alone would clear my money worries and leave me with something left over. Maybe I could use it go abroad to a place where they'd never find me."

By lunchtime, he was exhausted. Everyone in his diary had given him a knock back, most citing the current economic climate or the usual year end slowing down of sales. He had booked a space at a local boot sale, but after fees, that wouldn't bring in enough to make a dent in his debts.

Picking up the whisky bottle, he tipped it up and swallowed the few drops that remained. He opened his wallet and checked for notes and saw none. The change in his pockets didn't add up to enough to buy another bottle and opening a desk drawer, he removed an empty cash box and took out the business credit card.

The weather was lousy, the morning fog had failed to lift, and pulling on a jacket, Andrew made his way to the convenience store on the corner where he silently prayed the card payment would go through.

Relieved, he walked back to his warehouse and barely inside; he broke the seal and took a swig of the whisky.

Putting the bottle down on the desk, he made his way to the sink. He was rinsing a glass when a deep voice behind him said, "Trick or treat."

Andrew turned, and the glass fell from his hand, shattering on the floor. In front of him stood two figures in black, both wearing clown masks. Fear stole the scream from his throat and the two men moved apart and walked towards him from opposite sides. The terror he felt caused him to tremble noticeably, and he was doing his utmost to hold on to his bladder. One mask was inches away from his face when it was removed to reveal Nigel, who laughed.

"You... You..."

"Language, Andrew," said Nigel, wagging a finger as if

at an errant child.

"You scared the shit out of me."

"I wondered what that smell was." Andrew turned to see Velvet Jacket had removed his mask, however he hadn't laughed. Andrew was unsure which was the most disturbing, the mask or his pitiless gaze.

"What do you want?"

"As if you didn't know," Nigel said, picking up the bottle of whisky and unscrewing the cap, he picked a posy vase from a nearby shelf, blew out the dust from inside and poured himself a measure. Lowering himself into Andrew's chair, he took a mouthful, exhaling as the liquor hit his throat. "Do you have the money?"

"You know I don't."

"That's a shame." Velvet Jacket added, his monotone elevating Andrew's anxiety.

"I've already told you I've got a prosperous sale in the pipeline."

"Yes, I remember," Nigel said. "What was it you said… Eighty grand?"

"That's right."

"Where is it then?" Velvet Jacket moved around the table to face Andrew.

"I… I'm finalising the sale with the vendor."

"And when is that likely to be?" Nigel asked as he flicked through pages piled on Andrew's desk.

"Very soon. And then all I have to do is sell it on."

"There'll be no need for that." Nigel put down his drink and stood up. "If the goods are as you say, then we'll handle the sale."

"But…"

"But what?" Velvet jacket threw his mask onto the table and patted his inside pocket to imply he had a gun. Andrew swallowed and just nodded. "We can be reasonable men, can't we, Nigel?"

"Of course we can. There's no need for bad feelings."

He smiled, seeing Andrew's shoulders relax a little. "We'll give you a little more time."

"Thank you," Andrew mumbled. "I won't let you down. I promise."

"Sadly, your promises aren't worth shit." Nigel's smile faded. "You have until the fifth."

"That only gives me five days. I can't –"

"Well, you'd better get on to it." Nigel picked up the bottle of whisky and walked over to the sink. "And this won't help." he poured the whisky down the sink and his smile returned, but this time there was no warmth to it.

Velvet Jacket made a gun with his fingers and said with a smirk, "Remember, remember the fifth of November."

38

~ Manchester ~

Emilia was emptying the tumble dryer when one of Iain's socks fell onto the floor. She picked it up and an unwanted wing of emotion flapped inside her. It was like nothing she had felt before and, unaware of where it had come from, she dropped the sock into the basket with the rest of the laundry and opened the utility door and stepped outside.

The garden was glum. It carried the sadness that November brought, where many things were dying off or preparing for their winter slumber. Without a warning, an image of Paul lying on the floor of the Roebuck entered her head like a spilling wave slowly breaking upon the shore of her mind's eye. It hadn't happened before, and she wondered if Iain's sock had been the catalyst for the thought.

What was it? Grief? Guilt? Relief?

Sitting on one of her patio chairs; the cold of the metal seat gnawing at her legs, she broke down her thoughts logically.

It can't be grief; she hardly knew Paul and had formed no attachment to him. Guilt, maybe a little, but she hadn't killed him. It had been a fortunate accident.

Unfortunate for Paul, yet fortunate for her.

Perhaps, she thought, it's relief. Relief that my part of the pact is over.

That only leaves one thing, her mind told her as she shivered in the frigid breeze. Iain. Maybe he was the trigger for this anxiety.

She had thought her resolve to be resolute, but maybe now she was having doubts. Had her initial desire started sagging?

"Get a grip," she told herself and made her way back into the house where she fixed herself lunch.

Sitting at the table, her sandwich untouched as she cradled a mug of cold coffee, this conundrum had stolen her appetite.

She wondered what the others were thinking, particularly Melanie, as she'd – as far as she knew – already lost her husband. Iain was still alive, but what about Andrew? "I can't risk looking at news reports on the internet," she said as the realisation that their agreement to cut further contact had been a mistake. "We must meet again."

Tipping the cold coffee down the sink and disposing of the sandwich, she went upstairs to retrieve her burner phone from its hiding place. Glad that she hadn't followed her own advice, she switched it on and composed a text.

> Nothing to worry about, but we need to meet.
> What dates are you free?

Her finger hovered over the smiley face emoji before she felt it inappropriate and pressed send and waited.

Selena replied first, telling Emilia she was mostly free apart from the next day as she was visiting the art exhibition in Manchester. She scrolled through the museum website on her phone, checked the times, and fired off a new text to Melanie.

> Tomorrow. Manchester Art Gallery?

~~~

After parking her car, Emilia walked the five minutes to Primark on Market Street, where she selected a suit and changed into it.

In the changing room, she removed an auburn wig, shook it out and slipped it over her hair and, taking off the sales tags, walked over to the cashier. "Bloody kid in McDonald's spilled tomato ketchup on me this morning," she said as she explained away her wearing the clothes she was purchasing.

Outside the art gallery, Emilia felt that the façade of the Charles Barry designed building with its multiple columns looked incongruous beside modern glass offices, tramlines and a Greggs. How the modern architecture dilutes its magnificence, she thought as she walked towards the entrance.

Selena had said to meet at an exhibition of work illustrating global warming, and as Emilia entered the hall, she spotted Melanie first. Dressed in her combats and boots with the baseball cap pulled down over her eyes. She was looking at a painting of a withered tree casting a yellow shadow over a skeletal child. sidling over to Melanie, she said, "So what does the painting say to you?"

"Bloody hell, you made me jump." Melanie's reply was less hushed than the question, but her eyes told Emilia that she'd recognised her. Lowering her voice, she replied, "It's all rather grim."

"That's man-made climate change for you."

The conversation ended there when Selena stood beside them and said, "There's a more disturbing painting behind us."

Without turning around to look, Emilia said, "Outside. Café Nero in fifteen minutes." Before walking away.

When Selena and Melanie arrived at the coffee shop, they expected Emilia to be sitting inside already, but she was standing outside. "Are we going in?" Melanie asked. "I'm gagging for a drink."

"It's very crowded and the tables are so close together I'm not sure we'll have the privacy to talk openly."

"Follow me," Melanie said and strode off with the others in tow.

Outside The Seven Oaks public house, Selena looked dismayed. Pointing to the A-board outside, she read the advertisement in chalk for a football game. "It's a sports bar."

"Exactly," said Melanie. "That means the punters will be watching the game, not us."

"You sure we won't draw attention to ourselves?" Emilia asked.

"I doubt it. They must get lots of people just dropping in off the street during the day, so who cares if we stand out like a fish in a boiler suit? Come on." Melanie walked up the steps, opened the door, and breathed in the enticing beery smell of the interior.

Behind the bar stood a young man with a pierced nose and hair tied back in a ponytail. He looked up as they entered and furnished them with a wide smile. "Good morning, ladies." He glanced up at the clock across the room and corrected himself, "Or rather, good afternoon. It's past midday."

Emilia was happy with his welcome. It proved he was used to people dropping in who weren't obvious sports fans. "You two get a table and I'll order the drinks."

As Selena led Melanie to a table in a corner, away from the television screen and the main door, Emilia leant on the polished surface of the ornately carved bar. "Can I get three vodka and cranberry juice, please?"

"Would you ladies like food?" the barman asked as he poured their drinks. Not sure if the others had made plans for lunch, she just ordered a large bowl of chips and asked for three forks.

"Take a seat and I'll bring everything over for you." The barman said with a smile.

Joining her companions, Emilia shrugged off her jacket and dropped onto a stool. The initial conversation was mundane, reviews of their journeys, the extortionate cost of car parking and how the trams gave the city a continental vibe.

Their drinks arrived, and the barman told them to give him a nod if they needed anything more. Taking the bowl of chips from a kitchen worker, he placed them on the table and said, "Condiments are over by the bar." They all thanked him, and with a flick of his ponytail, he walked away.

"I need this," Melanie said, picking up her drink and taking a sip.

Emilia studied her face, looking for any changes since they'd last met. She'd thought about how her friend's reactions might differ now that Paul was dead, but so far, she'd seen no change.

"Your text surprised me," Selena said before she stabbed a chip with her fork.

"I'm glad I hadn't thrown the phone away yet."

"But the outfit's changed," Melanie said, biting the corner off a sachet of mayonnaise.

"I donated my old one. This one's care of Primark this morning, but this wig itches like a child with chickenpox."

"I'll be glad to see the back of mine," Selena said.

"Anyway, I didn't ask to see you both to talk about wigs and cheap fashion." Melanie and Selena leant in, and Emilia continued. "I don't think it's a good idea to sever contact yet."

"Why?"

"Because, Melanie, if something unexpected happens, we need to alert the others."

"Has something happened?"

"No Selena. It's just I was thinking also that once we've achieved our goal, we'll need to make plans to meet up again."

"To celebrate," Melanie said, and Selena huffed loudly and shook her head. "Come on, Selena, why can't we be happy? I know I am. Now that –"

"We get it," Emilia interrupted.

"So, what do you suggest?"

Emilia opened her mouth to respond when the barman appeared at their table. "Everything all right?" They all nodded. "Top up ladies?"

"Please," Melanie said.

"Just an orange for me," added Selena, and he walked away.

Emilia glanced around, making sure he was being occupied behind the bar, and said, "When this is all over, we'll need to regroup. I think we should wait a couple of months and meet up somewhere safe and yes, as Melanie said, 'celebrate' if we think it's appropriate."

"Let's meet in Milan. Go full circle." Melanie said excitedly.

"Are we all agreed?"

Selena nodded as the barman delivered their second round of drinks to the table, and Melanie lifted her glass in a silent toast.

Back on the street, Selena said goodbye and headed off towards the art gallery, and as Emilia took her car keys from her bag, Melanie placed a hand on her arm and whispered, "Thank you."

39

~ Hart Holdings ~

Vinnie had borrowed a car and drove past the entrance to Astley House, slowing down to look up the driveway, the length of which made it impossible to see anything more than trees and lawn. He pulled over, got out, and walked over to the hedge that bordered the property. However, trees still obstructed his view. It's a long way from the road, he thought. He went back to the car and reversed back to the entrance. "I'm not walking that far," he said as he drove through the gates.

He slowed as the house came into view and he let out a low whistle, "Someone's got some brass," he mumbled, then hearing a beeping behind him, he moved to the side to allow a flatbed truck laden with plants to pass.

Nearer the house, a collection of vehicles had parked randomly, with no sense of order. A pallet of plaster and boarding was standing beside another stacked with bags of bark chippings. A cement mixer stood idle, a hardened grey mass around its wheels, with empty cement bags lying crumpled beneath it.

The flatbed pulled over and men jumped out and began unloading the plants, which put Vinnie in mind of one of those makeover programs where a celebrity gardener pitches a design to homeowners whose gardens have gone to seed.

Vinnie parked his car behind the mess of white vans and watched as a youth appeared at a side door, selected a length of wood, and returned to where he'd come from.

He sat watching the men unload the plants before stepping out of his car and causally strolling around trying to look like he belonged there.

He walked up to the main entrance; the door was open, and he craned his neck to look inside. The hallway was clear of building materials and a beside what looked like a new reception desk was a stack of boxes containing computers and other office hardware. Vinnie's mind clocked these, and he was already thinking about the gear he could buy if he came back later and took them. There was always someone on the estate looking to buy electronics.

"Can I help you?" a voice behind him said.

Turning to see a man in brown overalls, he replied, "I'm looking for work. Do you know if there's any going?"

"Don't know mate. I'm contract, I don't work for the company."

"What is the company?" The man pointed to a sign and wandered off without giving Vinnie a second glance.

The temporary sign contained a large green circle with a double 'H' logo and the name Hart Holdings Ltd. A lower strapline read, 'a new eco-friendly development'.

Having never heard of the company, Vinnie took out his phone and snapped a quick photograph of the sign, telling himself he'd Google it later.

The plants were now being wheeled around the side of the building and seeing the youth from earlier, Vinnie sidled over. "You okay there?" the lad said.

"Yeah mate," Vinnie said. "Do you know if there's any casual work going?"

"You'd need to speak with the boss, mate."

"Where can I find him?"

"You won't. He's not here today."

"So, what is this place?"

"A hotel and wedding venue. Proper lush it is inside, Mr Hart's spent a mint on the place."

The youth selected a length of wood from a pile when

Vinnie asked, "When will the boss be here?"

"Not sure. He's going abroad for a couple of weeks."

"No doubt on a jolly while you lot do all the work."

"Yeah probably." A half-hearted laugh. "I need to get on, mate." And with a nod towards the house, he walked away.

Vinnie took another look inside, and smiling, made his way back to his car.

~~~

Vinnie lit the roll-up hanging out of the corner of his mouth before lifting the lid of Cyndi's laptop. "Any chance of a brew, Cyn?" he called from the sitting room.

"Can't you do it? You're next to the kitchen?"

"I'm busy."

Cyndi entered wearing rubber gloves and her cardigan sleeves pushed up her arms. "I'm doing some hand washing; we can't afford to waste money at the launderette."

"You're good to me, Cyn. Make a lovely little wife, you will." He tossed her a wink, which was met with a scowl. She clicked the switch on the kettle and lifted the mugs out of the sink before wiping a teaspoon on the leg of her jeans.

"What is so important that you can't put the kettle on?"

"Research Cyn. Research." His eyes closed, watering as a trail of smoke rose from the skinny cigarette.

"What kind of research? For a job?"

"Don't be daft, Cyn," he laughed. "A job."

He tapped the keys, and Google brought up a selection of options. At the top was Hart Holdings Ltd. He scanned the home page with an artist's impression of a commercial building surrounded by trees with pedestrians walking past with smiles on their artificial faces.

After scanning an overview of the company's history, he

opened the page, featuring photographs of key personnel. He studied the CEO's face, took in the flawless portrait. The confident stare and well-groomed appearance. Vinnie had to admit that Iain was handsome. "Why is this guy paying you for sex?" he said aloud.

"Who?" Cyndi asked from the kitchen.

"Iain Hart, the guy who's restoring Astley."

Cyndi looked over Vinnie's shoulder at the image of Iain on the screen and said, "I don't know."

"Look at him," Vinnie said. "Would you say he's good looking?"

"I guess so." Cyndi tried to make her response sound matter of fact and went back to stirring the tea bags in the mugs.

"You guess so. He could have any woman he wanted, yet he pays the agency."

"Leave it, Vin. You know I don't like to talk about work."

"You've hit on a good earner there, Cyn. Best keep him sweet." Vinnie winked at his girlfriend but failed to notice how uncomfortable she looked. He clicked back to the search page and saw a link for the company's estimated worth. He opened the window and whistled. There were so many noughts he couldn't read what the number was. "You're shitting me," he said to himself, then to Cyndi, "Not only is he good looking, but he's minted too."

Placing a mug down beside him, Cyndi said, "Why are you so interested?"

"I just am."

"Whatever. If there's nothing else, I'll get back to washing your clothes."

Cyndi left the room and Vinnie carried on opening windows before he said to himself, "Now I know who's been putting the food on our table and topping up our electric meter."

He closed the lid, picked up his drink and said, "I look forward to meeting you, Mr Hart."

40

~ Dragon ~

After applying a stroke of black kohl under her eyes, Melanie straightened her baseball cap and slipped her arms inside the army surplus jacket. She grabbed her car keys from their hook in the hallway and headed out to meet Andrew.

He'd left another message, and she'd thought his voice had sounded desperate and so decided that to make a success of dispatching him, she'd need to give his warehouse one last look over.

The journey was relatively quiet. The darker months always seemed to cut down the traffic on the roads. This gave her time to think about her plan and how, when the time came, she would use the element of surprise to gain the upper hand.

The November sky changed from pewter to slate and the first drops of rain flecked her windscreen. "Oh, brilliant, just what I need. Who'd have thought two days ago I was in Manchester and it was sunny," she said, turning into the road towards Andrew's warehouse. Pulling up outside, the gloomy weather made the dilapidated building look more depressing than it had seemed on her first visit.

A stagnant smell from the canal hung heavily in the air, and deliberately holding her breath, she locked her car and opened her umbrella. The rain was still light but coated everything it touched and it was dripping from the umbrella spokes as she opened the door and stepped inside.

Inside the showroom, the air carried a new aroma, a combination of mildew and linseed oil, replacing the scent from outside and creating a feeling of both decay and renewal. The room was empty, and as she walked around, she mapped it in her head. She ran a gloved finger through the dirt on a Victorian dresser and swirled a pattern across a dust covered sideboard.

Intricate oriental patterns adorned the many vases and jars displayed behind glass cabinets, and an enormous wall hanging caught her attention. A silver dragon holding a pearl against a scarlet background. How apt, she thought, looking at the rain deity holding the Chinese symbol of power and wisdom.

"You like it?"

She swivelled around to see Andrew standing in the doorway of his office. "Very much, yes," she said and turned back to study the wall hanging.

"I might consider selling it." Now standing beside her, she could smell him, unwashed clothing and a hint of sour alcohol. She looked at his unshaven face and hair that looked like it hadn't seen a comb in many days and wondered what had happened to him.

"Coffee, tea?"

Melanie nodded and watched him as he walked back into his office. He was a complete contrast to the smartly turned out man she'd first met. Studying him, she noticed the rucked up shirt tail hanging over his belt, his creased trousers, and dull shoes. He looked as grimy as his furniture.

Following him into his office, she could see him in the small kitchenette, rinsing mugs under the tap before he spooned instant coffee into them.

"Are you having a sort out?"

"Sorry?" he replied, his gaze catching her looking at his desk, strewn with papers, printed images and invoices. "Yes. Getting ready for the end of the year. VAT returns, etc."

"Accounts. A right pain in the ass, I bet."

"Tell me about it." The kettle clicked, and he returned to it.

"You should get yourself a woman in to do all that for you."

"A woman?" he handed her a mug. "Tut-tut Charlotte. I didn't have you pegged as someone prone to promoting stereotypes."

She noticed the phantom smile, an attempt at jollity, and placed her mug down on the corner of his desk. "I believe women make better bookkeepers. Attention to detail and multi-tasking. The politically correct police can arrest me now." She held up her hands and gave him a smile.

The room fell silent and Melanie felt uncomfortable; she thought about picking up her drink to give her something to do, but having seen him just rinse the dirty mug, she chose not to drink from it.

"How's business?" she hoped the question would break their conversational standstill.

"It's been good. But it usually slows down, as we approach Christmas."

"I'd have thought sales would increase. People looking for that special gift."

"You'd think so."

Silence again, with the two of them looking in opposite directions. He feels awkward, Melanie thought. Either that or I'm missing something.

"As luck has it, I have a buyer lined up to take your pieces." He said, "he wants to buy them quickly. In fact, I think we could lose the sale if we don't act fast."

"That sounds good. I hope you'll make a good return."

"Sadly not, the resale value is quite lean. If you remember, I told you the objects were quite common."

Liar. She hoped her face didn't reveal her thoughts. You said nothing of the sort.

"Did you bring them with you?"

"No. I didn't."

"What!"

"I said I didn't bring them. I wasn't planning on coming. I was just passing on the off chance."

He dismissed her explanation and jumped in with, "So, when can you get them to me?"

"I'm not sure. As you say, the festive season is rapidly advancing and I'll have a lot to do. Maybe the New Year."

"The New Year," he moved towards her and, standing too close, he said. "Charlie, I'm not sure you realise how much work I've put into this opportunity for you. I've already told you we could lose this sale if we don't act fast."

Melanie was feeling uncomfortable. Was this how things were at home with Selena? Minor irritation, invading personal space, before he exploded with rage?

"Until just now, I wasn't aware there was an urgency."

"Really?"

His voice rose to an unprofessional level and Melanie could see his face fight against the anger his tone was displaying. Now she went from uncomfortable to scared.

"I… I… wasn't aware you'd be in a hurry for them."

"Charlotte, in this game, speed is often the difference between a sale or no sale. Understand?"

Melanie didn't like the way he'd spoken to her, patronising and clipped and she wanted to leave, but he was standing between her and the exit and so her only chance was to get him to calm down.

Hoping to distract him, she stepped back and picked up a trinket box. "This is nice. How much is it?"

His demeanour changed, and he instinctively moved into sales mode. He took the box, telling her its age and provenance.

Melanie nodded and asked more questions as she walked around the room, looking at the few items that were stacked on shelves rather than in the main showroom. She felt safe once she had manoeuvred herself between Andrew and the door and said. "Will it be okay for me to drop by with the pieces over the next day or so?"

Andrew made a show of consulting his diary and then said, "Yes, I'll be here most days, if not the only appointments I have are quite local. Maybe you can call me first?"

"Okay, I'll do that." She took her phone out of her pocket and looked at the screen and said, "Goodness, is that the time? I'll be late if I don't get a move on. I'll call you tomorrow."

"Thanks. Yes, do that."

Melanie said goodbye and turned to walk away. She imagined his eyes burning into her back, a quashed rage behind them. She picked up her umbrella from beside the door where she had left it and, after a quick smile to Andrew, she stepped outside.

Thankfully, the rain had stopped and after she'd slid a CD into the player; she turned the engine over and drove home with music so loud it pushed her thoughts to the back of her head.

After closing the front door, she fixed herself a vodka and cranberry and went to sit at the dining table. The meeting with Andrew flooded her mind, and before she realised it, she was shaking. She scrabbled around inside her head, trying to remember a time she'd felt as unsafe as Andrew had made her feel but couldn't recall anything.

"Now I know a little about the hell that Selena is living in."

She downed her drink and prepared supper. Such was her anger that she chopped an onion with such vigour that, when she finished, it was shredded.

Looking down at her efforts, she said, "I'll have no doubts about killing you, Andrew Cavendish. In fact, I'll be doing the world a favour." She slammed the knife down on the counter, forgot about supper, and went to fix herself a second drink.

41

~ Gun Club ~

Selena removed her phone from its hiding place and, as she turned it on, it instantly pinged with a text notification. With Andrew away, she was still cautious and looked out of the kitchen window, checking his car wasn't outside. She couldn't assuage the fear of his returning without warning and catching her.

Opening the text, she saw Emilia had asked her to call.

nothing to worry about

Selena dialled Emilia's number and connected to her voicemail. After leaving a brief message, she went back to rinsing her breakfast dishes before loading the dishwasher.

An hour later, because Selena couldn't risk having the ringer switched on, the phone vibrated in her pocket.

"Hi Selena," Emilia's voice sounded breezy, calming any fears Selena had built up in her head about the impending call. "It's nothing to worry about. I just wanted you to know that Iain will be away for two weeks."

"Thanks for telling me. Where's he off to?"

"Spain, looking at some proposed development over there."

"I didn't know the company built abroad."

"We don't. It's a proposition that he says he's considering."

"I always thought the Spanish property market was risky. I've seen news reports about land being taken back and expat villas being repossessed."

"Iain's too savvy to get involved in anything unprofitable. He'll weigh everything up more than once before he invests any money. He's always chasing a healthy percentage. Said this idea looks like an excellent investment, at least that's what he's telling me. I think there's more to it."

"Just a minute Emilia. There's a vehicle pulled up outside." The line went quiet for a while until Selena returned. "Sorry about that. Amazon delivery, something Andrew's ordered."

"How are things with him at the moment?"

"Well, that's the thing. He's not here."

"Not there?"

"No, he came home, packed and left several days ago, said he'd got business to attend to."

"Does Melanie know?"

"I've not called her. I just assumed she's in contact with him, so will know where he is."

"Aren't you curious?"

"Somewhat. But to be honest, I'm preferring his not being here." Selena heard Emilia chuckle and added, "I'll be able to relax fully once he's out of the picture."

"Do you mind if I ask you a question? Just between the two of us."

"Not at all." Selena instinctively closed the door to keep the conversation contained, then smiled, realising what she had done. "As if the air fryer and kitchen scales would be interested."

"Pardon… Air Fryer?" Emilia said.

"Sorry, I got a bit distracted. Okay, you have my full attention."

"I've been thinking. Ever since Paul died, I wondered if any of us had considered if our men warranted being killed."

Panic in Selena's voice raised the timbre. "Are you saying you don't want to continue?"

"Not at all. The die is cast, there's no going back. I guess now my part is over. I've had more time to reflect."

"Do you have any regrets?"

"Not at the moment. Who's to say they won't come further down the line? I know out of the three of us, you have a more valid reason to want to see the back of Andrew. Are you're still intent on continuing?"

"Too right I am. For the first time in longer than I can remember, I can see beyond the prison bars of my marriage."

"I understand. I hope you didn't mind my asking?"

"Not at all. And don't worry, this will stay between the two of us."

"I appreciate that," Emilia said, and Selena could hear relief in her voice. "Tell me, do you have anything planned for tonight?"

"Nothing. What about you?"

"Iain booked us tickets to a charity firework display. Not really my idea of fun, standing about with cold feet, drinking warm wine."

Selena laughs. "Pack yourself a hip flask of vodka to help you get through it."

"I may just do that."

~~~

Melanie vigorously fastened the laces of her Doc Martens. "Why am I still annoyed?" She asked herself. "Because he's an arsehole." Picking up the box at her feet, she grabbed her jacket from off the back of a chair and made her way out to the car.

At her destination, she retrieved the box, walked through the familiar doors and signed in. "Nice to see you, Mel. How long has it been?"

"Too long, Jack," she said to the man behind the reception desk.

"Sorry to hear about your fella. Tragic news."

"Yeah tragic." Melanie dipped her eyes and hopes Jack wouldn't dwell on Paul's death.

Thankfully, he didn't.

"I've got you booked into lane three, but we're not busy today, so if you fancy another?"

"Lane three will be fine, Jack."

After he'd checked her revolver, Jack handed her the rounds and ear protectors and Melanie made her way through to the shooting area.

It took her less than a minute to get back into the rhythm of firing at the target further down the lane and within another she'd relaxed, shooting off the anger she felt towards Andrew. How dare he invade my personal space, she thought, taking aim and imagining the target to be his head. "Take that shithead," she muttered as she blasted the paper rings into confetti.

After her session at the gun club, she said goodbye to Jack, promising not to leave it so long next time, and drove into town.

Feeling energised, she walked towards her favourite bistro and, after ordering a chicken Caesar salad with extra anchovies and a large glass of chardonnay; she mulled over the events of the morning. It had been nice to see Jack after so long and de-stressing at the range had done her a power of good. But most importantly, it had given her the solution to the problem that had been plaguing her for weeks. Now she knew exactly how Andrew Cavendish would meet his end and providence had delivered her the perfect day for it.

42

~ Fireworks ~

With its headlights turned off, the car slipped around the corner silently. Two doors opened, and the sky became illuminated by a rocket. Stars in red and green flashed and fell to earth as Nigel and Velvet Jacket got out of the car.

Standing for a few seconds, they looked around, checking for anyone on the street. Luckily, Andrew's business wasn't on a major thoroughfare, and the chance of a random person passing by was rare. The only people who walked by were anglers heading to the canal in search of fish.

The warehouse windows were lit up and a shadow moved behind the glass, signalling that someone was inside. Nigel pulled on a pair of gloves and tried the door. It was locked.

"I don't think he's expecting us to call," Velvet said.

"He knows today is the deadline. I'm guessing because it's late, he thinks we're not coming."

"He'll get a surprise then." Velvet took a pair of gloves out of his pocket and chuckled, a low growl punctuated by pauses, giving him a guffaw that sounded like a pantomime villain.

Removing a small wallet, he selected a steel pick and tension bar and inserted them into the mortice lock. Experience had taught him he didn't need a light to see what he was doing. In the darkness, he felt as the pick and bar manoeuvred the lock open.

Quietly, he pushed the door open and stepped inside as soundless as a jaguar.

Nigel followed him and closed the door without allowing the latch to click.

The showroom was in darkness, the only light coming from the office window. Display cases stood against the walls in shadow, like hushed soldiers. The two men peered through the darkness at the tables covered in trinkets. Should any of them fall, they'd alert Andrew to their presence.

Velvet signalled to Nigel to follow his lead, and with their backs towards the display units they slowly shuffled their feet, moving sideways like crabs, avoiding touching anything unstable.

As they reached the office door, they heard music playing; it sounded lost inside the room, as if it wasn't large enough to fill the space. Opening the door, they saw Andrew's phone on the desk and discovered where the sound was coming from.

Andrew was in his chair. He'd fallen asleep, his head slumped onto his chest, a soft snoring coming from him. On the desk was a bottle of whisky and a takeaway carton of half-eaten food. Velvet reached over and lifted the phone from the desk and Andrew's eyes snapped open as Nigel clapped his hands, "Wakey, wakey."

Andrew's eyes, despite sleep, were now wide and staring, fear creeping across the irises. He opened his mouth to speak, but seeing the gun in Velvet's hand, no words came.

"I think you know why we're here," Nigel said.

"I... I..." stammered Andrew.

"Are you trying to tell us you don't have the money?"

"The seller is coming here very soon with the goods."

"Sadly, very soon, isn't right now," Velvet said, and scratched his temple with the revolver's barrel.

"Look I can promise..."

"You're not in a position to promise anything."

Nigel stepped around the desk leant into Andrew and said, "You see, Andrew, you've annoyed too many people. Not just me. Milton-Cole, his clients and, dare I say it, important people in high places."

"I didn't know."

"That's beside the point. How do you think we get some of the high-profile pieces for our clients? We don't use tin-pot thieves or amateurs, like your good self. We don't piss about on the dark web. You see, Mr Chan, or rather Hugh, has connections with people in power. Leaders of countries that need a cash injection to… let's say purchase other items on the quiet. It's people like these that don't want you to live longer than is necessary."

"I won't say a word. I'll get the money and disappear."

"We can't take that risk. Stand up." Velvet said.

"Why?"

"I won't tell you again."

Andrew did as he was told, and Velvet pointed to the right with the revolver and Andrew moved away from the window behind his desk. "You were going to kill me regardless, weren't you?"

"Yes." Velvet smiled and nodded.

"Please…"

"Begging won't work with me."

"Nigel, can't you do anything?"

He shook his head and said, "It's not up to me."

"But surely you ca –"

The bullet pierced his chest before the last word had fully formed and his body fell against the sink unit before dropping to the floor.

Velvet unscrewed the silencer and put the revolver away, selected a Spotify playlist on Andrew's phone and placed it back on the desk.

"We have one more task. Take his arms."

Afterwards, Velvet picked up the whisky bottle and Nigel followed him out of the building.

~~~

Earlier in the day, Melanie had been inside her garage. She'd cleared the items from the bottom shelf of a cupboard and slid the shelf out of its housing and reached down inside the hole it exposed and retrieved a bundle of rags before taking them into the house.

Opening the rags, she revealed the revolver that had once belonged to her grandfather. Unregistered, she had kept it hidden away and after spreading a newspaper on the dining table; she checked it over, cleaning and oiling where required.

She showered, scrubbed all traces of oil from her hands and, wrapping a towel around herself, said. "November the fifth, the perfect day. There'll be so many bangs and explosions tonight, no one will think a gunshot is unusual." She had already laid her clothes out before she showered and, now, just needed to transform herself into Charlotte 'Charlie' Allen.

She checked herself out in the mirror before looking at the clock. "This should all be over in three and a half hours, then I'll be back here enjoying a vodka and cranberry."

Melanie had planned the journey precisely. She would head north via the M6 and the toll road before she returned on the M42.

Through the car's open window, she could hear the glut of explosions that grew in the darkness and occasionally disrupted the sky with multi-coloured stars.

To take her mind off the task in hand, she tried to imagine families with happy children at organised displays and the smell of hotdogs and fried onions.

Parking two streets away, Melanie patted the revolver in her jacket pocket and made her way to Andrew's warehouse.

She walked with a confident gait – a gun in your pocket can do that – and so wasn't worried about running into anyone intent on harm.

Oh, the irony, she thought as a firework exploded nearby. Walking around the corner, the street was in darkness; she hadn't noticed the lack of streetlights before. "What luck."

The door to the warehouse was ajar, and she gingerly pushed it open further, hoping Andrew wouldn't see her. She wanted this to hinge on the element of surprise. She stood still, holding her breath for a second, and listened. "Is that Bon Jovi?" she said to herself and crept toward the office, where a single light burned. Seeing the room was empty, she stepped inside and grinned as Jon Bon Jovi launched into the chorus of 'Shot in the Heart.'

On the sink unit, a smear in brick red caught her attention, and as she walked around the desk and realised it was blood, she followed the crimson line across the floor towards the rear door.

The dank smell from the canal reached her as she crossed the paved area. The trail of blood was no longer visible in the darkness, but she felt it must lead towards the water. Looking at the flat surface of the water, as black as the revolver in her hand, she saw nothing. Suddenly a squeal filled the air and above her a rocket exploded, illuminating the body lying motionless, half-submerged, before once again it became enveloped in darkness.

Melanie stumbled, grabbing onto a wheelie bin as she bent over and gasped for air. She'd recognised the jacket and knew the person face down in the canal was Andrew.

Shock cause her to almost stumble, she pulled back from the water's edge and slowly walked back to the warehouse, mindful not to step in the trial of blood.

"Shit. Shit. Shit," she said back behind the wheel of her car as it travelled out of the town. Unable to organise the thoughts colliding inside her head, she pulled over before the slip road for the motorway and opened her door, clambered outside and vomited on the roadside verge.

Back home, she'd hidden the gun inside a biscuit tin before she poured herself a drink, downing neat vodka in one mouthful before pouring a second.

Questioning who had killed Andrew, she said, "How dare they? It was my job to kill him."

43

~ Police ~

Selena had woken feeling refreshed. She had always slept better when Andrew was away, but on waking her thoughts came back to him and thoughts that he may return home today invaded her mind. Opening the curtains, she had looked out over the garden. The post bonfire night skies were grey, and a mist clung to the lawn, reminding her of the fog in Milan five months before. She had read somewhere, that after a thunderstorm, fog drifted off the river Po because of the city's low elevation and was a daily occurrence in the colder months. The thought made her shiver, not because of the eeriness of fog but because she now realised that so much had happened in a brief space of time, and now her life and her outlook on it had changed.

Placing her shopping into the boot of her car, she had a sudden craving for something sweet and locking the car; she walked towards the high street.

While waiting for the green man at a crossing, she spotted a sign posted in the window of her favourite bake shop. Selena squinted and from across the road could make out the words, 'part time'.

The pastries and cakes with coloured icing displayed behind the glass, along with an array of sausage rolls and quiches, tempted her, but today Selena was more interested in the poster advertising a part-time vacancy.

The advert said to call a phone number listed below and Selena took out her phone and took a photograph before stepping inside and selecting two iced fingers. Two are indulgent, she thought, but I don't care.

"I see in the window you have a vacancy."

"That's right, duck," the woman serving her said. "You interested?"

"I would be, but..." She remembered Andrew and his aversion to her working. He would never allow her to take a job. "I don't think I'll have the time." Smiling, she watched the woman spin the paper bag to twist the corners and place it on the counter.

"Shame. Most applicants are teenagers or school leavers."

"Is that a bad thing?"

"In essence, no, but they don't stay for long. Usually they see a job in a cake shop as a stopgap until something better comes along."

Handing over her payment, Selena said, "But what could be better than working surrounded by cakes?"

"Exactly," the woman said, handing her the change, and the two of them laughed together. "Have a lovely day."

"You too," Selena said, opening the door.

Although the day had brightened, it was chilly and she pulled her scarf tighter around her neck as she made her way back to her car, stopping once to look at a dress with butterfly sleeves in a shop window that she knew wouldn't be suitable. Nowhere to hide the bruises, she thought and walked away.

Turning back to her car after opening the front door, Selena watched as the police car came around the corner, closely followed by another, obviously unmarked. She walked back towards her car with its open boot and was lifting out the first of her shopping bags when the cars pulled up beside her gate.

Turning around, she watched as both cars ejaculated their occupants. From the first, a uniformed PC and from the second, two men in suits.

"Mrs Cavendish?" the shorter of the suited men said.
"Yes."
"Can we have a word, please?"
"I'm just unloading my shopping."

Shit, she thought, why did I say that? The taller suited man wordlessly signalled that the PC should empty the boot, which he began doing as Selena led the officers inside the house.

"What can I do for you officers?" Selena suddenly felt warm and pulled her scarf away from her neck. "Would you like a drink? Tea? Coffee?"

"We're good, thank you. If you'd like to take a seat, Mrs Cavendish."

Observing the shorter man as he removed a notebook from his inside pocket, she thought his suit looked lived in, whereas the other man's looked smartly pressed. "Mrs Cavendish…"

"Please. Call me Selena."

"Selena," the smarter one said, "My name is DS Obasi Adebayo, and this is my colleague DC Dan Malpass. I'm afraid we have some bad news."

Adebayo explained to Selena that they had found a body that morning, causing her to sit with a blank expression and an open mouth. "I'm afraid I have to tell you we believe it to be Andrew Cavendish."

"My Andrew?" instinctively her hand went to her mouth.

"It appears he's been shot."

"Shot!" The word snapped her out of the trancelike state she was slipping into. "How?"

Both officers looked at each other, not knowing how to answer, when the PC looked into the room and coughed. "Yes?" Adebayo said, looking at him.

"I've put the shopping on the kitchen counter."

"Thank you," Selena said, and the tears started.

Malpass lifted a box of tissues from beside a table lamp

and handed it to her, her whispered thanks inaudible.

The PC retired back into the kitchen and she heard her kettle hum. Blowing her nose, she looked up at Adebayo and without speaking, her eyes demanded more information.

"Someone discovered his body in the canal behind his shop."

"What was he doing in the canal?"

Malpass cleared his throat and said, "We're unsure. Our investigation has only just begun."

"Investigation?" The tears had ceased, but she continued to sniff and use the tissue to rub at her nose.

"Sorry, but Andrew's death is a murder enquiry," he said.

The PC walked in carrying a mug of tea and placed it on the side table beside Selena.

She smiled her thanks as Adebayo started speaking again. "Mrs ... Selena, I have to ask. Are you aware of anyone who would want to harm your husband?"

Yes! Her mind screamed, but her voice said, "No." She took a sip of tea and grimaced at its sweetness. "I'm sorry I'm not being very helpful, am I?"

"That's okay. There's a lot to take in." Malpass said.

"In time, you might remember something that could help us." Adebayo said, "Until then, we'll assign you an F.L.O."

Selena placed the mug back on the table. "F.L.O?"

"A family liaison officer. Her job is to support you."

"You'll like her," Malpass interrupted, "She's called Gayle, she's..." A stern glance from Adebayo silenced him.

"I'm not sure I'll need her. But thanks for the consideration."

"It is standard procedure in an investigation of this magnitude. Just give it a few days and we'll take it from there. Until then, DC Malpass and I will take our leave. PC Corbett will remain here until PC Moran arrives."

Selena went to rise from the sofa, but Adebayo told her

there was no need as they'd see themselves out. The sitting room felt vast after they'd left, and grasping the fact that Andrew would not return home today, the tears returned.

~~~

Melanie had a restless night and woke in the early hours. Trembling, she pulled the duvet up to her chin and closed her eyes, but try as she might, sleep eluded her. Feeling the effects of too many vodkas the night before, she shuffled into the bathroom. Sitting on the toilet, she peed as she drank a tumbler of tap water.

Not caring that she was naked apart from a pair of knickers she'd headed into the kitchen and as the kettle heated, she searched the cupboards for pain killers. Sliding two slices of bread into the toaster, she busied herself selecting a knife and a jar of peanut butter only to leave the toast untouched, cooling in the toaster.

Breakfast became paracetamol and a black coffee on the sofa.

The sound of knocking woke her, and Melanie wrenched herself upright and made her way into the hall. In the frosted glass of the front door, she saw the outline of a figure, black and pixelated. "Just a minute," she called as a shiver reminded her she was naked.

Bolting into the bedroom, she grabbed a pair of jeans and buttoning a blouse she looked out of the window to see in her drive a police car. "Shit, shit, shit." Panic crept up her body. Her legs felt unable to support her and her heart felt like Phil Collins was playing his famous 'In the Air Tonight' drum fill in her chest.

Tucking the blouse into her jeans, she took a deep breath and opened the front door to reveal a uniformed police constable. She gave Melanie a smile and introduced herself as PC Khan. Melanie returned the smile and invited her inside.

"Sorry it took me so long; I was still in my nightclothes." PC Khan nodded and followed Melanie into the sitting room. Spotting the empty vodka bottle and solitary glass on the coffee table, she chuckled and said, "Bit of a session yesterday. You know how it is… or rather not… umm… I mean… because… well."

"That's okay, Mrs Rothman. No need to explain."

Calm down, you stupid bitch. – The words bounced around Melanie's head as she offered to make coffee.

"I'm fine thanks," Pc Khan said. "I'm here to deliver this." She held up a jiffy bag. "I must apologise on behalf of the force for the delay in returning these to you."

Melanie's face must have shown her confusion.

"It's the items belonging to your husband. They were sitting in a cupboard overlooked, I'm afraid."

"My fault. I received a call to tell me they were available to collect, and it just slipped my mind."

"No harm done. Shall I leave them here?" Melanie nodded, and PC Khan placed the jiffy bag on a table. "I'll let you get back to your day."

Melanie walked the PC to the door and, turning, she thanked Melanie for her time and climbed into her car and reversed out of the drive.

Closing the door Melanie breathed out forcefully, her relief obvious, and noticing she was sweating she peeled off her blouse and made her way to the bathroom, removing the jeans she turned on the shower and stepped inside allowing the hot water to wash away the smell of fear.

In her kitchen, she took down a china cup and saucer and fixed herself a chamomile tea to calm her nerves. Sitting at the breakfast bar, she thought about how she'd expected the worst, seeing PC Khan on her doorstep. Her mind had been racing and now images from the night before invaded her consciousness.

The sight of Andrew floating face down was still there when she closed her eyes, as was the smear of blood where someone had dragged his body from the office.

Speaking aloud, she said, "What could have incited emotions so extreme that someone had killed him?"

She discovered she was shaking; the cup was rattling against the saucer, so she placed it down gingerly and breathed deeply to quell what she assumed to be delayed shock. Another thought entered her head, this one condemnatory. *But you, despite having no feelings for Andrew, were intent on killing him too.*

"But we had an agreement," she told herself, and her face crumbled into tears.

~~~

Selena opened the door to find PC Gayle Moran on her doorstep. Out of uniform, she held up her warrant card to establish her identity, her face expressionless.

Standing aside to allow her visitor inside, Selena walked through to the kitchen before speaking. "Tea? Coffee?"

"Tea please. Milk, no sugar."

As Selena made their drinks, Gayle pulled out a stool and sat at the breakfast bar and explained her position.

"I'm not here to cause you any stress. It's purely to make sure you're coping. Crime can affect people in a variety of ways. Mostly shock and anger. And my job is to answer any questions you may have."

And to ask questions. Investigating me, Selena thought. "Your being here. Does this mean the police think I'm involved?" – *Shit why have I said that,* – "because it's usually the partner you investigate first, isn't it?" – *Shut up, you stupid woman, and just make the tea.*

"No one is thinking anything of the sort."

Selena placed two mugs on the worktop and poured the tea that had barely had time to brew. She moved to the fridge and removed a carton of milk and placed it down beside Gayle's mug.

"Will you be staying overnight?"

"Only if you'd like me to. I've a bag packed in the car."

"I don't think it'll be necessary."

"If you're certain."

"I am."

They drank their tea in silence, each scrutinising the other.

The afternoon passed slowly. Awkward silences followed awkward conversations until Gayle said, "Right, I'll make tracks. I'll see you tomorrow morning."

Selena smiled, a weak half-smile, before leading the PC through the hall. At the door she said goodbye and closing the door, she felt like she was exhaling for the first time in an age.

44

~ Press ~

Selena assumed the knock at the front door was Gayle. She didn't check through the window and turned the lock. The door opened and a flash temporarily blinded her. As the dancing colours faded, she saw a man on the step holding a camera.

"Warren Tate. Derbyshire Record. I'm here to ask you a few questions about your husband's death."

"Excuse me?"

"Our readers will be interested to hear your feelings about this unfortunate incident." He pushed his mobile phone towards her. "Do you have a comment you'd like to share with us?"

"No…"

"Come on, Mrs Cavendish, give me something I can use."

Gayle's car pulled into Selena's drive and, seeing her, she broke down and tears streamed down her face.

"Do you have any idea who would want to shoot your husband?"

"Can I help you?" Gayle said, walking towards the house.

"We're busy here, love," Warren said, "if you don't mind." His attitude and face dropped when Gayle flashed him her warrant card. "I'm just trying to do my job."

"Are you okay?" Gayle said to Selena, who nodded. "Now sir, I'd like you to leave, please."

"People have a right to know…"

"I shan't ask you again, sir. Please vacate the property."

Warren huffed and stomped away.

Gayle put a hand on Selena's shoulder and said, "He's gone now. Come on, I'll fix us both a hot drink."

Selena sniffed through her thanks and allowed herself to be turned around and directed inside.

Gayle carried two steaming mugs into the sitting room and placed them down on the coasters on the coffee table. "How are you feeling now?"

"I'm okay. It was a shock to find him standing on the doorstep."

"Some of these journos have no tact or manners."

"Do you think he'll come back?"

"I can't say, but if he does while I'm here, I'll send him away with a flea in his ear."

"What if you're not here?"

"Just close the door on him."

They sat quietly, both hugging their mugs until Gayle broke the silence. "Is that your wedding photo on the windowsill?"

Selena glanced across at the image in the silver frame. "Yes. I always found it a creepy seeing myself. Andrew put it there."

"It's a nice photo. You both look happy."

"We were." Selena hoped her reply didn't give away the unhappiness that had seeped into her marriage.

"Where did you get married?"

"The little church on Oaks Lane."

"So, have you always lived here?"

"No. Andrew used to come with his parents as a child and loved the village.

"So, was it his idea to marry and move here?"

What are you getting at? – "No, it was a joint decision." Frightened that she could say something that Gayle might misread, Selena raised her guard.

"Did Andrew have the antique shop when you got married?"

Here we go, Selena thought. She's fishing. "It's not an antique shop."

"Sorry, my mistake."

I bet it was – "It's a warehouse. He's a dealer… Sorry, he was a dealer. He supplied auction houses and personal clients."

"So he didn't get passers-by calling in?" Gayle replaced her mug on the table and smiled. "People off the street."

So you're trying to look relaxed and friendly – "He may have, but he never spoke of it."

Selena placed her mug down and stood. "I'm going to make myself a sandwich. Would you like one?"

"I'll give you a hand."

"No. You stay there; you've done enough already." Selena walked away, choosing to take a break from Gayle's questions.

45

~ Trapped ~

Melanie stopped at the charity clothing bin and looked inside the carrier bag she was carrying. She was reluctant to part with the Dr Martens; they had been so different from the designer shoes she typically wore, and they had been practical and comfortable.

In two minds whether to keep them, she imagined Emilia telling her not to be stupid. If they're that important, I can always buy another pair, she thought, and hoisted the bag through the hole, pulled the handle, sending her alias into the metal container.

Walking away without the disguise, she felt a sudden freedom, like a yoke being removed after a long day's labour. She walked into town with a confident stride, looking to anyone who observed her, like a woman with a purpose.

The shock she had felt days ago had faded, and she'd come to terms with the events that had transpired at Andrew's office. She'd returned the old gun to its original hiding place. Fearing any DNA traces, she'd burned the wig she'd worn under the cap in her log burner and now, with the clothes disposed of, she felt like she could be herself again.

The person she'd been before. Before the madness of promises and pacts.

Pushing the door of the shoe shop open, she made her way over to the assistant, who looked up as she entered and said, "I'm interested in buying a pair of Dr Martens."

~~~

Emilia wandered around the supermarket, shopping on autopilot. She'd had a niggling thought that nibbled at her like a mouse with a biscuit. Keeping busy kept it at bay, but routine tasks like shopping brought it to the fore. She turned into an aisle and on the shelves were canned goods. She stood staring at row upon row of tin cans, looking but not seeing. Shoppers passing, glanced at the woman staring into space, then continued with their own business. "Excuse me," a voice beside her said. She stepped aside to let a young man take a can from the shelf.

"Sorry," she whispered to herself. The man had moved on.

It wasn't until she got home that she thought about how she'd walked away, leaving her trolley stacked with goods at a display of tinned carrots.

Emilia couldn't stop thinking about how she felt a fraud. The others believed she'd delivered on her promise. But Paul had died because of an unfortunate accident. That was how the coroner had determined his death.

"I'm the one that's supposed to be the stronger of the three of us," she told herself as she stood looking out over the garden. "I have been in control right from the start, so why am I allowing these feelings to disturb my life?" She knew the answer. Correctness and truth.

"Maybe..." she said, "Maybe I should come clean before things go any further."

This wasn't anything she hadn't told herself many times before, the chief obstacle being how would Melanie feel? She'd already lost *her* husband; would it cause problems for the three of them if she reacted badly? Then there's the danger of being arrested for conspiracy to murder.

"Would Melanie put us all at risk?"

This was a question she couldn't answer. A question that showed how little they all actually knew about each other. The ringing telephone disrupted her thoughts.

~~~

Back home, Melanie admired her new boots, cherry red and shining. She remembered her father showing her a picture taken in the 1970s of himself surrounded by youths, all shaven headed wearing them. The image had looked menacing, but he'd assured her the lads were his friends. Friends frowned upon by his parents and schoolmasters.

"Maybe I should shave my head?" she laughed, dismissing the stupidity of the idea. However, she knew, had she still been a teenager, she'd probably have done it, just for effect. Rebellious intention never went far away.

Her stomach rumbled. She'd missed breakfast in her eagerness to get out, and it was now past lunchtime. She grabbed a pack of bacon from the fridge and slid a couple of rashers under the grill to cook while she removed the ketchup from the cupboard and two slices of bread from the bread bin.

Devouring the sandwich, she switched on the kettle and took a sponge from the sink to clean the board. The smear of ketchup left behind reminded her of the blood in Andrew's office.

Closing her eyes, images from bonfire night floated behind the lids and she knew she had to sort herself out or the fact that *she* hadn't killed Andrew would continue to haunt her.

"Who can I talk to?" she told herself as she finally pulled herself together enough to make a coffee. Stirring, she mumbled possibilities, "Dad, what would I tell him? – Oh by the way, I made a promise to kill a friend's husband if she killed mine. – Fuck that."

Carrying the coffee over to the breakfast bar, she

suddenly said, "Emilia." She put the mug down and reached for her bag and took out her burner phone. "Makes sense. I'll explain that I had arrived, and he was already dead, so I couldn't carry out my intention. Surely, she'll understand. Why should this alter our agreement?"

Scrolling through the contacts was quick. There were only two. She was about to press the call button, but paused, reminding herself that it was Emilia who had drawn the straw to kill Paul. So would this information throw a spanner into the proverbial?

~~~

Adding sunshine into her voice, Emilia answered her ringing phone. "Hello Selena, what a pleasant surprise."

"I might not have much time, so listen."

"Very well."

"Melanie has done it…"

There was a pause, as if Selena was waiting for her to respond. None came and Selena told her that the police had come four days ago to inform her about Andrew's body being found in the canal with gunshot wounds,

"And how do you feel?"

"I'm not sure, numb. Frightened. Bewildered."

"That's understandable. What's happening now?"

"Like I said, I might not have much time to speak fully. There's a family liaison officer coming to my house every day, and she's making me nervous. Honestly Emilia, I'm worried I'll say something I shouldn't. She is being supportive, but in the background she's fishing. Mixing pointed questions with mundane ones. It's as if she suspects me of being involved."

"It's plausible to be jittery, but unless they have something concrete, they won't suspect you."

"And yesterday, I had a visit from a journalist. Bold as brass, knocking on my door with a camera in my face, asking questions. I was so stressed I just broke down into tears."

"What did you tell him?"

"Nothing, Gayle dealt with him."

"Gayle?"

"The family liaison officer. She got rid of him. I don't feel like I have time to absorb everything because she's here. I feel trapped." The line went briefly silent, then Selena said, "There's her car now," and disconnected.

Emilia continued to hold the phone against her ear as the connection died and wondered if, when this was over and done with, would they all feel trapped by their actions?

46

~ Cyndi ~

Cyndi dragged her feet as she walked home. The flat where she lived looked bleak as it came into view. She was tired after having worked an overnight assignment with a businessman old enough to have been her father. The lack of a regular income forced her lifestyle choices, that and Vinnie's requirements. She would usually switch off her feelings while on a job. But last night, as the obese but wealthy man had sweated and pawed over her, she had thought about her situation.

She exhaled loudly as she slid the key into the lock and opened the door to be welcomed by her untidy home. Discarded clothing littered the sofa, its cushions lying on the floor alongside empty beer cans and the trappings of Vinnie's habit. Foil food trays and used cutlery, and a pair of boxer shorts lay on the floor. Looking across the room, she could see that the kitchen was in a similar state. "Welcome home, Cyndi," she muttered to herself.

She dropped her keys into the bowl by the TV and picked up Vinnie's boxers and carried them into the bathroom and dropped them into the laundry basket. The bathroom was tidy, apart from a shaving ring around the sink. She'd cleaned it the previous morning and now, taking a deep breath, she rinsed the soap scum and stubble away.

Glancing into the bedroom at the unmade bed, dirty plates on the floor and the open wardrobe door spewing out clothes that really should have been hanging up, her mind jolted. She walked back into the sitting room and picked up her keys and let herself out again. No longer tired, she headed into town; she knew she had to make a decision.

With last night's tip inside her purse, she scanned the properties for rent in the local area. I must get out, she thought. Staying any longer will just mean more of the same. She had grown tired of Vinnie's needs. Yes, she'd known he liked a smoke and dropped the occasional tab when she had met him, but things had progressed, and now Vinnie was no longer the man she'd met two years before.

"Shit," she said aloud as she read the details in the agent's window. "The best I can afford is a room in a shared house."

Her experience of HMO living was based on Vinnie's friends, this being houses filled with single men, loud music, and more drugs. She wanted a fresh start and although she had enough money to fund a deposit and a month's rent, she'd need more cash to live on. "A few more jobs like last night could set me up for a month or more." But no sooner had the words left her mouth than she remembered she would have to look after Vinnie in the meantime. This meant financing his habit and running the hovel they called a flat.

Making her way to another agency, Cyndi's mobile beeped and expecting it to be Vinnie asking where she was, she ignored it.

While looking in another window, she ignored the images of property that were deliberately doctored to make them look more appealing, and instead read the costs printed beneath them first.

Again, the prices were prohibitive.

There was nothing on display that she could afford. Maybe, she thought, if I lived alone and worked a couple of extra days each week, I could eke out a decent living. And possibly look at changing my life.

Her mobile started ringing and taking it from her pocket.

She didn't recognise the number and was about to ignore it when she pressed the connect button. "Hello."

"Cyndi?"

"Speaking."

"Hi, Iain here. I was curious to know your availability."

"When were you thinking of?"

"I'll be in Banbury for a few days from tomorrow. It would be nice to see you again."

Cyndi couldn't believe her luck; this is just what she needed. The extra cash Iain would give her would help enormously. "I'm free for the next few days."

"Good. How about we make a weekend of it?"

"A weekend?"

"Yes. My surprise if you're up for it."

"What will I need to pack?"

"Just a couple of outfits fit for dining out." He chuckled and added, "You can pack knickers, but you won't be wearing them for long." His voice became distant as he spoke with someone, "Listen, I have to go for now. If the dates are okay, text me on this number and I'll let you know where to meet."

The call ended, and she smiled, thinking that fate was her BFF today. But fate has a way of throwing obstacles in your path, and before she could put her mobile away, it rang again. This time, Vinnie. "Where are you?"

"I'm on my way home. I had to pick up some shopping."

"Grab me a couple of cans on your way," and he was gone.

~~~

Vinnie was also planning a new future. He'd woken in a combination of comedown and hangover; his bones ached and felt heavy while his eyes found it hard to focus through the pulsing beating in his head. His breakfast had been a cigarette, cold curry and some funky flavoured milk he'd left out of the fridge.

Scrabbling around in the pockets of jeans, down the back of the sofa and taking the few pounds put aside for the electric meter, he was gone. Out searching for his next fix.

His addiction was the first thing that entered his head each morning, and it was now a full-time occupation planning where the next journey into oblivion would come from.

He knew he was lucky to have Cyndi. She'd helped him out when his need had been greater than his ability to pay for it. The stories he'd heard from others in his social group, and the things they had to do to pay for a hit.

Spanner had taken great joy in telling him what his girlfriend had done to help him out and, although he knew he should have been angry, the emptiness in his veins had overridden it and he'd accepted it. It wasn't any different to the work she did to look after him, and in moments of lucidity; he wondered if they could ever have a life away from the darkness, they both lived in.

Vinnie had no luck finding Spanner or any of his other suppliers and so turned to Joff, a dealer whose product wasn't always of the best quality. But needs must, thought Vinnie as he approached him.

Sliding alongside him beside the litter bin, Joff whispered, "What you in for, Vin?"

"What's in the shop?"

"Jet. Green. Rail. Wings."

"What's your wings cut with?" Vinnie asked, knowing it could be anything from rat poison to dishwasher powder, knowing Joff.

"It's clean man," Joff said. "Tenner a wrap."

"I'm short," Vinnie said. "Can you sub me?"

"Not sure Vin, man."

"It's only two quid. Come on Joff, I need my morning flight."

"Maybe if your lady does for me what she did for

Spanner."

"What? No."

"Okay, laters."

Vinnie started to saunter away, but Joff called him back. "Look man, for two quid, I'll settle for a blowie." Vinnie nodded, his eyes looking at his feet. "Tell your lady I'll be round later."

Vinnie palmed Joff the cash and the wrap was delivered and they broke apart and walked away in opposite directions.

"Fucking Spanner," Vinnie muttered to himself, "telling everyone."

Cyndi was home when Vinnie returned. "Did you get me some cans, babe?"

"They're in the fridge."

Vinnie was about to mention the arrangement he'd made with Joff earlier, but he chickened out. Knowing Joff was both a user and a dealer, he told himself, "He'll probably be off his face all afternoon."

As he lifted a can of unbranded lager from the fridge shelf, he asked. "Good payday last night?"

"It was okay, but the client paid the agency, so I'll have to wait a couple of days to get my wages. At least he gave me a good tip. That'll cover things for the next couple of days."

"Sweet," Vinnie said as the ring pull clicked and the beer fizzed before he put the can to his lips.

"I'm going for a shower," Cyndi said. "There's a pack of noodles in the cupboard if you're hungry. I'll tidy up when I've finished in the bathroom."

"No worries."

Cyndi walked out of the room, and after checking she had stepped into the shower, Vinnie picked up her handbag and rummaged around inside until he found her purse. He opened it and took out a fiver, pushing it into his jeans pocket. He turned his attention to her phone and saw the call she'd answered earlier. "So," he said, walking into the bathroom. "Do you have any more jobs lined up?"

"Not at the moment."

"Do you think you'll hear from the guy who has the big house on the Tadmarton Road again?"

"Maybe. We could do with the extra cash."

"Sure babe." Vinnie left the bathroom and headed off to the bedroom and oblivion. There'll be time to make plans later.

47

~ Legacy ~

Selena was the only person in the bookshop. She ran her fingers over the book spines in the art department and selected a volume and flicked through the plates of artworks without actually looking at them. She just needed to get out of the house.

The autopsy findings were conclusive. "Death by a gunshot wound," was how DS Adebayo had worded it when he'd informed her that the coroner had said Andrew's body was being released and she could arrange her husband's funeral. She'd thought about it and recalled it hadn't been something they had discussed. She didn't know his preference and although she'd instructed a local undertaker, she'd made no firm decisions regarding coffins and services, or between a cremation or burial.

She took the book over to the till and the assistant smiled as she took it from her. "Some nice photos in here," she said, making small talk.

"Yes," was the one-word reply from Selena.

Walking slowly through town, dragging her feet, earned her withering looks and tutting from the people she slowed down as they walked past. A poster advertising a theatre production caught her eye, a man lying on the floor, a pool of blood beneath him and a gun by his side. The image pricked at her consciousness and her inability to move as her eyes glazed with tears resulted in further tutting and stares. Selena didn't care.

There was one free table when Selena entered the café. She ordered a cappuccino and took a seat in the corner, waiting for it to be delivered. The room was rich with the hubbub of conversation and looking around, people were sitting chatting over their drinks, some dipped biscuits into mugs, while others became engrossed in their phone screens. Her drink arrived and she thanked the young waitress, declining anything further.

A couple holding hands snapped up a vacant table nearby. She watched as the girl removed her jacket and passed it to her lover, who slipped it over the back of his chair before he placed a kiss on her cheek. Selena watched him walk to the counter and place an order, and he gave her a smile on his return before sitting down and entwining his fingers with his girlfriend's.

Memories flooded Selena's mind. Andrew holding her hand as they walked through a meadow filled with cornflowers and oxeye daisies. His arm across her shoulders while they looked up at the sky through the oculus of the Pantheon in Rome. Why was she remembering just the good times? Making love under the stars on a Croatian hillside. Heads bobbing in unison at a concert.

Suppressing a smile, Selena thought, how before, when I tried to recall our life together, it was only the hurt and fear that rose to the surface? Now I remember there had been happy times, but sadly, the unhappy ones outweighed them.

Do I miss him? Another thought.

No, the answer came.

She knew she should have some feelings of sorrow, but no matter how deep she searched her heart, she couldn't find any.

Was she glad he was dead?

No.

Would she have preferred if the marriage had ended in divorce, no matter how unpleasant?

Yes.

But what is done is done, and she had to live with it, but she was certain of one thing. The legacy of having been married to Andrew would not dictate her future.

She drank her cold cappuccino and noticed that during her thoughts the couple had left the café, and picking up her bookshop purchase, she left and headed home.

The house seemed quieter. Larger now she was on her own. Selena had spent many days and nights alone in the house, but now, knowing no one was going to come through the front door unannounced made it feel like a vast, open space. Silly really, she thought, how could her end of terrace cottage have grown, but it certainly felt that way.

Gayle no longer visited daily. She'd explained a few days before that her time as her family liaison officer. was ending, and she'd was to be assigned elsewhere. Selena had disliked having Gayle. in her home. In fact, she thought more than once that the officer had suspected her of being involved with Andrew's murder. Technically, she knew she was, but pushed that thought to the back of her mind. Despite her fear of Gayle finding out, she had appreciated the help she'd received. The trip to identify Andrew's body was made easier with her support. The initial ringing around of funeral directors had been down to her and even fending off friends and well-meaning neighbours who had arrived with dishes of stews and casseroles.

Selena made herself a sandwich and moved into the sitting room, where she picked up the remote. She was about to wake up the television when her burner phone rang. "Hello Heather. Iain Hart, from Astley House. I hope I'm not disturbing you."

"Not at all. How are you?"

"I'm very well, thank you. I've just recharged my batteries during a brief Spanish break."

"What can I do for you, Iain?"

"I was calling to say we'll be releasing some images of the new orangery at Astley House next week and we're going to make a start on constructing a spa in the grounds. I wondered if you'd like me to send you the details?" he paused, and she heard him throw in, "or if you'd like to come and see the work so far for yourself. I'd be happy to show you around."

"Let me consult my diary and I'll get back to you."

"I can email you the plans if you like. Just let me have your email address and I'll get someone to send them over today."

"There's no need," Selena said quickly. "I don't use email." It was her turn to laugh. She hoped it was convincing. "I'm what they call a techno-dinosaur. Imagine running a business nowadays without it. My assistant deals with that side of things."

"Not to worry," Iain replied. "I'll look forward to your call."

"I'll be in touch soon."

Selena disconnected the call and thought it was about time she stepped up to the plate.

48

~ Max ~

Cyndi stood up and stepped back, looking at the space where she'd just been kneeling. She had to make sure no one would find the vanity case she'd pushed behind the community waste bins.

The collection wasn't due for another three days. By then, she'd be gone. Embarking on her journey to a new life.

Pushing open the flat door, she peered into the bedroom. Vinnie was on top of the bed, but somewhere else, as the rubbish in his veins carried him to unconsciousness.

She found it harder with each day to look at him without scowling. His presence grated on her.

In the kitchen, the washing machine was sloshing its load and Cyndi watched her clothes mixing with Vinnie's, shirts hugging and trouser legs entwining something their bodies hadn't done for so long that she felt they had ceased to be a couple.

She couldn't remember the last time Vinnie had shown her any affection. She could recall every minute of whining when he needed a fix. Every forced embrace and skin stroke as he'd pleaded for her to sort him out. Now all she felt was resentment.

She'd not forgiven him for Joff. That had been the final hammer stroke that sealed her heart shut.

Looking in on Vinnie again, she walked back into the sitting room and pulled back the rug and, lifting a broken floorboard, she took out the purse she'd hidden there. She slid the notes she'd earned the previous evening out of her jeans pocket and, removing a tenner from the bundle, she stowed them in the purse and replaced it, making sure the rug was back in place.

She kept herself busy with housework until Vinnie surfaced, rubbing his stomach, complaining he was hungry. "I thought we had Pop Tarts in here," he said, rooting through the kitchen cupboards.

"There's a tenner in the pot if you want to nip to the shop and get some."

"Sod that, I'll have these." Taking Cyndi's box of Rice Krispies, he plopped down, eating them straight from the packet, spilling those that failed to reach his mouth down his front and over the sofa.

Picking up the stray cereal, Cyndi fussed around him, a smile plastered on her face. "Don't forget, I've got another job tonight. A weekender."

"With the big shot from Tadmarton?"

That's the second time Vinnie has mentioned the road name, Cyndi thought. How does he know? She'd never told him; always keeping her work destinations to herself.

"Yes, it's a big earner. We'll make a packet out of this gig. Maybe we can go away together for a few days."

"Nah," he shook his head. "Better pack a jumper. It'll be cold in that big old house."

His knowledge of Astley House chilled her. She didn't know why, but it tied her heart in a knot. "Will you have enough gear while I'm away?" She tried to make her voice sound light. "Do you want me to call Spanner and get you some?"

"Just leave the cash, I'll be okay… oh, and some extra for beers."

"I'll fetch you some, save you the hassle of getting them."

"Sweet."

Cyndi picked up a canvas tote bag and her other purse and asked Vinnie if there was anything else he wanted. He shook his head and then said, "How much do you reckon we'll make this weekend?"

We'll make? Cyndi thought, The face on him. "About a grand, I reckon."

Vinnie whistled. "A grand, eh? Well, change that from beers to a bottle of scotch. Might as well celebrate if I'm going to be home alone."

Cyndi gave him a fractured smile and pulled the front door behind her.

~~~

Vinnie picked up his mobile, searched the contacts, and pressed the call button. "Hi mate, it's Vin. You around this aft? …Cool, see you later."

After he ended the call, he cupped and sniffed his armpits. "Bloody hell, Vinnie, you stink like an unwashed dog," he laughed to himself and stripped off and made his way into the bathroom, turned on the shower and stepped inside the bath and under the tepid water. He used Cyndi's shower gel, not bothered that it was a jasmine scented brand.

He reached an arm out of the shower curtain and grabbed a toothbrush – Cyndi's – and after holding it under the stream of water; he rubbed it around the inside of his mouth and let it fall into the bath landing where he stood lazily urinating.

Naked, he walked into the sitting room as Cyndi entered from outside. "Bloody hell, Vinnie, put some clothes on."

Grabbing his genitals he scoffed, said, "I know loads of skirt who'd be gagging for this."

Cyndi ignored him and placed the bag on the countertop. and unpacked the bottle of scotch and cans of beer. "This should do you until I get back."

"When will you be back?" He grabbed a beer and popped the ring pull.

"Sunday."

"What time?"

"Around 10:30 – 11:00 as usual."

"Cool," he said, taking a swig of his beer, "Bring us a kebab back if there's anywhere open," and disappeared into the bedroom.

Picking up a pair of boxer shorts, he checked the inside before stepping into them, grabbed a T-shirt and pulled a pair of jeans from the open wardrobe. He dressed, finished his beer and, he entered the sitting room and said, "I'm off out."

"Where you going?"

"Just seeing who's around. Got a fiver, I might nip to the Shoes?" Cyndi handed him the money and without a word, he left the flat.

Pushing open the door, the bar of the Three Horseshoes was quiet. Old men with disconsolate faces sat at tables with half-empty glasses of beer in front of them. The younger patrons ranged from the visibly skint to those dressed in designer copies and gold plated chains; youths who lived by their wits with a scam or two on the go.

Vinnie heard his name called and turned to see Max, the friend he'd called earlier. He motioned to the bar and his friend held up his glass to let him know he had a pint already.

Joining Max at the pool table, they watched a skinny tattooed lad thrash his opponent. "What did you want earlier?"

"Any chance I could borrow your motor again?"

"I'm not sure. Last time you returned it empty." Max finished his pint in a couple of swallows and waved the empty glass at Vinnie. They walked over to the bar, and Vinnie ordered two more drinks before bending down to remove a twenty-pound note from his sock, he handed it to the barman.

"I promise, I'll put petrol in it."

"You'd better. When do you need it?"

"Sunday night." They took their drinks over to a table and sat down.

"It's not for anything dodgy, is it? Last thing I want is the cops coming to visit."

"No, nothing dodgy. Got to pick Cyndi up from her friend's place."

"Can't she get a taxi?"

"She would normally, but it'll be late and I don't like her being on her own in the early hours."

"Bloody hell, Vin. When did you become so gentlemanly?" Vinnie gave Max a friendly punch. "Okay, you can have it as long as I get it back before lunchtime on Monday. I've got my Universal Credit interview at two."

"Brilliant, thanks, mate. Another pint?"

Vinnie walked back to the bar, smiling. If his plan worked, he'd be earning himself a tasty wedge of cash.

49

~ Malmaison ~

Hitching the backpack onto her shoulder, Cyndi took one last look into the bedroom at Vinnie lying in a starfish position, his head tilted back as if he was gazing upwards at something she couldn't see. The whisky bottle was on the floor, half-empty. He'd started drinking it as soon as she'd bought it home. All that remained now were two cans of beer, which would have to suffice when he came back to the land of the living.

She opened her purse and was about to leave him a ten-pound note to cover more supplies when she screwed it up, and said, "Stuff him," and returned the note to her purse. "I've given you too much already, Vinnie, and now I owe you nothing."

Cyndi left the flat and walked down the stairs for one last time. She knew she wouldn't miss the sound of neighbours' arguing or their televisions and sound systems blaring at all hours. The outer door closed behind her and she moved around to the side of the building and retrieved her case from behind the bins and walked towards the town centre.

As usual, Iain's car was on time. The boot opened automatically, and she placed her things inside before joining him, sitting in the front passenger seat.

"No driver tonight?"

"I gave him the weekend off, it just the two of us." His hand squeezed her knee and silently the Bentley pulled away from the kerb.

"I've a treat for you," Iain said. "I hope you'll like it."

"What is it?"

"Wait and see."

They continued the rest of the journey in silence until the car pulled into the car park of Malmaison and Iain said, "You're going to prison."

Cyndi looked out at the austere façade of the redundant prison converted into an exclusive hotel. "Does it still look like a prison?"

Iain popped the boot. "Let's find out."

Walking towards the entrance, Cyndi had butterflies in the pit of her stomach. She was used to entertaining clients in hotels, but Malmaison had a reputation for being the epitome of luxury. An enormous window above the double doors gave the perfect view of a gigantic chandelier, its bulbs bathing the lobby in a golden glow.

Once inside, like an excited child, she wanted to run from room to room checking out the bar and dining room, the dark walls and wooden panelling, the comfortable seating. She felt like she'd walked onto a movie set. Containing herself, she waited for Iain to check in.

The old prison landings were still intact, however now carpeted and welcoming. They walked past cell rooms converted into bedrooms that she assumed now housed more than a metal bunk bed and toilet in the corner.

Iain had booked a suite, and she tried to drink it all in at once, the king size bed, earthy toned walls and subdued lighting. The split level stairs leading up to a seating area overlooking the centre of Oxford where she knew she'd enjoy sitting. "I'll order us some drinks," Iain said as Cyndi looked in awe at the roll top bath double sinks and sparkling tiles. It was a far cry from her damp and black mould decorated bathroom at the flat.

Back in the bedroom, she watched as room service delivered a bottle of champagne and she thought, I'm going to love this.

She watched Iain as he removed his jacket, his strong

shoulders visible beneath his shirt. Cyndi was feeling something she'd never felt for any of her clients before. She wanted to admonish herself but didn't, deciding instead to allow herself a weekend living in a fantasy. A memory to cherish when she'd moved onto her new life.

Stretching out, enjoying the feel of the clean mattress, Cyndi lay looking up at the ceiling. The sound of Iain in the shower and the aroma of fresh coffee drifting over from the espresso machine filled her senses with satisfaction. She knew she was going to enjoy the remainder of her time.

They'd made love before dinner, not the usual frantic, secretive sex she usually experienced with married men away from home. Iain was gentle and attentive. She hadn't thought things could get better until he escorted her into the dining room. Waiters whose sole intention was the delivery of excellence served her, pandering to her and ensuring that her dinner wasn't just a meal but an exquisite experience.

Over brandies she'd reached across the table and placed her hand on Iain's and he had removed his, giving her an ineffective smile. Perhaps he's a little shy in public, she thought. He's certainly not in the bedroom.

Back in their suite, he was once again focused on her enjoyment; he had ordered two more large brandies to be delivered and stood in the doorway as she lay in a bath of bubbles sipping hers. "Why don't you join me?" she said. "There's plenty of room."

"No. I'm allergic to highly perfumed products." She thought his voice sounded flat until he said, "You enjoy them. I'll order more drinks. What do you fancy?"

"Can we have champagne?"

"Why don't I surprise you?" Iain left the bathroom and picked up the telephone in the lounge area, and she heard him speaking to reception before submerging her head beneath the bubbles.

Wrapped in a white robe, Cyndi watched as the waiter

delivered a wooden box and two long stemmed shot glasses on a highly polished tray. Iain thanked him and handed over a tip before he picked up the small wooden box and opened it.

Cyndi watched as he removed an aquamarine coloured bottle with a gold lid. "Wait until you taste this," Iain said. "Rochelt, it's Austrian."

Cyndi took the offered glass and watched Iain taste it first, noting that it was to be sipped and not swallowed like the shots she was used to. This wasn't a common tequila. The plum brandy smothered her tongue, and she did her best to hide her displeasure. It wasn't to her taste. How she wished he'd ordered champagne – Cyndi liked bubbles. Iain's phone indicated a text message and as he read it she looked at the ticket on the tray beside the bottle. "Bloody hell, one hundred and seventy-six pounds for something not much bigger than a perfume bottle."

"I'm going to have to go to a meeting tomorrow for an hour, maybe two, so can you keep yourself amused until I return?"

"I could come with you."

"No." he said sharply, then his voice softened. "I'll give you some cash. You can have a shopping expedition in town." Cyndi smiled, but it failed to reach her eyes. "How about tomorrow I order us a late lunch in the room?"

Cyndi nodded, and Iain slipped the robe from her shoulders.

~~~

Cyndi found she enjoyed shopping when she didn't need to count the pennies and she soon forget about Iain's sharpness the day before.

Room service at Malmaison brought their lunch, just as Cyndi had seen in movies. They wheeled a table covered with a white cloth into the room and placed plates covered by silver cloches on it. The waiter popped the champagne cork and poured two half flutes before bowing slightly and leaving the room with a generous tip in his fist.

The salmon was moist and the butter bathing the tiny herby potatoes glistened and cutting a spear in half, Cyndi said, "I've never had asparagus before." Iain didn't respond. "Did your meeting go well?"

"As expected, how did you fill your time?"

"Window shopping."

"Did you get yourself something nice?"

"Yes, let me show you." She pushed her chair back, ready to leave the table.

"Later, it can wait. Eat your lunch first."

"I've never paid so much for lingerie before."

Silence covered the rest of their lunch, the only sound that of cutlery on china.

This isn't how I imagined the weekend would pan out, Cyndi thought. He's bored with me.

Attempting to lift the mood, she asked, "How are things going with Astley House?"

Iain became more animated. "Everything's on schedule. We're adding a spa."

"A spa. Sounds lush. I bet I'd love to work in a spa."

"The roles have already been filled," he replied, again quicker than she had liked, so she changed tack.

"Not that I could work there. I'm hoping to move away."

"Really. Where?"

"Back up North. My family is quite close to Blackpool. I'd like to be near them again."

"I understand."

Shit! Cyndi thought, why did I tell him that? He might not give me a tip now, thinking I won't be available in the future. "But I don't have to move away." Iain raised his eyebrows. "Not if you'd like me to stay in Banbury, or maybe I could move to London." A smile cut across her face.

"Why would I want you to stay?"

"Because of this... Us."

"Us?" His eyes narrowed. "There is no us. This," he motioned between them both with his hand, "is just a business transaction. Paid companionship."

His words stabbed her and she swallowed hard before, with bluster, she replied, "Yes, of course. I know. I wasn't implying –"

"Come on," he cut her off and, taking her hand, led her towards the bed. "You can show me what you bought today."

50

~ Headlights ~

Iain was on his phone while Cyndi was sipping champagne, propped up by soft white pillows luxuriating on the bed. The newly purchased lingerie discarded at her feet.

"I have to go," Iain said suddenly, "A last-minute appointment."

"But you had one this morning." As soon as she'd spoken, she regretted it and his look of disapproval confirmed she had spoken out of turn.

"Would you like me to come with you?" Cyndi asked.

"That won't be necessary. I'll only be an hour, ninety minutes, tops."

"I don't mind coming."

"No!" his voice once again was hard. "Order anything you want or take a trip down to the bar," his voice didn't soften this time and still had an edge to it. "Charge it to the room. I'll see you back here later." She watched him pick up his jacket and briefcase and leave the room before she slumped back and swallowed the remaining champagne in her glass. "Who has business meetings at night?" she said sulkily.

~~~

Vinnie was happy Tadmarton Road was unlit. The darkness hid the black hatchback he'd borrowed from Max and, luckily, the annoying rattle only alerted the nearby wildlife.

He hoped there would be no security guards to see him arrive. If there was, he'd already planned to tell them he'd pulled in for a slash.

A fox scooted across the road, its eyes briefly lit up by the headlights, and Vinnie saw the entrance up ahead. Cutting the lights, he drove the last few metres in darkness before turning into the driveway and stopping.

Peering into the dark, he saw no sign of a guard and crawled up the drive until the house came into view, black and ominous, against the ash coloured sky. Dark, irregular shapes caught his attention, giving the impression they were creatures hiding in the gloom, casting no shadows. Briefly, as he opened the car door, its interior bulb illuminated the area with a meagre yellow light, showing him that the shapes were just pallets of building materials. Some discarded waste pipes resembling a dragon's tail.

Briefly the clouds parted, and the moon lit up the drive in silver and Vinnie saw that the only vehicle parked up was a transit van. He walked back to the car and drove it behind the van, hiding it from anyone who may arrive.

He walked around the perimeter of the building, tripping occasionally on debris left behind by the trades people working during the day. Around the rear he felt safer and using the torch on his phone, he scanned the windows and tried the doors, looking for a place to enter.

Discovering an unlatched sash window, he lifted it and kept it open by sliding a house brick underneath the frame.

Vinnie found himself inside a room where the smell of fresh plaster hung in the air. Turning on his torch, he saw that apart from a bucket and paddle mixer; the room was bare. His footsteps rustled on the plastic floor covering as he walked towards the door.

Outside the room, he was standing in a corridor. He picked up a discarded screwdriver from a window ledge and made his way towards the front of the property until he reached the main hall.

He walked around, opening doors and looking inside the rooms off the hallway. At one point, he used the screwdriver to cut a groove into the freshly decorated plaster. He grinned at the stupidity of the act and was about to carve another when headlights filled the room.

Standing back from the window, he saw a car had parked in the drive. He ducked down and shuffled towards the stairs and launched himself upwards to a bend where he could stoop and observe without being seen.

The main door opened and as Iain stepped inside, the hall became flooded with light, and he instantly saw the scratch in the plaster. Vinnie heard him swear under his breath as he removed his phone and took a photograph of the vandalism before walking into the old caretaker's rooms.

"So here's Mr Bigshot," Vinnie muttered to himself and started walking down the stairs. He was halfway down when the office door opened again and Iain entered.

"Who the fuck are you? What are you doing in here?"

"I'm here to speak with you."

"Then make an appointment with my secretary." Iain opened the main door and said, "Now get out."

"What if I don't want to?"

"I shan't tell you again, you need to leave before—"

Vinnie cut him off. "Before what?"

Now at the same level, Vinnie saw Iain was a good four inches taller than himself. "Look, I just want to talk."

"I'm not interested in what you have to say. Get out before I call the police and have you removed." Iain's voice was raising in volume.

"Don't piss me off, old man," Vinnie held out the screwdriver.

Iain sensed danger and lowered his voice and said. "So, what do you want to say?"

"That's better. No need to be an arsehole."

"Okay, I apologise." Iain put his hand inside his jacket pocket, looking for his phone, then remembered he'd put it inside his briefcase. "Look, I have an appointment. In ten minutes, a client will be arriving."

"Do you think I'm going to fall for that old trick?"

"Very well, get on with it."

Vinnie shuffled, thinking hard about where to start. He had gone over this in his head several times, and now it was difficult to get the words out.

"Come on, we haven't got all night."

"Very well... I know what your game is."

"My game?"

"Yes. I know what you're up to and I'm betting it's not something you'd like to get out."

"Why don't you enlighten me?" Iain folded his arms and leant back against a doorjamb.

Vinnie shifted from one foot to the other and took a deep breath. "I know all about your thing with Cyndi."

He noticed that Iain's' face didn't move, no twitches, no flicker of recognition. "I'm sure your wife would be interested in your affair with a girl old enough to be your daughter."

"Affair?" Iain said blandly. "And how do you know I'm married?"

"Because I've checked you out... Okay, not so much an affair. How do you think it would look if people knew you paid for sex?"

Iain shrugged.

"Well!" Vinnie raised his voice.

"So you know Cyndi?"

"Yeah... she's my... I know her, okay?"

"Let's cut to the chase. Why are you here? What is it you want?"

"You need to buy my silence."

"Blackmail, eh?"

"Call it what you like. You need to see me right if you want to keep your reputation."

Iain laughed, "Reputation. You're out of your depth, young man. Now, like I said, get out before I have you forcibly removed."

Vinnie lunged at Iain, grabbing at his jacket, and the two men struggled. Iain was getting the better of his weaker opponent until Vinnie pushed the screwdriver up under his chin and he froze.

"You're going to sort me out with… let's call it a bonus to keep my trap shut."

"How much?" The point of the screwdriver was painful against the soft skin of his throat.

"Ten grand should do it."

"Ten thousand, you've got to be–" The screwdriver's pressure increased. "Okay, I'll see what I can do."

"You'll see what you can do. Don't play games. Laying your hands on that sort of money would be as easy for you as pissing in a bucket."

"It's not that simple… I'll need to make some arrangements. Why don't we meet tomorrow and –"

"Do you think I'm stupid? I want the money now… in cash."

"Very well, but I'll need to make a call. I can't just draw that much from a cash machine."

Vinnie suddenly grasped he hadn't thought it through fully and relented. "Okay, make your call… but no funny business."

Iain gestured to his briefcase, and Vinnie removed the screwdriver from his neck and allowed him to pick it up. In an instant, before he could react, Iain slammed the briefcase against his head, sending Vinnie flailing across the room. His back came into contact with the wall and Iain was on him rapidly, his fists raised and ready to land on Vinnie, when he froze.

For seconds, they both stood like statues until Iain's body slid to the floor, the screwdriver sticking out of his abdomen.

Vinnie couldn't move. Shock took his mobility. He watched as blood pooled beneath Iain's body until he heard another car approaching.

Again, headlights filled the room. "Shit!" he pushed himself out of his paralysis and raced through the door he'd come through earlier and slipped out of the window and running towards his car, he heard a scream.

51

~ Blue Lights ~

Selena had pushed the open door further and stepped inside the hall where rooted to the spot, she had screamed.

Iain lay on the ground with blood oozing from a wound in his abdomen, where a handled spike appeared to be embedded. He groaned, and she rushed to him, bending down. "Heather," he said as his eyes flickered shut.

Selena's head shot around as she heard a car drive away, its wheels spinning on the gravelled drive. There was almost no rise and fall with Iain's chest and so she leant into him and tried to determine if he was still breathing.

His eyes were still moving behind his eyelids. He was still alive. Forcing herself to look down, she saw that the implement sticking out of his body was, as she had thought, a screwdriver.

She knew she should do something.

CPR was her first thought, but what if it made things worse? He was, after all, not having a heart attack. Should she remove the weapon? Somewhere in the depths of her mind, she recalled being told it would be dangerous to remove it.

"Think, Selena, think," she said aloud and instantly regretted using her real name. "What a mess this is."

Knowing there was only one thing she could do, she opened her handbag and rummaged for her phone.

"Where is it?" she cursed, tipping the contents out onto the floor.

Grabbing up the phone, she punched in three nines and waited for the operator to answer.

"Ambulance," she replied to the question asked. "Astley House. A man has been stabbed. Yes, he's still breathing… almost."

"Can I take your name?"

"My name… My name is…"

Selena disconnected the call and scrambled around, collecting her items and stuffing them back inside her bag. She looked back down at Iain, his eyes had stopped flickering and although she wanted to feel for a pulse she stood up and raced back to her car and drove away, waiting further down the lane in darkness until the blue lights and sirens turned into the drive of Astley House.

52

~ The News ~

The detective who had first broken the news to Emilia called and asked how she was feeling and to ask if she needed anything. She told him she was okay. "A little numb, but on the whole, I'm fine."

"That's the shock," he said. "I also wanted to let you know that from today, Mr Hart's murder will appear in the press. With him having been a high-profile businessman, it was inevitable."

Emilia nodded, 'having been', she thought, now it begins, Iain is in the past. Used to be. Formerly. Once was and having been.

"Mrs Hart?"

She crawled out of her thoughts and said, "Yes, it was inevitable." Repeating what the detective had just said. "What happens now?"

"Now that you've formally identified Mr Hart, we have to wait until the coroner releases the body."

"Should I contact a funeral director?"

"It won't do any harm to let one know the situation. I'm sure most will have experience in this situation."

He gave her a small smile, made his excuses, and left.

Emilia closed the front door behind him. She didn't smile nor frown. With her face fixed, she walked into the sitting room and slowly lowered herself into a chair. Although she had expected Iain's death, the reality had still come as a shock.

Sitting, her eyes focussed on the wall opposite, she was

unaware of how she felt. Should I be angry? Should I be sad? She thought, it's inappropriate to be happy, but I am. Well, not exactly happy, as part of me wishes there'd been another way. – Had there been? – Her mind tripped off on a tangent before returning to her previous thought. "At least I'm not doing cartwheels of joy," she told herself. "Now I need to get on and make sure everything is in order and then decide what to do about the future."

She made her way into the kitchen, dropped a coffee pod into the machine and picked up the phone and called Iain's office.

~~~

With Vinnie lying on the bed, his mind soaring, Cyndi studied her black eye in the bathroom mirror. To pay for the rubbish currently flowing through his veins, she'd had to take her trade out onto the street.

Vinnie was agitated when she had returned to the flat, his addiction contributing to the shakes that ravaged his body. "I need some junk."

"I don't have any money," Cyndi had told him.

"Why not?"

"He didn't pay me. He went off to a meeting and never returned."

"What do you mean, he never came back?" The deception fell easily from Vinnie's mouth. Of course, Iain hadn't returned. He knew that, but pretended he didn't understand what Cyndi was telling him.

"Can't you get any? I need it, babe."

"I've not got any work booked with the agency." She had already told them prematurely she was leaving. How stupid she had been to confuse Iain's financed affection for reality.

"Shall I put the kettle on?"

"Oh, yes!" his voice rising. "let's have a fucking cup of

tea. That'll make everything better."

The argument had continued until he'd lost it and given her a slap and after grinding her down further, she'd gone out to earn enough to feed his arm.

She turned on the television and the newscaster was finishing a story about the lack of government funding for social housing when Iain's face filled the screen and a story about how Hart Holdings had three years before donated two houses to a homeless charity. "The death of Mr Hart is being treated as murder and an investigation is underway."

"What did she just say?" Cyndi said. Flicking through TV channels looking for news reports. Her eyes wide, she held her breath until another image of Iain appeared. She listened to the man behind the desk. "Paramedics found Mr Hart's body inside an Oxfordshire property, his London based business owned. Police sources say that they have strong forensic evidence and are confident that an arrest will be imminent."

"So that's what happened," Cyndi said under her breath, and her mind slipped back to Malmaison.

She'd been in the bar and fended off a businessman who, after buying her a couple of drinks, had become touchy-feely. She'd waited in Iain's room until she had got hungry and ordered room service and a bottle of champagne. The following morning she'd woken up beside the empty bottle and he wasn't there. She continued to wait until reception had called to tell her that the room needed to be vacated.

"I was drinking champers, and he was being killed," she said as tears tumbled down her cheeks.

~~~

"What?" Selena screeched at the television screen. "They have forensic evidence. What shall I do?"

Panic shook her body and without thinking about the time of the day, she opened a bottle of Andrew's whisky and took a deep slug from the bottle; the spirit burning her throat.

She reached behind the sofa where she'd dropped her handbag after returning from Astley House. Removing her burner phone, she noticed the blood that had dried on the screen; she glanced at her bag and saw spots of dark brown where it had dried there too.

She dropped it and rubbed her hands down her jeans, then ran into the kitchen and washed them, fear pushing her breath down inside her. She continued scrubbing under the running tap until the ringing drilled through her panic.

Grabbing at the phone, she answered the call and before Melanie could say anything; she started gabbling, almost incoherently.

"Selena, slow down. Tell me what's wrong."

"Iain's just been on the news."

"Yes, I saw it."

"They said the police have forensic evidence. What if it leads them to me? We're all finished then. It'll all come out."

"Take a deep breath… Have you been arrested before?"

"No."

"So, you've never given the police a DNA test?"

"No."

"That means there's no link to you if you're not on the police database." Melanie's words calmed Selena, and pointing out obvious things eased her fretting mind. "There's always going to be forensic evidence, but the police will need something or someone to link it to."

"But what if they come to arrest me? What do I say?"

"There's no point worrying about something that might never happen. You need to relax, chill out. Would you like me to call Emilia and ask if she knows anything?"

"Will you?"

"Of course. Now make yourself a coffee, take a few breaths and sit down and relax. I'm sure everything will be all right."

Selena did as she was told and sitting on the sofa cupping a mug of coffee, her breathing returned to normal.

~~~

Emilia turned off the television. She'd seen enough. Iain's murder had been journalistic fodder for the past week. Every newspaper had an opinion, a gory headline. Every station kept the public up to date on police activities, excluding sensitive information.

She'd spoken with Melanie and asked her to put Selena's mind at rest. "The police say they are waiting on DNA tests. I'm not sure what that'll prove, considering that builders and tradespeople have most likely left an abundance of samples all over the house."

The inspector had kept her informed at every stage, told her about how the specialist team had searched for forensic evidence. He'd even told her that a bottle of ladies' liquid foundation had been near his body, but there was no suggestion it was important. The last thing he told her was, "I'm confident the coroner will release Iain's body soon."

Over the past week, she'd got used to her husband being gone, and if she was honest with herself, the last thing she wanted was to have his body back at home. She'd left all the arrangements with the funeral directors; it was up to them now to liaise with the coroner.

She had gone to the office to collect some of Iain's personal items and, while she was there, had informed everyone that their jobs were safe and she'd appreciate it, considering the circumstances, if they could carry on as normal.

She had requested all the company accounts and came home with old-fashioned ledgers and CDs containing digital information. At least if she was busy at home, it would take her mind off the endless waiting.

53

~ Leaving ~

It was early in the morning when the police knocked on their door.

Cyndi had been making a pot of tea and Vinnie hadn't yet had his morning fix. There were two officers in uniform and a further two in plain clothes. One, a serious-looking woman, introduced herself and Cyndi was part way through asking what the problem was when the officers delivered their well-rehearsed script and, along with Vinnie, they handcuffed them before they began the search of the flat.

Vinnie said nothing throughout the process, although his morning shakes appeared more pronounced and when his bloodstained jeans and trainers were located under the bed, he shook like a sapling in the wind.

Cyndi's packed case aroused suspicion, and they were both taken away.

Video evidence from Malmaison confirmed Cyndi had been there with Iain and the time stamps proved she hadn't left the hotel on the night of his death.

Vinnie crumbled during his interviews his need for the daily medication his body craved, made him pliable. Foolishly thinking he could exchange it for a fix, he willingly offered the evidence needed to charge him.

~~~

After her release, Cyndi spent just an hour collecting her things from the flat.

Sitting on the train heading north and looking out of the train window. She cried silently.

54

~ Milan ~

Six months later.

Swaddled in a fluffy white robe with the hotel name, *Il Viale Tre* embroidered across the breast, Emilia walked out of the bathroom and picked up the glass of prosecco on the dressing table, took a sip and looked out over Milan.

From her room she could see the spire of the duomo in the distance, and she remembered months ago Selena telling her about the roof tour and the annoying couple from Wigan.

Earlier that morning, she'd received a text from Melanie telling her she'd checked in and was looking forward to dinner that evening.

The phrase, *"Servizio in camera,"* followed by a knock at the door. An elegantly dressed young man in a burgundy two piece suit with gold braiding entered and silently wheeled the lunch trolley out of the room.

Emilia poured herself another glass of fizz before selecting a pair of lime coloured Capri pants and a simple white blouse, teaming them with a pair of Valentino Garavani sandals.

Before leaving the room, she'd tied her hair back and applied her trademark slash of red to her lips. And picking up a lemon coloured Gucci bucket hat and sunglasses, she walked out into the corridor.

The June warmth was the equivalent of a loving hug and, looking up, Emilia let the sunshine bathe her face. She'd booked a ticket to tour the world renowned opera house, La Scala, and from the hotel it was a short walk that took her through the Indro Montanelli Gardens. Stopping to look at the cream-coloured façade of the Palazzo Dugnani, she thought about Astley House. Not as large or as grand as this palace, but it reminded her she needed to make a decision about its future.

As she continued on her way, the sounds of Milan became almost muted in this vast open space of greenery. She could hear birdsong over the roar of modern life, and she thought that even the local population slowed down as they strolled along the paths. She stopped to study the statue, which was dedicated to the controversial journalist and writer whom the park took its name from.

I can't believe that I was last in this city a year ago, she thought as she exited the gardens at Piazza Cavour. So much has happened in the twelve months since Selena tossed her matter-of-fact comment across the dining table. "Oh well," she said, quoting Lady Macbeth, "*What's done cannot be undone.*" She hoped that the madness the character had succumbed to didn't visit either of the three friends.

~~~

Selena had enjoyed her second rooftop tour of the cathedral and now sitting in the side street gelateria where she'd enjoyed prosecco the year before with Emilia, she watched tourists being funnelled down the narrow vico.

Wearing a green polka dot dress with capped sleeves, she smoothed a hand down her arm, marvelling at how quickly she had become used to not choosing clothes that would hide bruising.

Looking back, that sad period in her life now felt so far away that she rarely thought about it, but the sun and Milan reminded her it was okay to show a little skin, albeit with a covering of a high-factor sunscreen.

After finishing her drink and ice cream, Selena wandered off exploring and soon found herself in a street market, nothing special, just local people shopping for provisions; she'd heard Italians prefer to shop for their ingredients daily.

She enjoyed sauntering along, looking at trays filled with vibrant oranges and zesty lemons. Lettuces stacked up, red bitter ones alongside peppery rocket and not a single piece of plastic in sight. Tomatoes of every size and colour were abundant and Selena watched women fill shopping baskets as they bought vast quantities.

At a flower stall, a cheerful man offered her a stem of lilac-coloured dianthus. She accepted and thanked him, following his instruction to smell it. The perfume was subtle but spicy, and the stall owner gave her a beaming smile before turning to serve a customer.

Skirting through the fish section where the smell teased by the warm weather was far from welcoming, she emerged into an area which was a handful of stalls selling second-hand goods. An hour passed as she picked up photo frames, vases and other trinkets, picking her way between the narrow paths between the tables. She stopped at one when she spotted a pot with a Chinese design. Memories flooded back, and she was staring at it when her concentration became broken by the stallholder, telling her the price. "*Mi dispiace. sono non interessante.*" Using her phrase book Italian, she wasn't aware that she'd actually said, 'I'm sorry, I'm not interesting', but the stallholder seemed to understand her meaning and bade her a good morning.

Leaving the shaded street with its market and out into the open air, the sun lavished her with heat and she placed the sunhat she had been carrying on her head. Checking her shoulder bag for her camera, she headed off towards the 15th century fortification, Castello Sforzesco.

~~~

Melanie wasn't interested in ancient buildings, culture, or sightseeing. She'd pulled on a wraparound skirt and sleeveless blouse. Melanie didn't worry about her shoulders being uncovered; she had no plans to visit ecclesiastical attractions, unless you considered shopping her religion.

Armed with her credit card, sunglasses and a bottle of water, she was ready to do battle in the boutiques of Galleria Vittorio Emanuele II.

Melanie was a savvy traveller; she'd flown in with a cabin bag holding a couple of items of clothing, mostly high street and the requisite amount of knickers and shoes needed for her stay. She would fill her hand luggage with her purchases during her stay, but her first job was to find an outfit for dinner that evening, something that would look good alongside her cherry red Dr Martens.

Showered and refreshed after her shopping marathon, Melanie fingered the feathered ruffle of the Dolce and Gabbana mini dress she had found before sitting at the dressing table and unwrapping the towel around her head. Giving it a blast from the hairdryer. It had to be crafted with precision if she wanted to give the impression of messy random spikes. She'd had her blonde hair tipped with a purple dye and when she was satisfied with its appearance, she resembled a thistle.

Naked, she padded across the room to where she had put away her underwear and selected a tiny black thong and was stepping into it when there was a knock at the door. Opening it, she saw a young waiter who had arrived with the half bottle of prosecco she had ordered. With his eyes averted away, he walked inside, placed the tray holding the bottle and a glass on the dressing table, and left the room. Melanie chuckled at her topless reflection in a mirror and popped the cork. "What are you like?" she asked herself.

With her make up finished and wearing just her boots

and thong, she studied herself in a full-length mirror. Giving herself an approving nod, she surveyed her gamine appearance, accentuated by small breasts and a trim waist, she said, "For a forty-one-year-old you're not doing too bad, Melanie. I reckon you could easily pass for thirty."

Stepping into the dress and marvelling at its fit. Her slender legs beneath the tulle skirt, the cupped bodice and cinched waist gave her the look of a prima ballerina. "Tonight I shall be the black swan," she said before downing the last of her bubbles and heading out.

Making her way through the hotel lobby, Melanie spotted Selena and wolf-whistled at her tall, lean frame swathed in a Missoni metallic knit dress, the gold and silver threads reflecting the lighting. "You look the dogs–"

"Language Melanie," Selena laughed. "I love your hair."

"I'm channelling my inner punk."

"Shall we?" Selena said, directing towards the restaurant.

The maître d' led them to a reserved table that gave a view of the whole dining room. "I can't wait to see what Emilia is wearing," Melanie said as a waiter delivered a bucket holding a chilled bottle of prosecco to the table.

"This table is perfect for a dramatic entrance," said Selena.

Selena was right. Emilia's entrance made an impact. Heads turned as she stood in the restaurant doorway. She knew what she was doing, allowing the room to see her. Wearing a scarlet gown that matched her lipstick and Louboutin's, she sashayed across the room, the white streak in her tar-coloured hair shining as it draped across her shoulders.

"Evening ladies," she said as the silence in the room returned to muted conversation.

"Wow!" Melanie said, "Is that a…?"

"Oscar de la Renta," Emilia replied and raised a hand, beckoning over a waiter.

"Do you know how much that dress cost?" Melanie said, leaning into Selena as Emilia gave the waiter an instruction, "You wouldn't get much change out of seven thousand pounds."

Before leaving, the waiter pulled out the remaining chair at the table, and Emilia lowered herself into it.

"So, what have we all been up to today?" Selena poured Emilia a glass of prosecco, and the three of them clinked their glasses and sipped. "Melanie went shopping."

"Too right. What did you do Emilia?"

"I had a guided tour of La Scala. It was very interesting; we were treated to a few minutes of a rehearsal for a forthcoming performance of Tosca."

"I did the Duomo rooftop tour again, then spent some time just walking around a local market." Selena said, looking up as the waiter returned with a bottle of vodka, three glasses, and a jug of cranberry juice. He placed them down and Emilia slipped him a fifty euro note as Selena continued, "This afternoon I visited the Sforzesco castle." The conversation was polite, if a little stilted, as they all seemed to skirt around the elephant in the room.

Emilia opened the vodka and poured three glasses with the cranberry juice after the main course had been cleared away. "To the vodka and cranberry club," she said, offering her glass aloft. The others took theirs and the glass rims met in a toast as they all smiled across at each other.

"I guess it would be fair to say that we all achieved the goals we set a year ago."

Melanie nodded, but Selena's eyes dipped towards the table and she put down her glass and said, "I... err... need to say something."

Melanie looked across, first at Selena, then at Emilia. Concern shadowed her face, and she wondered if maybe now was the time to come clean as she said, "I also need to say something."

Emilia took a sip of her drink and took a deep breath and

said, "I think after our endeavours we all must have things we need to get off our chests. I know I do."

The conversation paused as a waiter delivered their dolce; he gave each of them a practiced smile before departing.

The women watched his tightly clad bottom as it traversed the floor, and then unrehearsed, but in unison, the three of them said, "I have a confession…"

The End

Author Notes

I've always been drawn to feel-good stories; quite frankly there's too much doom and gloom in the world and because of this my readers will know me for uplifting tales. A style I like to call, 'Life-Lit' and this book slots into this genre as it's about people with real-life issues that they want to overcome – albeit in this story more extremely.

Originally, the story outline was for a dark comedy, but over time and consecutive drafts, the comedy elements faded to become a more contemporary storyline. This led to some criticism from fellow writers and my beta readers. The first was a question about genre change. I don't believe this is a genre change. The Vodka and Cranberry Club is not intended to be a thriller or a crime novel per se, it's an exercise in taking control and facing up to adversity and therefore still sits within the 'Women's Fiction' category.

Some beta readers asked me if it is morally right to want to kill someone when there are other avenues to go down? I answered that, (1) The decision I took is morally wrong, but it's used solely as a device to tell a story. (2) This is fiction, not real life and I believe readers can distinguish between the two. (3) The wives are foiled in their attempts because their husbands are the engineers of their own downfall.

I enjoyed writing about Emilia, Melanie and Selena. They are an unlikely collection of friends which kept me on my toes, switching between each of them and maintaining their individuality – which I hope I have achieved.

I hope you enjoyed the story and if you had a favourite wife, send me an email to let me know who it was as I'd be interested to know. I'm always happy to hear from my readers with questions, opinions and suggestions.

I need to thank the following people: The inimitable Jan Edwards, for tips on writing crime and how not to give too much away too soon. The fabulous Misha Herwin, for keeping my tenses and waffle in check. To all the Renegades for feedback and criticism, my beta readers for their honesty. Eternal thanks go to my wonderful editor Georgie, who's work I always appreciate, even at those times when I disagree but always with good humour.

Will there be another story like this one? I can honestly say I don't know. Never say never – let's wait for the feedback. This type of story has lots of plot points to remember, many minor details to keep in mind, and also research into procedures outside my skill set. I have enjoyed creating the Vodka and Cranberry Club, but I can't at present see a follow up – any ideas? Let me know at **barry@barrylillie.com**. Perhaps I'll stay with Italian relationship drama (notice I didn't mention the R word) and novels that tackle dark issues and add to them my brand of comedy.

If you've enjoyed this book, I'd really appreciate your support; please consider leaving a review or a simple star rating on Amazon or Goodreads. Small publishers don't have the extensive advertising and marketing budgets of the big boys and so reviews are so important for creating awareness and helping to spread the word. For updates automatically from Amazon, go to my author page and click on the +Follow button, and don't forget you can get news and free offers by signing up for Lillie's Letters at **https://barrylillie.eo.page/yz39v**

Finally, I'd like to take this opportunity to say a huge thank you to my readers in the United Kingdom, the United States, Italy and Canada and also my newly emerging markets in Australia and New Zealand. Thanks, I really appreciate everything.

"'Thank you' is the best prayer that anyone could say."
Alice Walker

Printed in Great Britain
by Amazon